SHADOWS OVER FULHAM

PAUL ASLING

Published by Independent Publishing

DEDICATION

Dedicated to my friends in Fulham
What great days we had.

Bernie Montgomery - Martin Billham
Jimmy Adams - Alan Hopkins
Micky Coomber - Gary Ives
Terry Gibson - Roy Knight
Steve Noakes - Ronnie Galvin
Ronnie Bennett - Pete Doherty
Mark Adams - Geoff Hurren
Jimmy Gadd - Peter Barker
Dave Payton - Gary Cutts
Richie Brown - Billy Dent
Paul Coomber - Reg Wise
Johnny Greenaway - Billy West
Richard Phillips - Dave O'Leary

CHAPTER ONE

Moonlight sliced through the gaps between buildings, turning the Fulham streets into a checkerboard of light and dark. Her heels clacked against the pavement, the sound ricocheting off the walls around her like an alarm she couldn't silence. Each step tightened the knot in her gut. She gasped for air; it felt like inhaling needles.

She plunged her hand into her bag, sending lipstick and keys flying. Her fingers met the mocking fabric at the bottom—no Oyster Card. Her eyes shot from side to side. These streets, once as familiar as her own name, now twisted into a maze under the night's dark veil. Did she misplace it? Or was it stolen? Her mind raced, her thoughts sinking in the quicksand of rising panic.

"Why didn't I double-check?" She muttered, her voice barely rising above a whisper as she remembered leaving her friends at the Kings Road pub, their laughter now a haunting echo.

Stranded and phone-dead, her only option was to walk. Her footsteps took on a purposeful tempo, each echo bouncing off the walls as if taunting her. A bus stop loomed ahead, its fogged glass obscuring the adverts like a blur over her judgement. She scanned behind her—nothing but more mist, eating the road alive. Yet, she couldn't shake the feeling of unseen eyes on her.

Her heart drummed in her chest. It wasn't just the streets or the dark pockets where light couldn't infiltrate. There was a taut string in her gut that told her she wasn't alone. She quickened her pace, forcing her mind to focus, each click of her heels cutting through the static of her anxiety.

At the top of Wandsworth Bridge Road, she stopped, a slight grimace betraying her discomfort. Her eyes darted to the heels of her shoes. A deep breath and she moved again, determination cutting through her every step.

A silhouette cut through the mist from an alley, a man tall and imposing. Every footstep announced his intent, confident yet furtive. As he neared the streetlight, the briefest flash revealed a keen eye, scanning, always alert. As quickly as it was noticed, his collar shot up, shrouding the shadow of stubble that hinted at days without rest. Closing the distance, he stopped her, the gravelly depth of his voice holding a touch of desolation. "Got a smoke, love?"

She halted, her heart racing, feeling the weight of the gaze of the looming stranger. Her handbag swung from her arm, and for a heartbeat, she considered sprinting, but the pain in her feet anchored her to the pavement. Digging into her bag with fingers trembling ever so slightly, she produced a near-empty packet. One cigarette left, its lonely presence mirroring the desolation that seemed to grip her. Lighting it and taking a hesitant drag, she offered it to him. His fingers, coarse and stained, grazed hers as he accepted the cigarette. The smoky tendrils curled around them, forming a fleeting bond in the cold, uncaring night.

For a moment, the world seemed suspended, her misery becoming an unspoken language. "Why here?" he mumbled, the smoke swirling from his mouth, his eyes not meeting hers. "Of all the rotten places."

Her eyes, pools of weariness, regarded him with a mix of suspicion and understanding. "What are you talking about?" she whispered. Nodding, he took another drag, letting the silence stretch. Around them, Fulham's sleepless shadows seemed to be watching, bearing witness to her despair.

Confusion gripped her mind like a vice, squeezing out coherent thoughts and replacing them with a paralysing fear. It was as if the world around her had morphed into a distorted nightmare. Just as panic began to tighten its grip, a blood-curdling scream formed on her lips, ready to shatter the eerie stillness. But before the sound could escape, his forceful hand propelled her backward, stumbling toward a gleaming white van by the curb. In that moment, a searing pain erupted within her chest, shooting through her veins like a relentless surge of electricity.

The agony consumed her, pulsating through every fibre of her being, rendering her helpless and weak. With a tremble in her limbs, she crumpled to the unforgiving ground, feeling the cold pavement under her trembling body. Struggling to catch her breath, she tilted her head upward, her vision blurred and hazy. Through a disorienting haze, her gaze fell upon the man who had led her into this nightmarish predicament. His features were etched with an unsettling blend of determination and malice. In his hand was a syringe, a sinister instrument of unknown substances and intentions. Desperation clawed at her, urging her to cry out for help. But as she scanned the empty street, a desolate realisation settled in. There was no one around to rescue her from this hellish nightmare.

The once-familiar road seemed eerily deserted, devoid of any signs of life or salvation. Instead, her frantic eyes were met with a hallucinatory spectacle—an otherworldly kaleidoscope of swirling patterns and vibrant colours that danced before her, mocking her desperate plight. As the world around her dissolved into a chaotic mess of disorienting colours, her eyelids grew heavy, weighed down by a profound weariness. Her head listlessly fell back, the impact with the unforgiving pavement reverberating through the silence of the night. In those fleeting final moments, she clung to the flickering hope of help, her heart wrenching with the knowledge that her fate lay at the mercy of the man with the clenched syringe, and the enigmatic shadows that cast their menacing embrace upon her crumbling reality.

The tyres screeched against the worn tarmac of New Kings Road. With every jolt and jerk inside the white van, the silent form in the back gave no protest. A swift turn onto Munster Road, the city's hum faded momentarily. A hundred yards on the right, the discreet sign of a builder's yard beckoned. With a sharp swerve, the van found its sanctuary. The rusty gates groaned shut, embracing the van in its shadowy confines.

The driver's chest heaved; the humid air within the van made his shirt cling to his back. The heady cocktail of fear and thrill pulsed at his temples. He leaned closer, eyes darting to a sliver of the outside world through a gap in the gate. The streets of Fulham beyond seemed indifferent, un-watchful. For now.

The ropes dug into her wrists as he tightened the knots, gauging the tension with practised hands. He lifted her, each step creaking underfoot as they descended into the stifling darkness of the Victorian building's basement. The sound of fabric brushing against skin punctuated the silence. Time stretched taut in that subterranean space. An hour later, he ascended alone, emerging from the building's shadowy depths.

The night outside was deceptive, only half-giving in to the encroaching mist. The moon, high and cold, cast its pale light on Munster Road, while distant lampposts shed pools of amber that hinted at the existence of concealed spaces. The muted hum of distant cars, the echo of footsteps — all betrayed the presence of Fulham's restless souls. A few silhouettes skulked about; their collarbones sharply raised against the cold. Their movements were deliberate, as if the night whispered secrets only they could hear.

As he ambled along Munster Road, his gaze was sharpened by the eerie luminescence that fell upon a shadowy figure sitting on the pavement on the corner of Colehill Lane. The man, dishevelled and worn, seemed to carry the weight of the world upon his shoulders. Dirty jeans and torn grey top clung to his thin frame. Beside him sat a woman; her sunken cheeks mirrored the desolation that echoed through their shared existence. Tears flowed relentlessly down her face, leaving trails of anguish etched upon her cheeks. The scruffy man, sensing his presence, rose with a mixture of anger and resignation etched upon his weathered face. But as he laid eyes upon the hulking figure standing before him, an unspoken understanding passed between them. A flicker of fear danced in the depths of his eyes, causing him to retreat into the shadows from which he had emerged.

Continuing his solitary journey, Munster Road stretched out before him. Each step brought him closer to the sanctuary he sought, a refuge amidst the chaos of the night. The Aintree Estate, a collection of modest flats tucked away from prying eyes, beckoned him. Behind those walls, he would find respite from the relentless darkness that encroached upon his world.

With a mixture of weariness and hope, he finally reached the door of his humble abode, his hands fumbling for the key. As he stepped inside, closing the door behind him, the weight of the night's encounters slowly lifted from his shoulders. Within those walls, he would find temporary respite from the struggles and sorrows that seemed to haunt the very air he breathed.

CHAPTER TWO

Luca Rossi sat in his Parsons Green Lane home, the only illumination a single, lamp casting drawn-out shadows on the opposite wall. His eyes locked onto an old photograph, of him and Julia in Venice. Smiles wide, gondolas in the backdrop. He looked away, his eyes stinging. His gaze shifted to his hands, fidgeting restlessly in his lap. The room was quiet except for the rhythmic tick-tock of a clock that hung just above the television, each second falling like a weight, dragging him deeper into a silence that felt both loud and suffocating.

In those empty hours before dawn, questions swirled through his mind, each more distressing than the last. He touched his temple as if he could physically push away the thought that this agony was just some grand illusion, a mirage his brain concocted.

To have known pure love and then lose it was a wound that defied healing. Losing a love like Julia's was like taking a bullet, sharp and sudden, its mark irrevocable. He regretted not saying those three words to her one last time, not feeling the warmth of her embrace as fate cruelly took her away. He never held her close as she slipped away, never beheld the radiance of her beautiful face that had brought him immeasurable joy. The very essence of her, which once filled his days with laughter, was now a haunting absence.

Every dawn brought a familiar weight, dragging him deeper into grief. As he'd begin to find some semblance of normality, another memory would blindside him, pulling him back. The pain was tangible, like a blade cutting through him, robbing him of rest and hunger. He felt alone, adrift in a city that bustled around him, increasingly conscious of life's impermanence and the uncertainty ahead.

With his tall stature, Luca naturally drew attention wherever he went. His body possessed a balanced combination of strength and grace, highlighting his lean physique and well-defined muscles. However, it wasn't just his physical appearance that captivated observers; there was an elusive charm that radiated from within him. His hair, a rich shade of midnight black, framed his face effortlessly. His eyes were particularly striking, resembling sapphires filled with an enchanting quality. They held a captivating power, capable of mesmerising anyone who met his gaze.

Following the tragic loss of Julia, Luca found himself presented with numerous opportunities to pursue new connections and seek comfort in the company of other women. But despite the potential for new romances, his heart steadfastly clung to the memories of his lost love.

As he gazed into the mirror, his heartbreak stared back at him, a haunting reflection of his pain. His throat tightened, and the all-too-familiar sadness settled deep within his chest. Raising his gaze, he caught sight of Julia's silver-framed photograph hanging in the hallway. Her smiling face humbled him. It took a man of true humility to admit he was broken.

For the past two years following Julia's death in a car crash, Luca had been too consumed by her death to care. Pressing two fingers to his lips, he tenderly placed them on the photo, returning the smile.

Clad impeccably in a navy suit with a crisp white shirt unbuttoned at the collar, Luca retrieved his handkerchief from his pocket and polished his Ray-Ban sunglasses before perching them upon his nose, hiding eyes glistening with more than the day's light. As he walked away from his home on Parsons Green Lane, Fulham, the house faded into the distance behind him.

Luca was born and bred in Fulham, but Fulham had now changed significantly. There is now no mirror big enough for the ever-growing self-obsessed population of Fulham. They will stop at nothing to find any activity that helps to reflect their own wealth back to them or brag about their life so they can perpetuate the Fulham myth. Fulham now has more fake vegans per square inch than any other town in the UK.

Fulham used to be a friendly, welcoming place where one could enjoy and relax, but it is now blighted by narcissists. If you're not being mowed down by passive-aggressive parents unloading their children from their vast and badly parked cars on a Saturday morning. You also might find yourself in the way of hordes of steely-faced runners, yoga mat-carrying mid-lifers, or dogs wearing coats all marking their territory on Fulham’s bustling streets.

By the time Luca reached the entrance of Parsons Green tube station, the station clock read 10:30 AM. His polished shoes tapped a steady beat against the station floor. Worn tiles led him up to the eastbound platform, their patina shaped by years of footsteps. Commuters flowed downward, narrowly avoiding collisions, their shoulders occasionally brushing against his. Undeterred, he moved with purpose, carving a path through the hum of city life.

The east-bound platform buzzed with the low hum of chatter and announcements, occasionally punctuated by the screech of a train. Screens flickered with incoming train schedules.

Luca's every move was deliberate. There was no hurried glance at his wristwatch or the overhead monitors; he knew the timings by heart. Nearby, a newspaper vendor shuffled the day’s headlines. A few metres away, a barista at a small kiosk poured steaming coffee into takeaway cups, the aroma blending with the distinct scent of the underground. Though these were familiar sights and sounds, Luca seemed detached, focused only on the journey ahead. A train approached and the platform vibrated subtly underfoot, building in intensity until the train roared into the station. The doors slid open, revealing a smattering of passengers inside. Luca stepped in, finding an empty corner to lean against. Around him, fellow passengers engaged in their own world – headphones plugged in, books open, or gazing blankly.

Luca's shoes struck the pavement rhythmically as he navigated the bustling streets of South Kensington. Bright sunlight dappled through overhead leaves, casting long shadows on the pavements below. Around him, voices of tourists chattered excitedly, their cameras clicking and maps rustling, all eager to capture London's history tucked away in its museums.

London's heartbeat, constant and loud. He glanced around, letting the wave of people, colour, and noise wash over him. London had changed a lot since Luca's childhood in Fulham. London had become a place full of problems, with traffic that suffocated and stress that never let up. Luca was disappointed to see that the enchantment and magic he once felt in London were gone.

Luca remembered a time when London was a wonderful place, with its charming streets and impressive landmarks. But now he longed for the simpler days of his youth. The colourful and whimsical atmosphere had been replaced by dull skyscrapers and corporate monotony.

Every day was a struggle for Luca as he moved through the crowded streets, filled with rushed people and blaring horns. The landmarks he used to know were hidden among the towering buildings, overshadowed by the constant noise of urban life. The parks, once peaceful retreats, were now crowded with people seeking a momentary escape from London's demands. Luca missed the peaceful beauty of the Thames, where he could watch the boats and reflect. Now, the river was just a backdrop to a city that never slept. The vibrant energy of the streets had turned into a chaotic and restless rhythm that bothered Luca.

Cromwell Road stretched before him like an ominous runway. Martina's words pounded in his ears: her friend's daughter, vanished, two weeks ago, somewhere between the Kings Road, Chelsea and Putney. A couple with a pram weaved past him; he sidestepped, nearly stumbling. His feet carried him faster towards the flickering sign of the Cortana Club—part of his family's business. A quick nod from the bouncer, familiar and yet tinged with something unreadable. What would he find tonight?

The door swung open and a burst of rich coffee aroma ambushed him. He barely took a breath before his sister Martina swooped in, her eyes like dark clouds, heavy with unshed rain.

"You alright, Luca?" Her voice trembled, almost imperceptible.

His lips brushed her cheeks. "I'm fine sis? Where's Franco?"

"He's at the restaurant. We're sorted here." Her head tilted slightly, gesturing to the staircase, shrouded in plush red carpet.

As they reached the top of the stairs, a slim, blonde woman stood from her seat, her posture rigid. She wore a white, tight-fitting dress that cut sharp lines against her brown boots. "Luca? Nice to meet you; I've heard a lot about you."

His mouth stretched into a half-grin. "Hope she saved the juicy stuff for you."

Martina flagged a passing waitress. "Three cappuccinos, love." Inhaling deeply, her gaze flicked to Grace. "About Emma..."

Luca's forehead tightened, creasing like folded paper. "Who's on it, Grace?

"Rick James." She paused, watching him.

"Rick was on my team when I was in The Met. Any blokes in Emma's life?"

She hesitated, the pause hanging heavy. "Not serious ones."

“What about her father?”

“Died of a heart attack. Two years ago.”

He studied Grace, picking apart the lines around her eyes, the tautness of her lips. “And you?”

“No one, just Emma,” she whispered, her voice breaking like fragile glass.

His eyes locked onto hers. “Has Emma been acting differently? Anything out of the ordinary?”

“Nothing. She’d have told me. She’s not the kind to just leave. We are so close.”

He looked deep into her eyes, watching as they brimmed and overflowed.

“What else, Grace? Is there anything?”

“Nothing,” she choked out, her eyes finally spilling over. “Something’s happened. I know it.”

“I’ll talk to Rick James and get an update. Then I’ll call you.”

“Thank you, Luca,” she barely managed, her voice a thin wisp.

He nodded, a silent promise. "I'll do whatever I can, Grace. Whatever it takes."

CHAPTER THREE

After arranging a meeting with Rick James at a café back in Fulham, Luca made his way back to South Kensington Underground Station. The faint rumble of an approaching train vibrated in the distance. As the air gently stirred, a delicate perfume wafted towards him from a lady standing close by. It was unmistakable: the same perfume Julia used to wear. A flood of memories washed over him, each one more poignant than the last. Each thought seemed to tighten an already painful knot within his chest. His struggle was not only the void that Julia left behind but also the emptiness he had felt since resigning from the Metropolitan Police Force.

Every day, Luca felt the absence of Julia like a hollow space in his chest. Once filled with shared laughter and dreams, that space had turned into a void, a constant reminder of the life they'd never get to live. He moved through their home like a ghost, tracing the outlines of their past—the empty chair across the breakfast table, the untouched piano keys, the solitary cup of morning tea. The weight of his grief was palpable, pressing down on him until he could barely breathe. Yet, he didn't turn away from the pain; he knew he needed to feel it fully to grasp the magnitude of his loss. Even in the darkest moments, he understood that this agony was the price of love, and so he let it wash over him, as unwelcome but necessary as the rain.

In the darkest of nights, when solitude became his sole companion, Luca bravely confronted his anguish head on. With each passing day, the slow and arduous journey towards healing commenced, though not without leaving behind indelible scars as testaments to the boundless love he had once shared with Julia. The club was co-run by Luca, his brother Franco, and sister Martina. It served as the nerve centre for their collective projects, including Gianni's, a restaurant on Harrington Road in South Kensington.

Each day became slightly more manageable, even though he still navigated through an unpredictable emotional landscape. The thought of Julia remained ever-present, but it started to inspire a bittersweet comfort rather than a piercing pain. These changes, subtle as they were, indicated that his mind was slowly beginning to heal. The scars wouldn't disappear, and he didn't want them to. They would remain with him as signs of its depth, not as wounds that incapacitated him.

As Luca stepped out of Fulham Broadway Tube station, the immediate buzz of Fulham hit him: cars honking and people chatting. The sun was high, its rays casting a warm glow on the streets and glass fronts of shops. The city was a living, breathing spectacle, especially with the throngs of tourists bringing an array of colours and voices. It was a scene that always cheered him up. But for Luca, Fulham had changed so much in the last twenty years.

Beneath the canvas awning of a trendy Fulham café, a woman gripped her reusable bamboo cup, steam rising from her oat milk latte like tendrils of fog. Her eyes, encased in environmentally friendly mascara, darted from one person to another on the busy Fulham Road. Across the road, a Land Rover the size of a small yacht clumsily parked beside a line of hybrid vehicles. Its door swung open and a cascade of children spilled out, each gripping an iPad and sporting the latest eco-friendly school gear. The mother, a fortress of makeup and self-assurance, shouted into her Bluetooth earpiece while shoving the children forward. Her eyes narrowed— not a hint of awareness, not a single care about anyone but herself.

Luca entered the café, ordered a flat white coffee, and waited for Rick Stone to arrive. The doorbell of the café jingled, and a group of athletic runners swept in. Their faces were steely, eyes locked forward as if even acknowledging other people would slow their pace. They chattered about personal records and impossible marathons, filling the café with an audible tension that seemed to thicken the air. Another woman pulled out her phone, snapping selfies that featured the café's artisanal interior but excluded any human presence, including her friends. The quiet murmurs of approval seemed louder than any actual conversation, each nod as calculated as a chess move.

He watched another woman who had probably thought Fulham would be a sanctuary—an idyllic neighbourhood where like-minded people engaged in mindful living. Instead, she found herself enmeshed in a relentless charade, a daily performance where everyone seemed to be on stage but no one was in the audience. The aroma of freshly brewed coffee could no longer mask the scent of narcissism that seemed to hang in the air like smog. Even here, sipping a latte marketed as "guilt-free," she felt choked. She placed her cup down, the last remnants of her latte forming a pale heart at the bottom. For a moment, she considered taking a picture, a snapshot of her "perfect morning" to upload on social media. But who was she kidding? That would make her one of them.

With a sigh, she gathered her coat and her faux-leather bag, each item carefully chosen to reflect her ethics and social standing. Yet, she wondered how many in this crowd, with their perfect lives on display, would ever admit to the emptiness that sometimes crept up like an unwelcome shadow. And so, she left, searching for authenticity in a neighbourhood that had forgotten its meaning.

Luca then spotted an old man standing outside the pub opposite, his face etched with lines like a road map of life. His eyes darted from one woman to the next as they passed by. There was a keenness to his gaze that stood out in contrast to the casual enjoyment around him. As women approached, he'd lean in slightly, his eyes widening, only to pull back in evident disappointment.

Two young Henrietta's breezed by, lost in conversation. The older man's eyes lit up, tracking their movement. They walked on, never noticing him. Both seemed ensnared by their own form of quiet suffering.

Rick's footsteps echoed on the tiled floor of Gino's Café. Seeing Luca, his tense shoulders relaxed a notch, and the corners of his mouth tilted upward. "Luca." The two men met, hands clasping in a firm handshake, the weight of shared history momentarily pressing between their palms. Inside, the café hummed with life. The hiss of a coffee machine and laughter intertwined, while patrons bent in closer, their conversations a muted buzz of intrigue. Every so often, a glance or two would dart toward the café's newest entrants.

Rick slid a folder across the table. Luca opened it, his fingers pausing on a bank statement. His eyebrows drew together in confusion. "All this money... And she still hasn't used a penny of it?"

Rick leaned back in his chair, a hint of a smile on his lips. "Strange, right? If she was running away, you'd expect her to use some cash."

Flipping through the folder, Luca's eyes caught on a series of CCTV images. "This is Kings Road, isn't it?"

Rick tapped the image. "Right outside the World's End Estate. She's there, all smiles, no one tailing her. After that? A dead end."

Luca shuffled the papers. "Grace said Emma wasn't seeing anyone."

Rick's gaze hardened a bit. "We thought so too. But there's a guy from Hammersmith she'd been meeting. He checked out though."

Luca paused, taking a deep breath. "Has this happened before? Other girls in the area, I mean?"

Rick sighed, his voice heavy. "About six months ago. A girl from North End Road, went missing. We found her body by Hammersmith Bridge — it wasn't pretty. Throat cut, sexually assaulted, the whole deal. We got nothing: no evidence, no leads, even after grilling all the usual suspects."

Luca's fingers drummed on the desk, restless. "Have you looked at her social media and spoken with her friends?"

"Indeed, we have, and regrettably, they provided no valuable leads. All we gathered was that she was a carefree, fun-loving girl. We scoured her social media accounts, yet nothing hints at any underlying issues in her life," Rick replied.

Rick spread his hands out, frustration evident. "There's nothing. Everyone says the same thing: she was happy. It's like she just vanished into thin air."

Rick rubbed his temples, fatigue etching lines on his face. "Each disappearance, it's always a nightmare. But this is something else. I can't figure it out."

Luca asked, "What's our next move?"

"We're broadcasting on radio and TV. It starts tonight. I'll keep you in the loop," Rick said, his tone unwavering.

Luca nodded. "Mind if I update Grace?"

Rick met his gaze. "Go ahead." The unspoken promise to find Emma solidifying between them.

The weight of the situation weighed heavily on Rick's shoulders as he continued, "It's a parent's worst nightmare, the vanishing of their child. Countless children go missing each year, but as you know we usually locate the majority of them. Some are mere runaways who eventually return home. But this case, it's a conundrum. And I'm afraid the prospects appear bleak."

CHAPTER FOUR

Two weeks earlier...

Darkness swallowed the street, it's hold only loosened by the fading street lamps struggling to cast their last beams of light. In a small rectangular block on the Aintree Estate, windows flickered on and off like hesitant stars, breaking the early morning into a jagged landscape of light and shadow. The persistent growl and honk of engines reverberated, painting an auditory backdrop that signalled the city's impatience to get somewhere—anywhere—in the sprawling maze of London.

Amid the discord of light and sound, a solitary figure emerged from the door of one flickering flat. Johnnie Billham stepped out, his face momentarily lit as he passed under a sputtering street lamp before merging back into the shroud of darkness. His eyes darted too each fleeting pocket of light, like a nocturnal creature cautiously navigating its habitat.

On the pavement, a stray tabby cat prowled, its eyes reflecting a brief glimmer from a passing car's headlights before it disappeared into a narrow alley. Across the street, the tattered curtain of a second-floor flat fluttered through an open window, as if catching its breath from the stuffy room behind it. The sound of hurried and uneven footsteps came from around the corner, eventually revealing a young couple. As the couple turned the corner and vanished into another lit passageway, Johnnie shook his head and glanced at his wrist-watch, its face faintly luminous. He sighed, feeling the weight of time in that small, glowing circle.

As Johnnie Billham traversed the gloomy streets, he couldn't help but be stirred by a deep-seated exhilaration. Amid the sea of sombre faces that surrounded him, he detected an emptiness haunting these individuals. It was a void, he believed, that they desperately sought to fill, resorting to the numbing allure of alcohol, fleeting distractions, and trivial gossip. Their lives seemed entangled in a web of despair, where every step was steeped in a profound sense of desperation.

Johnnie, a member of a large family with six siblings, was born in 1965 and spent his early years living on a Victorian terraced street situated right next to North End Road Market. His father, a resourceful merchant specialising in household goods, tirelessly walked the streets of West London, selling his wares. Johnnie reluctantly accompanied his father most days and couldn't help but harbour a deep dislike for this particular experience.

In the world of boxing, where giants loomed and brute strength reigned supreme, stood a man named Johnnie Bill-ham. Standing just under six feet tall and weighing a mere

13.5 stone, he was an unlikely contender in the heavyweight division. Yet what he lacked in physical stature, he made up for with an unconquerable fighting spirit that few could match.

Johnnie's determination knew no bounds. He possessed a tenacity that propelled him forward, undeterred by his physical shortcomings. In the face of overwhelming odds, he willingly subjected himself to immense punishment, unyielding in his pursuit of victory. Each blow absorbed by his body only fuelled his resolve. For he understood that enduring such agony was the price to be paid for conquering his adversaries.

It was a paradoxical dance of pain and resilience that characterised Johnnie's style. Impervious to the blows inflicted upon him, he would absorb three or four punishing punches in order to unleash a single devastating strike. This calculated strategy separated him from the pack, for he knew that in the cruel world of boxing, the ability to withstand the storm was what set champions apart from the defeated.

Johnnie thrived on the thrill of uncertainty. He was a gladiator of the modern era, always ready to step into the ring at a moment's notice, regardless of the circumstances. The concept of fear was foreign to him, as he embraced the chaos and unpredictability that came with accepting fights on short notice. It was in these moments that he felt most alive, as the crowd roared in anticipation and he prepared to unleash his captivating show.

For Johnnie, boxing was not merely a sport; it was a profound metaphor for life itself. It represented an intense confrontation with one's own limitations and a relentless pursuit of greatness. In the ring, he found purpose and meaning, surpassing the boundaries of his physical stature and becoming a symbol of resilience and determination. So, as the world of boxing marvelled at the towering figures that dominated the heavyweight division, Johnnie Billham stood as a testament to the power of the human spirit, and embodied the essence of a true fighter—a warrior who faced the most formidable opponents head-on, with an unwavering spirit and an unbreakable will.

In his younger days, he was charismatic and amiable, and possessed a magnetism that drew people to him. With his quick wit and a seemingly endless repertoire of thrilling stories, he effortlessly captivated people. Yet, beneath the surface, this was all a façade. Johnnie Billham harboured an inflated sense of self-importance, akin to that of a narcissist, and was convinced that conventional rules did not apply to him. He harboured grandiose delusions about his own potential, firmly believing he was unmatched in every endeavour he undertook. Throughout his life, Johnnie had become an expert at deceiving people to get ahead. Although he never felt true emotions for anyone, he knew exactly how to mimic empathy and honesty. A master manipulator, he never took responsibility for the hurt he caused, always finding a way to shift the blame elsewhere. Continuing his charade, Johnnie seamlessly blended into social circles, using his fabricated charm to gain trust and advantage. At work, his colleagues admired his apparent dedication; in friendships, people were drawn to his seeming authenticity. Yet, behind the mask lay a calculated strategy to exploit these relationships for his own gain.

When things went wrong, as they inevitably did, Johnnie would identify a scapegoat or circumstance to divert attention away from his own misdeeds. Whether it was blaming a failed project on an "incompetent" team member or attributing a friendship's breakdown to "unforeseen life changes," Johnnie always emerged unscathed.

Unbeknownst to those around him, his lack of remorse and accountability were as calculated as his charming exterior. The web he wove was intricate, but to him, it was just the necessary groundwork for advancing his own interests, regardless of whom got hurt in the process.

Johnnie strode purposefully towards the far end of Munster Road, to his builder's yard. Until this moment, he had not spared a thought for his latest victim; now, however, he could hardly contain his eagerness for their second and final encounter.

In his mind, a monstrous tune played on an endless loop, incessantly grating on Johnnie's sanity. For him, it was not a melodic arrangement but rather a morbid contemplation of the imminent act that would end the life of the girl he had violated the previous night. Reliving the events in his mind, he vividly recalled her petite mouth, slightly pouty and delicate. When she smiled, her parted lips revealed a pristine set of teeth as white as pearls. Savouring the memory, he anticipated that her screams would soon pierce the air, filling the atmosphere with terror.

As he arrived at the entrance of his builder's yard, Johnnie fumbled with the gate's lock; it emitted a rusty screech as it swung open. Time had taken its toll on the once-proud Victorian structure, reducing it to a forlorn shell of its former glory. Distinct from their once-vibrant red, the bricks now bore swirls of muted colours, giving the three-story building a mottled appearance. Despite the height of summer, a chilling draft slithered beneath the doors, reminiscent of the relentless advance of the tide on a desolate beach. The condensation-covered windows rattled in response, drops of water cascading onto the decaying sills. In the dimness, spiders scurried through obscure corners; their ancient webs fluttered in dusty silence, clinging to the walls like ghostly fingers.

Within the gloomy confines of the house, Johnnie inserted a key into a door's lock in the hallway, causing it to emit a click before swinging open. He made his way toward the cellar rooms. Descending a creaking wooden staircase, he observed the ceiling marked by a labyrinth of old pipes, twisted at grotesque angles. The basement was more like a bunker than a liveable space, marked by cold, soulless concrete devoid of any trace of character. Near the ceiling, narrow windows stretched horizontally; their width was like the slits in medieval castle turrets, casting elongated beams of feeble light. Stagnant air filled the space with a putrid scent, reminiscent of a dungeon, triggering a sense of claustrophobic unease. The basement formed a maze of small rooms, crudely built from stone and timber.

Entering a modest chamber on his left, Johnnie flicked on the light, revealing his captive. A chilling smile stretched across his face as he observed her terrified expression, caught in the glare of the light. She froze, her mind struggling to process the horror unfolding before her. Bound with her wrists secured behind her back and her ankles tied to the chair legs, her screams were muffled by a cloth that he had forcibly jammed into her mouth, held in place by black tape since their encounter the previous night.

The room's walls and ceiling bore a sickly yellow, tar-like residue, while the once-cream carpet had succumbed to a dark grey hue, saturated with gritty filth. He shouted at her, contempt filling his voice, "If you want sympathy, you won't find it here. Look between 'shit' and 'syphilis' in the dictionary." He took pleasure in her torment, savouring her fear with a wicked grin.

Lurking behind his intended victim, consumed by agitation and nervous energy, Johnnie paced back and forth, clutching a gleaming aluminium baseball bat. Tears cascaded down her cheeks, transforming her once-beautiful face into something pitiful. "Well," he remarked, diverting his attention to the instrument of violence, "let's bring this to an end, shall we? The morning grows late, and I have matters to attend to."

Raising the bat high above his head, he swung it downward with relentless force, connecting with the crown of her skull. The resulting sound bore no resemblance to the crack of a bat striking a ball; instead, it reverberated through the room, shattering the silence. After dragging her lifeless body into an adjacent room, he covered her with old sacking, concealing his horrific handiwork. That night, he would return to dispose of her remains, erasing any trace of his gruesome act. Taking a few moments to compose himself, he wiped the blood from his hands and face, tucking the blood-stained handkerchief back into his pocket.

CHAPTER FIVE

Luca met Julia when they were both in their late teens. That night, the air in the Redcliffe Arms was saturated with the aroma of spilled beer and smoky perfume—a heady cocktail that swirled through the atmosphere. Luca's eyes were half-closed as he leaned back against the oak bar, cradling a half-empty pint of lager. The thumping bass of the music vibrated through the soles of his trainers, nudging him like a playful friend. Then she entered his line of sight: Julia.

She was on the dance floor, a fluid silhouette bathed in the oscillating glow of blue and red overhead lights. Each movement seemed to flow effortlessly into the next. Her eyes were closed, and a smile graced her lips, as if she were in a world entirely her own. She seemed both a part of and separate from the pulsating crowd around her. Luca felt a tightening in his chest, as if someone had reached in and squeezed his heart. A sudden clarity washed over him, turning the clamour of chattering voices and clinking glasses into an indistinct blur.

He couldn't tear his eyes away from her. The way she swayed to the rhythm, her arms lifted slightly as if to embrace the very air—Luca felt as though he was witnessing a form of magic, a manifestation of pure, untamed joy. The sensation tugged at him, a palpable force urging him to step away from the comfort of the bar. Without realising it, he found himself weaving through the throng of gyrating bodies, each step magnetically drawing him closer to her. As he neared, he felt both rising exhilaration and choking apprehension, like standing on the edge of a cliff with the sea's expanse stretching below. Finally, he stood there, just a couple of feet away from her. The proximity made him aware of the details: the subtle flush on her cheeks, the strands of blonde hair clinging to her forehead, the way her fingers seemed to trace invisible patterns in the air.

Her eyes fluttered open, sensing his presence, and met his gaze. The corner of her mouth twitched upwards, forming a knowing smile. Around Luca, the world seemed to mute; time stretched like a rubber band pulled to its limit.

For Luca, this wasn't just a random encounter on a typical Friday night. In that moment, amid the clamour of the pub and under the spell of its hypnotic lights, he realised he was besotted—utterly and irrevocably.

As the music played, filling the tiny gaps of silence between them, Luca felt as though the strings of his very soul had been tuned, aligning perfectly with the universe's frequency—all because of her, Julia. The air felt lighter, the room looked brighter, and his forgotten pint of lager on the bar seemed dull in comparison to his newfound intoxication.

As Julia's life neared its end, her weary body took its final breaths. In those fleeting moments, she gifted Luca a profound, timeless love. From their very first meeting, Julia had sensed a deep connection with him, as if their souls had recognised each other across lifetimes. Their love grew through joys and sorrows, surviving life's many challenges. Julia's love for Luca was not fleeting or superficial; it was a potent force rooted deep within her, an unwavering devotion that had weathered the tests of time. With each beat of her fragile heart, she poured her love into Luca's soul, leaving an indelible mark that could never fade.

Luca still longed for the tender touch of Julia's lips and the comforting warmth of her embrace. He sorely missed the love that gleamed in her eyes and the joy that radiated from her smile. In his bleak existence, he felt enveloped in darkness, as if the world had turned its back on him, devoid of anyone willing to cherish him. Whenever he faced trouble, no matter its scale, Julia had always been his first point of contact. Whether dealing with a trivial annoyance at work or navigating an urgent crisis, she was his sanctuary. Now, her untidy presence, her gentle snores, and even her off-key singing haunted his memories. The emptiness of his bed tormented him at night and greeted him with desolation each morning.

Upon returning to the Cortona Club, Luca took note of the crystal chandeliers hanging heavily from the ceiling, their brilliance eclipsed only by the egos of the influential and affluent clientele. Located on South Kensington's Cromwell Road, this prestigious family club had evolved to attract a new breed of elite and fashionable individuals, tailoring its offerings to their penchant for indulgence and permissive revelry. Despite its understated elegance, the club radiated an abundance of class and style, serving exclusively members who occupied the highest rungs of wealth and power. As Luca made his way to the bar, he spotted his brother, Franco, who was talking animatedly to Martina.

"What's going on?" Luca asked as he approached.

Martina spoke up before Franco could answer. "We ran into some trouble earlier. A couple of guys tried to order drinks before we opened. Franco handled it when he arrived."

"Are you, all right?" Luca asked his brother.

"I'm fine," Franco said, somewhat sharply.

"So, what really happened?" Luca inquired.

Martina filled him in. " As I said, two men walked in and demanded drinks. When I told them we were closed, one of them attempted to go behind the bar. The other started kicking stools. Franco arrived just in time and escorted them out."

"Did you recognise them?" Luca asked.

"I've never seen them before," Martina replied.

Franco added, "One looked vaguely familiar, but they're definitely not regulars."

"They seemed more interested in causing trouble than in having a drink," Martina noted.

Luca's eyebrows furrowed. "I was told, Bernie Montgomery faced a similar issue at his club last week. We might want to consider increasing security around here."

Franco signalled a waitress and ordered a double espresso. "I'll be on the terrace," he stated, then walked away.

Ten minutes later, Franco re-joined Luca and Martina at the table. "I've been pondering this. Do you think this is more than just a few guys causing a ruckus?"

Luca glanced at Martina. "Martina believes so."

Martina sighed. "That's what's strange—they weren't drunk. Completely sober, actually."

"I'll visit Bernie's place." Luca said. "To see if there's more to it."

CHAPTER SIX

Luca's eyes snapped open, his pulse a jagged rhythm throbbing in his temples. The ceiling above was a dull expanse of white, almost a blank canvas mirroring the chaotic thoughts swirling in his mind. The bedsheets clung to him like a moist shroud, a by-product of uneasy dreams and restless movement.

Swinging his legs over the side of the bed, his feet reluctantly touched the cool wooden floor. Each step toward the bathroom felt like a slog, as though he were moving through a thick fog. The mirror greeted him with a face he scarcely recognised—haggard eyes, unshaven stubble, and a furrowed brow weighed down by uncertainty.

By the time he stepped out of the shower, a monologue of internal questions had already begun to unfold. Did Grace know anything more? Could she provide any clues to the mystery of her missing daughter, Emma? His conversation with Detective Inspector Rick James had been unproductive—no answers, just an endless stream of questions and procedures.

Finally stepping out of his house, he felt the crisp morning air slap his face. The trees lining the lane stood tall, yet oddly forlorn; their leaves drooped like the heavy thoughts weighing on his mind. After boarding the tube train, he found the carriage to be a claustrophobic capsule filled with transient souls. Overhead lights flickered, casting uneven shadows across passengers' faces—each absorbed in their own world of smartphones, newspapers, or weary gazes. The air was thick with the exhaustion of the early morning commute, and a baby's cry clashed against the low murmurs and rhythmic clatter of the train moving along its rails.

As the train pulled away from the station, Luca leaned against the cold metal pole at the centre of the carriage. His eyes scanned the sea of heads bobbing in the confined space, and he felt a mild sense of relief—akin to loosening a tie after a long day. Closing his eyes briefly, he let the predictable, repetitive motion of the train lull the frenzy of his thoughts.

"Putney Bridge," the automated voice eventually announced, rousing Luca from his short-lived daydream. The doors whooshed open, trading a few drained souls for fresh ones, and he disembarked. Once outside, he was immediately engulfed by a throng of pedestrians. Around him, the streets came alive—shopkeepers adjusting their awnings, and cars navigating back streets like ants following a sugar trail.

Navigating through the urban maze, he could see the pedestrians weaving their way across Putney Bridge, their footsteps hurried yet rhythmic, like a well-rehearsed dance. The bridge itself was a jigsaw puzzle of exposed concrete and scaffolding, victim to a facelift in its old age. Construction workers in neon vests and hard hats occupied one lane, their machinery growling in the backdrop.

Turning right onto Lower Richmond Road, Luca's eyes narrowed slightly as he searched for the red-bricked façade of Grace's apartment building. Spotting it sandwiched between a pub and an ageing bookshop, its windows dimly lit like sleepy eyes, a surge of anticipation electrified his steady heartbeat. He stepped up to the intercom, its buttons worn and faded from the countless fingers that had pressed them before his. As he pressed the one marked “Lane” a brief silence ensued before the intercom buzzed—a static-filled sigh granting him entry. As the door clicked open, Luca felt the weight of the day lift off his shoulders.

The moment Luca stepped onto the plush cream-coloured carpet of Grace's second-floor flat, he felt as if he'd entered a sanctuary, a serene haven of sorts. Grace's eyes met his—sapphire pools shimmering with both hospitality and a flicker of anxiety she couldn't fully disguise. "Welcome, Luca. Please, come in."

The sunlight poured through the enormous glass windows that flanked two sides of the living area, casting gentle patterns of light and shadow on the floor. The Thames River meandered lazily below, a silvery serpent framed by the architectural marvel of Putney Bridge. For a fleeting moment, Luca lost himself in the view, as if the beauty outside could dilute the unease settling in his stomach.

Grace led him through to the open-plan kitchen-diner. The walls were as white as untouched snow, contrasting with the dark steel of the modern appliances. Venetian blinds hung elegantly in the windows, their slats minutely adjusted to let in just the right amount of daylight. The entire space seemed calculated for comfort but also precision, like a canvas waiting for the stroke of a brush.

"Would you like some tea or coffee?" Grace inquired, her voice as smooth as the surface of the marble countertop.

"Black coffee would be great," he replied. His eyes met hers, and he forced his lips into a taut line, a physical manifestation of the knot tightening in his gut.

"Grace, I need to be honest with you."

Her eyes searched his face, as if probing for a precursor to the words that would follow. Her hand, midway to the coffee jar, paused in the air, arrested by his tone. "I don't have any news about Emma. Rick informed me that the investigation involves aerial support, police dogs, the tactical support group, community rescue service, and local volunteers."

The air seemed to thicken, each word hanging heavy between them like a suspended droplet, quivering but not falling. Grace lowered her hand, her grip visibly tightening around the counter edge. For a moment, her eyes clouded over, as if misted by the weight of unshed tears.

"Rick James called me earlier and shared the same information," she finally said. Her voice was softer now, a fragile whisper laden with a sadness so palpable it was almost tactile. Yet, she didn't crumble, didn't break down; she simply stood there, embodying a strength that was both humbling and heart-wrenching to witness.

In that moment, as they stood in the immaculate room, each understood that the walls around them could offer no refuge from the storm of emotions churning within. All they had was the bitter brew of uncertainty and the shared ache of a name unspoken yet deeply felt—Emma.

Grace felt her fingertips grow cold, clutching the coffee mug as if it were an anchor to the reality she desperately wanted to escape. Her eyes met Luca's, a churning pool of urgency and concern. The room seemed to constrict around them, photos of Emma grinning from the mantelpiece. Her laughter now served as an echo haunting the hollow spaces.

"No news," she whispered, each syllable laced with a heaviness that sank to the pit of her stomach. "Her friends know nothing. It's like she's vanished into thin air."

Luca asked. "What about her college?"

"I went but he police got there before me. No leads," Grace said, feeling the gnawing dread tighten with each fruitless inquiry. "They said it's not unusual for students to go AWOL for a while."

Luca kept his eyes fixed on her, drilling past her facade, trying to unearth something—anything—that might lead them to Emma. "Is there anything you remember? Anything, however minor?"

A wisp of memory floated through the fog of Grace's thoughts. "She came home late one night. She'd tried marijuana. We talked until sleep overtook us." Grace's eyes shimmered; the dam holding back her emotions finally broke. "Since her dad died, it's been just us. I know my daughter. She wouldn't just disappear. Something's wrong; I know it." She wiped her eyes, smearing the wetness across her cheeks. Tears were useless, she told herself. She needed to be strong —for Emma.

"Was she close to her dad?"

"She adored him," Grace said, her voice faltering. "My feelings for him... they changed. I didn't love him the way I used to. I tried, but the heart rebels. It doesn't listen to reason. Before he died, I told him I loved him."

Luca reached across, his fingers gently closing over hers. His touch was warm, offering a brief reprieve from the icy grip of her despair. "I'm meeting with Rick again. I'll find something, Grace. We will bring her home." For a moment, in the hushed air between them, Grace allowed herself the fragile luxury of hope—a flickering flame in a sea of darkness. It was enough, for now.

CHAPTER SEVEN

Johnnie had known her father and for weeks, he'd occupied the same corner seat in the café, a half-finished cup of flat white growing cold beside his laptop. However, his eyes rarely met the screen. Instead, they were drawn across the room, captivated by her presence. She walked as if suspended in air, each step a calculation of grace, transforming the simple act of crossing the floor into a choreographed dance. A halo of golden hair framed her face, strands catching and refracting the café's light, virtually commanding onlookers to acknowledge their sun-kissed brilliance. As she laughed with her friends, her skin caught the light in a unique way, its fair tones glowing softly. It wasn't merely the way the ambient lighting played tricks, but rather how it seemed to subtly capture her vitality. The rosy hue of her cheeks was not applied artificially but was a natural manifestation, a testament to her youth. Her eyes scanned the room periodically, never hurried, as if bestowing upon each object they landed on a momentary significance. She spoke, and the world seemed to lean in, captivated.

Eagle-eyed, Johnnie slid into the streets of the Clem Atlee Estate, each step swallowed by the night, leaving neither trace nor echo behind. Tangles of alleys stretched before him like a twisted knot—inscrutable to the uninitiated, but familiar terrain for him. He moved with predatory resolve, every muscle fibre tensed, every sense on high alert.

Dull sodium-vapour lamps flickered overhead, their intermittent light dappled the pavement and cast ghoulish silhouettes onto the crumbling brick walls of the towering council flats. Their windows were like dead eyes—void of life, yet strangely watchful. The night was oppressively quiet, as if the very air held its breath in anticipation of his next move.

His boots barely grazed the pavement, like a predator too skilled to alert its prey. A stray cat darted out from a nearby skip, its eyes glowing momentarily in the lamplight before disappearing into deeper darkness.

His jaw clenched; his fingertips tingled—not with nervousness, but with a near-primeval excitement. As he delved deeper into the estate's bowels, the public realm faded away, replaced by an underworld governed by different rules—rules he both revered and exploited. A low, pulsating hum emanated from an unseen source, growing louder with each step he took. Whether it was an external sound or the internal drumbeat of his quickening heart remained unclear.

Up ahead, he saw her door. A dim light spilled from the flat next door, casting a narrow, glowing rectangle onto the dark pavement. His eyes narrowed, his pulse thrumming in his neck. As he approached, his hand gravitated toward the concealed pocket in his coat. The indistinct boundary between man and monster wavered. An eerie sensation swept over him—a shiver dancing up his spine, as if an invisible gaze were watching, judging. He hesitated, teetering on a precipice from which there was no return. He could turn back now, retreating into the obscurity from which he had come, leaving the monster within unfed. Alternatively, he could cross that threshold, letting the shrouded figure he was and the one he could become merge into one.

The night held its breath with him, waiting for the man to decide what kind of monster he would become. He hunted out of hate and excitement and succumbed to an insatiable urge to kill "certain" people. As his bloodlust consumed him, he moved stealthily from one victim to the next, leaving a trail of horror in his wake. His motives lacked rationality or vengeance; it was the sheer ecstasy of extinguishing life that fuelled his grisly campaign. For Johnnie, the act of murder wasn't a burden or a chore but a perverse joy. Disturbing glee coursed through his veins as he plunged a gleaming blade into the soft flesh of his prey. The twisted pleasure he derived from watching the light fade from their eyes offered a window into the depths of his fractured psyche.

Johnnie stood as a grim witness to the depths of human darkness—a haunting reminder that evil exists not only in the realm of monsters but also within the hearts of men.

The dim bulbs sputtered; their feeble light flickered as if gasping for breath, struggling against the suffocating darkness. Each beam managed to cut through the murk, though it did little more than carve a path of ghastly pale luminescence for Johnnie to tread. The buildings, giants of another era, loomed like silent sentinels, their facades marred by decay. In the muted glow, Johnnie could discern every fissure and crack, each one evidence to the relentless march of time. Every corner, every shadow, seemed to hold a secret, threatening to burst forth and engulf him. The weight of countless eyes—imagined or real—bore into his back, and Johnnie felt the prickling sensation of being watched, observed, judged. He swallowed hard; the cold air crystallised in his lungs, sharp and unforgiving.

CHAPTER EIGHT

Now, in the depths of the Clem Atlee Estate, Victoria Peters was alone. It seemed as if the world had frozen in time, leaving her to confront her fate alone, and the deserted estate offered no comfort. Lately, a disconcerting presence had infiltrated her life—a stranger lurking in the shadows, always watching her from a safe distance. At first, she dismissed it as a figment of her imagination, a series of coincidences holding no significance. But as the days turned into weeks, the feeling of being observed intensified, growing like a sinister vine, coiling around her thoughts and squeezing out any semblance of peace. Tonight, however, was different. Tonight, the weight of unease reached its breaking point. Every step she took, every breath she drew, felt heavy, burdened with the anticipation of confrontation. The stranger's relentless surveillance had taken a toll on her nerves, shredding the fragile fabric of her sanity. She couldn't bear the torment any longer.

Every corner she turned, every shadow that danced in the flickering light, amplified her terror. The sound of silence enveloped the dimly lit streets, broken only by the distant hum of a passing car. Her heart pounded in her chest as she darted through the alleys, her breath ragged and desperate. Fear clenched every muscle, urging her to push further, faster, away from the impending danger. She could feel the weight of his gaze, the predatory instinct driving him closer with each passing second. Sweat trickled down her forehead as she ran, her footsteps echoing through the estate. She dared not look back, fearing what she might see. Her mind raced, searching for an escape plan, but her options dwindled with each passing moment.

As the moonlight cast strange shadows on the street, she stood outside her front door, fumbling nervously with her keys. Her trembling hands struggled to find the keyhole, their movements betraying the turmoil within her mind. Paranoia and fear gripped her tightly, their icy tendrils seeping into every corner of her consciousness. With her heart pounding like a war drum, she finally managed to slide the key into the lock. The door creaked open, granting her access to the sanctuary of her home. Yet, even within the supposed safety of her walls, she couldn't shake off the lingering sense of dread that clung to her like a suffocating fog.

As she stepped inside, her senses heightened, acutely aware of the smallest sound, the slightest movement. The once-familiar surroundings now seemed alien, as if tainted by the presence of an unseen intruder. Her instincts screamed at her to be vigilant, to unravel the mystery that had consumed her days and haunted her nights. Once inside, she locked the door with trembling hands. She peered through the peephole, scanning the dimly lit street, but saw nothing out of the ordinary. Her breath caught in her throat as the realisation sank in—the danger could be anywhere. Her eyes darted around the room, searching for any signs of intrusion. Each creak and groan of the flat sent shivers down her spine. She thought about calling the police, but what evidence did she have? Just a feeling, a gut instinct that refused to be silenced.

As she advanced through the dark corridor, her pulse raced, matching the rhythm of her thoughts spiralling deeper into paranoia's abyss. And then, in the midst of her apprehension, she caught a flicker of movement—a fleeting shadow slipping through the corner of her eye. Her breath caught in her throat, and her entire body froze in a montage of dread. She held her breath, clutching her keys between her knuckles as a makeshift weapon. Her eyes darted from shadow to shadow, desperate for a hiding place, an escape, anything. But even as she focused on the looming threat, her thoughts betrayed her, drifting back to her dad.

In the fog of her fear, an image of her father appeared. In her mind, she saw him, a pillar of strength and comfort, standing in the familiar frame of their home's entrance. His voice, like a soothing lullaby, would promise, "I've got you, love." And she'd melt into his embrace, a sanctuary from the darkness lurking outside. But a brutal voice inside her snapped, "Dad can't save you now."

CHAPTER NINE

The sun took its final bow for the day, casting Fulham in hues of crimson and gold. Luca's eyes half-closed against the burst of colour, his body instinctively navigating the familiar pavement of Fulham Road. It seemed the universe had painted an oil canvas just for him—an ambiance that mirrored the nostalgia flooding his mind. His leather brogues scraped against the rough pavement, each step a resonant echo that brought a flicker of the past. Shopfronts flashed by in a blur, their signs delicate in the fading sunlight—mere spectators to Luca's nostalgic stroll. He inhaled deeply, finding the air—a peculiar mix of garlic and exhaust fumes—oddly comforting.

The sight of O'Grady's neon sign, flickering like an old film reel, beckoned from a distance. An involuntary smirk tugged at the corners of his lips. The place was a haven for poor decisions and lager-laden tales. Its weakly lit corners were practically woven into his friendship with Bernie Montgomery.

A sudden wave of anticipation interrupted his daydream, his heartbeat quickening to match the rhythm of his accelerating steps. Each step closer to O'Grady's felt like drawing a treasure map, where X marked not gold but a friendship weathered through storms and droughts.

He could almost hear Bernie's infectious laughter, as familiar as the chorus of a favourite song. It was laughter that erupted from Bernie's belly, filling the space and demanding to be heard—a laughter that had consoled Luca through heartbreaks, celebrated victories, and filled countless youthful daydreams.

Growing up as childhood friends on Kingwood Road, Fulham was more than their home; it was the fertile ground where their deep connection took root. Over the years, their friendship remained steadfast, resilient against life's trials and tribulations. Together, they faced whatever fate had in store, finding comfort and strength in each other's unwavering support. The streets and parks of Fulham bore witness to their shared experiences, their laughter echoing through its streets, their footsteps leaving imprints on its paths. These memories, now distant yet treasured, occupied a special place in Luca's heart, marking the deep bond they had nurtured. Although life had led Luca and Bernie down different paths, moulding them into the individuals they'd become, the strength of their alliance had not wavered.

Reaching for his phone, Luca glanced at the screen. Two new messages from Bernie appeared—likely some sarcastic quip about his lateness, as always. A grin formed, stretching across his face like a welcome guest. His fingers hesitated for a moment, hovering above the screen before deciding to leave the messages unread. Slipping the phone back into his pocket,

Luca's hand found the door handle of O'Grady's. For a moment, he paused, as if allowing time to catch its breath. Then, with newfound resolve, he pushed the door open, stepping into an ambiance of subdued lights and intense camaraderie.

A warm, amber glow enveloped him, a direct contrast to the twilight outside. There—standing behind the mahogany bar—was Bernie. As Luca walked towards the bar, he was instantly enveloped by the sights and sounds that recounted the rich narrative of the place. The walls, adorned with a blend of vintage photographs, faded newspaper clippings, and boxing memorabilia, told a timeless tale of the club's enduring connection to the noble art. The air resonated with the harmonious blend of coarse tones emanating from lively conversations and laughter. These sounds intertwined with the rhythmic clinking of glasses and the gentle hum of cheerful banter, forming a chorus that filled the room with warmth and friendship. Each sound was a vibrant thread in the fabric of connection.

Behind the worn, mahogany bar, ex-bricklayer Bernie stood tall. With years of service, he had become an integral part of the club's essence. The impressive array of colourful whisky bottles lined the bar, a testament to the craftsmanship and passion that flowed through these walls. Bernie, a guardian of tradition and a keeper of stories, tended to the needs of the club's patrons with a kind and knowing smile.

The low sun peeked through one of the windows, casting a soft glow on the weathered faces of the locals engrossed in lively debates. The lines etched on their faces spoke of wisdom gained through shared experiences. The worn, cushioned seats and sturdy wooden tables bore the honourable scars of countless conversations and the echoes of clinks from glasses raised in celebration. Each mark told a tale, a witness to the memories etched into the very fabric of this cherished place.

After some general banter, Luca leisurely swirled the rich amber liquid in his glass and asked, "Have you had any trouble in the club lately, Bernie?"

A deep sigh escaped Bernie's lips, casting a shadow over his eyes. Frustration tinged his words as he began to recount, "A few nights ago, a pair of troublemakers sauntered in. They were definitely out for trouble. They harassed the staff and started intimidating some of the regulars."

Luca's brow lined. "That's not something you normally tolerate, Bernie," he murmured, his voice reflecting his disquiet.

Bernie nodded, his jaw clenching with determination. "Fucking right," he replied, pride seeping into his words. "I had to summon a couple of the boys," he continued, his gaze shifting toward the robust figures positioned throughout the club. Their silent presence was evidence to their loyalty. "They swiftly threw them out."

Luca leaned forward, engrossed in Bernie's account, a shared understanding flickering in his eyes. "We experienced a similar thing at Cortana," he revealed, his voice resonating with empathy. "A couple of troublemakers stormed in and started to throw their weight around. Martina was alone. Just as things were getting out of hand, Franco showed up. You can guess the rest."

A half-smile played at the corners of Bernie's lips. "Ah, Franco. I bet they didn't come back?"

Luca smiled and shook his head. "I think we need to keep an eye on things and let each other know if there's any more of it." Bernie nodded in agreement.

A gentle smile adorned Luca’s lips. "I hope everything has been going well on the business front, Bernie," he inquired, his voice filled with genuine concern.

Bernie's eyes sparkled with a glimmer of amusement. "No complaints, Luca. Although I must admit, the place truly comes alive when Chelsea are playing at home. It becomes a fucking madhouse."

Inclining forward, Bernie's voice carried a blend of curiosity. He fixed his gaze on Luca, hoping to rekindle a distant memory. "Do you remember Ronnie Gadd?"

Luca furrowed his brow, searching his memory. "Of course, I do."

"I thought you might. Ronnie Gadd used to frequent the Atlee or the Wilton most nights, just like us, all those years ago. He was a regular drinking mate of Micky Coomber and Johnnie Bilham," Bernie explained, a tinge of nostalgia in his voice. Bernie's gaze drifted. "Something tragic happened to Ronnie's daughter, Julie. She went missing a few months ago. She had been on a hen do in Hammersmith but never returned home," he continued, his voice tinged with sorrow. "A couple of weeks later, her body was discovered beneath Hammersmith Bridge. Her throat had been slashed wide open."

Recalling a conversation, he had with Rick James, Luca added, "I spoke to one of my former colleagues from the Met a few days ago, who told me about the case. Unfortunately, they haven't made much progress in finding those responsible."

Bernie leaned over the table, a grin spreading across his face. "You won't believe it, mate. Micky Coomber and Johnnie Billham come in here throughout the week, along with some of the Fulham crew."

Luca's eyebrows shot up, a wry smile forming at the corners of his mouth. "Micky Coomber and Johnnie Billham? Here? Really?" He tapped his finger against the side of his glass. "What are they up to these days? Still running their scams?"

Bernie chuckled. "Nah, they've upgraded. They're both builders now."

Memories flooded back for Luca. Micky Coomber, built like a bouncer but always impeccably dressed, had a knack for being Johnnie's human shield—both metaphorically and sometimes quite literally.

Luca chuckled at the memory of a young officer attempting to slap handcuffs on Micky outside the Clem Attlee pub, only to find himself momentarily airborne before being pinned to the ground. All while Johnnie calmly walked away, of course. They were the uncatchable duo—always a game of cat and mouse with those two.

Bernie caught Luca's far-off look and waved a hand in front of his face. "Oi! Lost in the good old days, are we?"

Luca snapped back to reality, meeting Bernie's gaze. "Just thinking about how great the old times were, Bernie. The things we used to get up to."

They both burst out laughing, sharing a moment of camaraderie wrapped in nostalgia.

CHAPTER TEN

Rick James's hand hesitated over the tarnished doorknob before finally turning it with a resigned sigh. He stepped over the threshold, and the air inside the apartment closed in on him—thick and stagnant—a stifling blend of metallic scent and mildew that settled on his tongue like a bitter film.

This place was a tomb, a vault preserving its secrets in suffocating silence. The worn carpet muffled his footsteps as he moved cautiously forward, his eyes narrowing in an attempt to acclimate to the murkiness.

The moon forced its way through the gaps in the blinds, casting slender fingers of bluish light upon the chaos below. Rick felt the weight of that surreal light deep within him, as though it were pulling his very soul downward.

As they moved further in, their shoes murmured against the hardwood floor, each step disquietingly muted as though the space itself absorbed sound. The walls, once likely pulsating with the laughter and dreams of a young woman, now closed in with a suffocating stillness. There it was—the metallic, sickly odour that never quite left you. The smell of blood hung thickly in the air, merging with a sort of acrid aroma that pricked at their nostrils. Detective Scott looked over at Dr. Singh. Their eyes met, mirrors of exhaustion and grim determination.

The forensic team approached. There she was, in an almost poetic sprawl on the floor, a young woman now devoid of life. Her limbs were twisted into positions that made Rick wince instinctively, as if her very bones were screaming out the torment she had endured. Her arms and legs were as pale as the moonlight that washed over them, but her face—what he could see of it—was a mask of final agony, eyes vacant and staring into some eternal abyss.

Surrounding her head was a halo of blood, thick and almost black in the gloom, an appalling contrast to the pallor of her skin. The forensic team arrived at the lifeless figure sprawled on the ground; her eyes a scene of eternal horror. A momentary pause gripped the room, as if paying an unsaid tribute to the terror imprinted in the girl's dilated pupils. But within that silence lay a binding commitment—a silent oath to honour this life stolen too soon.

The forensic team moved in, a synchronised ballet of gloved hands, swabs, and little plastic bags. Each fragment of evidence—a fibber, a scrape of skin under the girl's fingernails, a cryptic scribble on a notepad—acquired solemn significance. These pieces were no longer just objects; they were torches in the murk, pinpricks of light that might eventually flood the darkness with truth.

The sterile latex gloves stretched taut over Dr. Harriet Scott's fingers as she picked up the tweezers, her eyes narrowing at the pale hand before her. The weight of the room hung heavily. She focused on the solitary strand of hair coiled around the girl's index finger—a near-invisible wisp in the cold light. The strand seemed so delicate. But in that fragile filament lay a maze of DNA, the unseen keys to a dark puzzle. She pinched the tweezers around the hair, her hand momentarily freezing in mid-air, petrified at the notion of compromising this fragile link to the truth.

With a barely perceptible nod, her colleague, Dr. Singh, manipulated the camera to capture the moment. Flash. The light momentarily spilled into the room. In one fluid, practiced movement, Scott transferred the strand into a sterile evidence bag, sealing it with a reverence usually reserved for sacred relics.

Detective Scott felt her jaw clench, her eyes stinging slightly. There was no room for sentimentality, yet her resolve tightened around a core of pure empathy. A life had been brutally severed, an existence reduced to case files and evidence bags. The nameless dread, the incalculable suffering the young woman must have faced—it fuelled her, anchored her to the haunting reality of the room. They would find justice. And as Harriet Scott looked down once more at the sealed evidence bag, holding the fragile strand of hair that seemed to scream silently from its plastic tomb, she knew they had no other choice.

In the midst of their meticulous examination, they swiftly discovered the identity of the victim. Victoria Peters, a mere 21 years of age, had been living in the flat on Clem Atlee Estate for six months.

Rick slid on his gloves, the latex snapping against his wrists, as he surveyed the modest flat. Every surface, every corner, seemed to hold its breath, waiting to exhale the secrets it hid. His eyes caught on the walls, adorned with a mosaic of photographs and doodles that seemed to dance even in the stillness. They were snapshots of smiles, of laughter, of dreamy landscapes, but to Rick, each frame seemed to pulse with the life force of the young woman who had lived here.

He moved toward the bookshelf, every step a muted echo on the floor. Books of varying thicknesses were neatly arranged, their worn pages sticking out like tongues eager to speak. His fingertips brushed over a dog-eared copy of "Love You Till I Die," its spine creased with love and attention. Victoria had read these, had travelled through realms and epochs within these pages, seeking, perhaps, the same solace he often did.

The scent of coffee still lingered in the kitchen, blending with the atmosphere. The aroma was almost thick enough to taste, like a cloud you could bite into. A coffee mug sat on the counter, its contents either half-empty or half-full, depending on your perspective on life. Rick imagined Victoria standing there in the mornings, the world still dim cradling her cup as she sifted through the complexities of her 21-year-old existence.

"Rick, come here. You should see this," Harriet Scott called from the bedroom.

Upon entering, he found her holding a sketchbook. As she turned its pages, the pencil lines sprang to life: portraits, land-scapes, abstract impressions. Each sketch seemed like an emotional X-ray, revealing layers of joy, despair, love, and loneliness. Victoria had laid herself bare on these pages, her fragile and tumultuous soul expressed in strokes of graphite.

In a corner of the room, tucked almost out of sight, stood a vinyl record player.

A collection of records sat nearby, their sleeves worn but carefully preserved. Rick picked one up, reading the title and the list of songs, each likely a chapter in Victoria's internal narrative. He envisioned her placing a record on the turntable, the needle dropping, and the soft crackle before the music filled the room—and her, swaying to melodies only she understood.

His heart constricted in a strange blend of sorrow and respect. In the midst of their meticulous examination, this flat had transformed from a mere crime scene into the sacred archive of a young woman's life and dreams. Victoria Peters was no longer just a name, an age, a statistic. She was a vivid tapestry of thoughts and experiences, a universe unto herself, now brutally extinguished.

"We need to find out what happened to her," Harriet's voice broke through his trance, tinged with a rare emotional quiver.

Rick looked at her, then back at the room. "We will," he affirmed, as if making a solemn vow to the lingering soul of Victoria Peters.

And as they left the flat, sealing the door behind them, a part of Victoria travelled with them. Each investigator, whether they realised it or not, now bore an invisible thread of connection to her. And in the depths of their minds, a resolve crystallised: they would follow this thread, no matter how tangled or frayed, to wherever it led them. They would discover the truth, and in doing so, offer the one thing they still could to Victoria Peters—justice.

CHAPTER ELEVEN

Luca sat in his cramped home office, buried under a relentless pile of paperwork. His phone shattered the silence, making him jump. The caller ID flashed "DI Rick James," and a feeling of dread washed over him. He knew that a call from the detective could only mean trouble.

"Hello, Rick," Luca answered, his voice tinged with apprehension.

"Luca, we have another murder on our hands," came Rick's urgent voice.

"What happened?" Luca inquired, his tone tense.

"A young woman was found dead in an apartment on the Clem Atlee Estate. It appears she was stabbed multiple times," Rick relayed tersely.

"Have you identified her?"

"Yes, her name is Victoria Peters. She had only been living there for six months. We're still piecing the rest together."

"Do you think this could be connected to the missing girl I've been looking at, or the previous murder near Hammersmith Bridge?" Luca asked.

"It's too early to tell," Rick replied. "I'll keep you updated. I have another call coming in."

Luca's thoughts immediately shifted to Emma, the missing daughter of Grace Lane. Grace had been living in a constant state of fear since her daughter disappeared. Knowing he needed to reach her before news of the murder broke, Luca dialled Grace's number, his fingers trembling slightly.

After a few rings, Grace answered, her voice tinged with a mixture of hope and despair.

"Grace, it's Luca. I've just received some news from Rick," he began, trying to steady his voice. Grace's breath hitched on the other end, and she waited in anticipation.

"There's been another murder, but I want to assure you, it's not Emma," Luca explained, hoping his words would offer some comfort.

There was a moment of silence, then Grace let out a sigh—a mixture of relief and sorrow—and then sank into the couch in her living room. Since Emma had gone missing, every ticking second had been agony. But Luca's words ignited a flicker of hope within her.

"Thank you, Luca. It's a relief to know it's not Emma, but who is the poor girl?"

"I don't have all the details, but as I said, I can confirm is that it's not Emma," Luca responded.

"I can't shake this feeling of helplessness. The police seem to be getting nowhere, and I just want my Emma back," Grace confided, her voice saturated with desperation.

"Grace, I understand how you're feeling. I promise you, I won't rest until we find out what happened to Emma. I have an idea, and I'll contact you as soon as there's any news," Luca reassured her, his voice brimming with determination.

Luca had always had a knack for improvisation, but this plan was teetering on the brink of madness. Faced with the potential loss of Emma, he felt compelled to turn to Eddie Ruben, one of London's most notorious criminals.

Merely uttering Eddie's name sent shivers down most people's spines, but the immediacy of the situation rendered conventional methods ineffective.

Eddie Ruben was more than a criminal; he was a clandestine expert on London's murky underworld. His network extended to places hidden from the public eye. As the police investigation faltered and the toll of unsolved murders of young women grew increasingly alarming, Luca—once a diligent detective—couldn't bear the thought of Emma becoming another statistic.

The course he was about to embark on would plunge him into a hazardous underbelly that most wouldn't dare approach. It was a perilous gamble to venture into this dangerous realm, but for him, the risk was worth it.

CHAPTER TWELVE

Nestled deep within the vibrant streets of Chelsea, where the scent of aged wine lingers and echoes of cultured conversations fill the air, stands an eight-bedroom, Grade II-listed Georgian house on Cheyne Walk. Its imposing presence commands attention, epitomising prestige and opulence in a neighbourhood dominated by multi-million-pound residences.

In this coveted enclave unfolds a hidden world where secrets intertwine with luxury. At the heart of this intriguing setting lives Eddie Ruben, a man seemingly shaped by timeless masculinity. His distinguished grey hair and air of sophistication belie his true nature. To the unknowing residents of this wealthy area, he is merely a neighbour. Yet, beneath his refined exterior, Eddie Ruben plays an extraordinary role in London's criminal underworld.

Unbeknownst to the local elite, Eddie serves as the kingpin of one of London's most feared modern crime syndicates. Like a maestro, he skilfully orchestrates his empire, always one step ahead of the law. His grand Georgian home conceals a complex network extending its reach throughout London and beyond.

Eddie is a man of contrasts; his aura masks the darkness within. His neighbours witness extravagant parties and glamorous soirées that adorn his residence, oblivious to the real reason behind the celebrations. While they sip champagne and bask in the glow of the chandeliers, Eddie's criminal enterprise flourishes in the shadows, expanding its reach and tightening its grip on London.

Like a chessboard, the streets of London have become the battleground for Eddie's calculated moves and strategic manoeuvres. Behind closed doors, he brokers deals, manipulates power, and ensures his name remains a whispered fear among those who dare to cross his path. His empire thrives on secrecy, and Eddie guards his secrets with unwavering vigilance. Few have glimpsed the true extent of his influence, and even fewer have lived to tell the tale.

Eddie Ruben is a name whispered in hushed tones. He has built a reputation of power and fear spanning three decades. From the moment he emerged from his tumultuous background in the backstreets of Fulham, his fate was sealed. The city would feel the impact of his rule, his iron fist forever etched on its streets.

Eddie's origins are shrouded in gritty tales swirling through London's underbelly, his enigmatic presence casting an ominous shadow over his deeds. Born into poverty and hardship, Eddie and his sister Lola grew up facing harsh realities. It was under these conditions that he began his journey to becoming a criminal mastermind.

By just twelve, Eddie was already initiated into the ruthless code of a gang, learning that survival required embracing his inner cutthroat nature. Each year drew him deeper into the perilous realm of crime, his thirst for power unquenchable. At sixteen, Eddie started working for a bookie, navigating through the shadowy maze of backstreet gambling where high-risk transactions set his adrenaline racing. A year later, he delved into the dangerous world of protection rackets, claiming Petticoat Lane as his grim territory. He learned the unwritten laws of the streets, mastering manipulation and coercion.

At twenty-three, Eddie's rise to infamy peaked. He became embroiled in a pub brawl on Greyhound Road in Fulham. Amid flying fists and the stench of alcohol, he confronted the enforcer of a West London gang notorious for brutal violence. With a single, devastating blow, Eddie took him down, cementing his status in West London's criminal circles.

From that point on, Eddie Ruben became a force to be reckoned with. Each day, his empire expanded, an intricate network of illegal activities crafted with care. Alongside his gang, he ruled over London's darkest corners, overseeing the flourishing vices of prostitution and pornography. Even the police, weighed down by the reality of his reign, conceded to his deep-rooted malevolence. They whispered his name, acknowledging that no other gang had matched the depths of his depravity in the city's history.

Eddie Ruben, a figure whose story will be told for generations, epitomised the dark magnetism coursing through London. As long as his power remained unchallenged, London would be under the grip of its most formidable kingpin.

Once a modest venture, the Ruben operation now boasts a network of six thriving nightclubs pulsing with life under cover of darkness. Yet behind this glamorous façade lies a corrupt web entangling judges, politicians, and even law enforcers. With over a hundred firm members, they are notorious for brutal assaults, leaving a trail of physical wreckage and devastated lives. Driven by an insatiable appetite for power, Eddie expanded his resources, importing Eastern European hitmen skilled in sowing a path of blood and terror. In this violent, treacherous world, he found an ally in his sister Lola.

Far from content with a supporting role, Lola had carved out her own infamy as a ruthless madam. Her string of brothels across London served as power bases, hidden away like dirty secrets. Employing seduction as her weapon, Lola manipulated her way to her goals. Bound by blood and a mutual drive for dominance, Eddie and Lola left an indelible imprint on the city. For a decade, they navigated its dangerous underbelly, spreading chaos and ruin. But their ambitions knew no bounds. As Eastern European syndicates became power players in Britain's drug trade, the Ruben siblings tightened their grip on this billion-pound market. London transformed into a cauldron of international crime, attracting Albanian cocaine moguls, African gangsters, and Turkish Cypriots skilled in robbery and contract killings. Brutality unfolded with shocking regularity: savage beatings, lethal stabbings on busy streets, impalements, and home invasions marred the cityscape. On the verge of collapse, Eddie and Lola devised audacious strategies to expand their empire, exploiting new business avenues and extending their influence into society's darkest corners. Once a bastion of culture, London has become a city shrouded in shadows, a place where law and chaos merge. At its core are Eddie and Lola Ruben, puppeteers of this dark transformation, their unquenchable thirst for power never satisfied.

CHAPTER THIRTEEN

The rain cascaded down the streets of West London, droplets pattering against the windowpane of Eddie Ruben's office. Luca stood outside the door, his heart pounding with a mix of anticipation and trepidation. He hadn't seen Eddie in years, not since leaving the police force and turning his back on a life of fighting crime. But desperate times called for desperate measures, and Luca knew he had to swallow his pride and seek the help of the one man who could make a difference.

As the door swung open, revealing a haze of cigar smoke and the silhouette of a formidable figure, a wave of nostalgia washed over Luca. Eddie Ruben, a notorious gangster and well-established businessman, peered at Luca through narrowed eyes. A glimmer of recognition sparked in Eddie's gaze, and he beckoned Luca inside with a nod.

"Luca Rossi," Eddie said, his voice gravelly yet tinged with familiarity. "Never thought I'd see your face around here again. What brings you to my doorstep after all these years?"

Luca stepped into the office, the scent of aged leather and polished wood enveloping him. "Thanks for meeting with me, Eddie."

"Take a seat, Luca," Eddie said, his voice a mix of familiarity and coldness, as he motioned toward a plush chair in front of his imposing oak desk. As Luca settled into the seat, he felt an undeniable pang of regret for the choices that led him away from serving in the Met Police, forsaking the profound camaraderie he had once cherished.

With a heavy sigh, Luca began, his voice betraying the weight of his burden. "It's about a friend of mine, Eddie. Her heart is breaking; her daughter has vanished without a trace. The police have hit a dead end, and she's left with an unbearable sense of despair, unsure of where else to turn." Luca's words hung in the air, laden with a profound sense of urgency and desperation.

In that moment, the atmosphere shifted. Eddie's typically stoic demeanour softened; his eyes revealed a glimmer of understanding and empathy. Despite their divergent paths in life, Luca and Eddie had forged an unlikely bond— a connection formed through shared experiences within the gritty underworld of London. They had witnessed each other's lowest lows and highest highs, a witness to the intricate ties that wove their destinies together.

Eddie's penetrating gaze seemed to cut through the layers of Luca's troubled mind, searching for a flicker of conviction. A palpable silence hung in the air, stretched thin like a taut wire, before Eddie's lips curled into a frosty smile—a reflection of his seasoned cynicism.

"You know, Luca," Eddie's voice resonated with a mixture of caution and world-weary wisdom, "helping others has never been my line of work." His words, laced with a tinge of resignation, hung in the air, daring Luca to comprehend their weight.

But Luca, undeterred, pushed forward, his tone brimming with unwavering determination. "I understand, Eddie. I know our paths have diverged, but you've witnessed the darker side of life and emerged with a unique perspective—a perspective that can shed light on the darkest corners, a perspective that can find what others cannot."

A flicker of uncertainty danced across Eddie's face, his resolve momentarily shaken by Luca's passionate plea. The two men locked eyes, each searching for a glimmer of assurance in the other's gaze. Luca continued, his voice infused with persuasive eloquence, his words designed to dismantle the fortress of scepticism surrounding Eddie's heart. "Imagine the comfort you could bring to a shattered mother's heart."

As Luca's words hung in the air, the room seemed to hold its breath. Time stood still, allowing the weight of the moment to settle upon their shoulders. Then, as if a spark had been ignited within him, Eddie's countenance softened further, his eyes shimmering with newfound resolve.

"You've always had a way with words, Luca," Eddie murmured, a touch of admiration colouring his voice. "Perhaps it's time for me to explore uncharted territories of compassion."

In that moment, the trajectory of their intertwined lives shifted again, bound together by a shared purpose. Fuelled by their past and their determination, Luca and Eddie embarked on a journey that would test the limits of their resilience, challenge their preconceptions, and unravel the secrets hidden within the shadows of a city they both loved and called home.

Luca swallowed hard and shared the details of Emma's disappearance, laying bare the desperation of Emma's mother. Eddie's expression remained inscrutable as he absorbed the story. "You're diving into dangerous waters," he warned, his tone heavy with experience. Eddie paused to process the situation. "I've heard about the recent killings in Fulham and Hammersmith," he began, his voice tinged with concern. "It's a sick world out there, my friend. Girls are disappearing; lives are being cut short—it's an evil that runs deep."

Luca nodded, his face etched with anguish. The murders had been plastered across the newspapers, each headline serving as a painful reminder of the urgency of his own quest.

"But there's something else," Eddie continued, lowering his voice to a hushed tone. "Several Eastern European gangs are trafficking young girls, Luca. They prey on the vulnerable, the desperate. It's a trade fuelled by pain and despair." A chill crept down Luca's spine as he considered the implications of Eddie's words.

"Look, Luca, I know this city, its secrets, and its villains. Give me time, and I'll see what I can do."

"Thanks, Eddie. If I hear anything at my end, I will keep you informed." Luca said, acknowledging that he had embarked on a perilous path by placing his trust in a criminal. Yet it was his only choice. He had put everything on the line for Emma, and now he could only hope that his gamble would pay off.

As he left Eddie Ruben's office, Luca cast a glance back at Eddie, the man who might hold the key to Emma's fate. The die had been cast, and their lives were now intertwined in ways that Luca could never have imagined.

CHAPTER FOURTEEN

DI Rick James stood in the incident room. Officers leaned over tables scattered with maps and evidence bags, their faces taut with the invisible force of urgency. Phone lines buzzed; computer keyboards clattered. An undercurrent of hushed conversations sewed the room together like an intricate web.

In the eye of this storm, Rick found himself transfixed. The walls around him displayed enlarged photographs of the young victims—girls from Fulham whose lives had been extinguished. It wasn't just their smiles, frozen in time, that haunted him. It was their eyes. Those eyes, once vibrant, now stared out from the walls as if pleading for justice. They cut through the fog of data and conjecture filling the room.

Footsteps broke Rick's trance—sharp, deliberate. Detective Amy Williams walked toward him, cutting a swath through the hubbub like a scalpel. The ambient noise seemed to dip as she arrived, as if granting her an unspoken authority. Her face was a locked vault, revealing nothing, yet withholding an immeasurable weight. "We've discovered another dead girl, boss. She was found in Bishops Park." she said, her voice neither wavering nor embellished.

The words didn't just hang in the air; they landed with a thud, embedding themselves into the tight knot of apprehension settled in Rick's gut.

The room continued to swirl around him, but for a moment, the faces blurred, the sounds muffled. All he could see were those eyes—more eyes to add to the wall, more souls demanding retribution. The urgency filling the room was no longer just a palpable force; it was a scream, a howl, a vow. And Rick felt it fuse with his bones, becoming a part he could no longer ignore.

Rick's jaw tightened, knuckles whitening around the edges of the desk. Each word from Amy's detached voice was like a stone sinking into the pit of his stomach. A young woman, just another face in a growing gallery of tragedy.

Bishop's Park, he'd walked there; he'd sat on those benches and played football there. And now it had become a stage for another grim murder scene. His gaze drifted to the map pinned on the wall; every red dot was a scar on the city he had sworn to protect.

Amy had kids of her own; beneath her professionalism, she was human. And this got to her too. Rick's eyes met hers briefly. The subtle arch of her brow was an unspoken question: "Are you alright?"

But he wasn't alright; none of this was. Yet they'd both go on, treading further down the same dark path they'd walked so many times before. There was a killer out there, and justice was the only balm for wounds that never quite healed.

Twenty minutes later, Rick found himself concealed amidst the dense foliage of Bishop's Park. Crouched in the foliage, he barely rustled as he moved. The white protective suit clung to him, less a barrier and more a grim reminder of what lay ahead. Moving closer to the body, her vulnerability struck him; each wound was a nauseating spectacle against her porcelain skin. His heart tightened, filling with an unspeakable sadness and an indefinable dread. It was as if the very air had thickened, saturated with her unspoken torment.

Why? The question roared in his mind, drowning out the distant rustle of leaves and the subdued murmurs of his team. What unspeakable horror had swallowed her life, leaving behind just these remnants of pain?

Rick stared at her shattered skull, her face a silent scream frozen in time. His mind groped for understanding, aching to find meaning in the senseless brutality before him. But her scars refused to reveal their dark secrets, taunting him with their silent indictment of the world's inherent cruelty.

The forensic team methodically spread out, each member engrossed in their tasks. The air filled with the sterile clicks of cameras and the muted rustle of gloves against evidence bags. With clinical detachment, they measured, observed, documented—each action chipping away at the unfathomable mystery that lay sprawled in this lonely stretch of park.

Yet as they worked, Rick couldn't shake the nagging emptiness that clung to him. Each piece of data collected, each photograph taken, felt like a sterile whisper in a raging storm of questions. The haunting emptiness of the scene seemed to mock their futile search for understanding, a grim reminder that some truths may forever elude capture.

Time pushed forward, yet the team's dedication never stopped. Each member worked with determination, their thoroughness serving as a guiding light through the darkest corners of the investigation. Every swab, every fibre, and every trace were handled with the utmost care, delicately catalogued and safeguarded.

One of the team called out to him, holding up what looked like a credit card or some sort of pass. "Her name is Karen Tibbs."

As dusk settled over Bishop's Park, casting long shadows over the crime scene, Rick couldn't help but feel a sense of urgency. He couldn't allow the darkness to triumph over the light. The haunting smiles of the girls in the photographs lingered in his mind, urging him to uncover the truth and bring justice to her and the other girls who had met similar fates. The road ahead would be arduous and riddled with problems, but Rick was ready to face it head-on.

CHAPTER FIFTEEN

Tears cascaded down Emma Lane's pallid cheeks, their salty tracks carving a path through the dust on her skin. Emma's wrists burned against the coarse rope, each tug sending a flare of pain up her arms. A dull ache settled in her chest, pulsing in time with the thumping of her heart. The walls of the basement were covered in mould, blurring through her tear-soaked vision. The air was laden, with the musty stench of rot and dampness. Each breath she drew tasted like despair.

She let her mind drift, briefly, to her mum—strong-willed Grace. A sudden image of her mum, lips quivering and eyes reddening as she sat alone in their living room, shattered Emma's heart more than her physical captivity did. She could almost hear her mum's voice, tinged with disdain, muttering about the police's ineffectiveness. "About as useful as Anne Frank's drum kit," she'd say, a line that once elicited eye rolls but now only fuelled Emma's dread. And Dad, forever gone but an indelible presence in her thoughts, offered no comfort either. He wasn't around to barrel through the door and tear apart this godforsaken place brick by brick to find her.

A creaking sound echoed from the top of the stairs, snapping her back to the terrifying present. Each footstep descending seemed calculated, designed to maximise her anticipation, to let the dread pool in her stomach. Her heart no longer merely pounded; it screamed, as if yearning to leap out and confront whatever—or whoever—was coming.

She tightened her fists, nails digging into her palms. Her body tensed, every muscle coiling like a spring. Emma Lane might be bound and desperate, but she wasn't defeated. Not yet. And as the footsteps drew nearer, the faceless terror looming ever closer, she steeled herself for whatever came next.

Within the dimly lit chamber, fluorescent lights flickered above, casting surreal shadows that danced along the walls.

Disturbing photographs and artworks adorned the once-innocent canvas of the walls, filling her vision with unimaginable horrors. Her eyes darted from one tormenting image to another, each triggering a new wave of terror that crashed against her fragile psyche. The weight of death hung heavily in the air, making it hard to breathe.

With senses heightened to acute sensitivity, she meticulously observed her surroundings, dissecting every small detail for a glimmer of hope. Her gaze landed on a rusted pipe, evidence of the basement's decaying infrastructure. It clung precariously to the wall, its unsteady hold hinting at its potential as a weapon or a tool for liberation. A flicker of hope ignited within her, a tiny ember in the darkness.

Summoning her dwindling reserves of courage, Emma inched closer to the pipe, dragging the ropes with her, as far as they could reach. Suddenly, the oppressive stillness shattered like glass as echoes of footsteps cascaded down the staircase above. Emma's heart seized in her chest, her breath suspended in a stranglehold of anticipation. The return of her captors was imminent, their arrival heralded by the ominous clack of shoes against the floor. Panic surged within her, threatening to consume every thought. She fought against its insidious grip, steeling herself against the impending danger.

The door creaked open, its rusty hinges announcing the entry of two men. They stepped into the gloomy room. Their smiles, carved into their faces like gross sculptures, sent shivers down Emma's spine. Their eyes—dark and unyielding—fixed on her, as if trying to read her. "Look what we have here," one murmured, his voice dripping with vile satisfaction.

The air stiffened; each spoken word created a heavy atmosphere that enveloped Emma, shrinking her space and freedom until she felt cornered, almost suffocated. They catalogued her, assessing her worth in muttered conversations, reducing her body and face to calculated figures and cold percentages. Not a woman. Not a human. An asset; that's all she was to them.

A knot tightened in her stomach, a strong reaction to their dehumanising stares. Emma clenched her fists. The words they spoke became background noise; their evil intent clear in their stares. They envisioned lots of money, a future in which she played a nightmarish role. Emma felt her worth fading, as if her humanity were disappearing, leaving behind only a hollow shell. She was slipping away, sinking into a dark pit they'd dug for her, her identity crumbling under the weight of their greed.

Across the room, her eyes, once windows to boundless joy and youthful wonder, stared vacantly at the cracked concrete walls. Her wrists bore the indentation of tight ropes; her spirit, the deeper scars of degradation. She felt like a hollowed-out husk, her essence draining away with every passing second. As they continued talking, unaware or indifferent to her presence, each word they uttered seemed to compress the air around her.

Escape? The idea had long become an elusive fantasy. Her limbs felt heavy, unresponsive—bound not just by physical restraints but also by the emotional quagmire that pinned her to this gruesome reality.

The room grew colder, as if absorbing the chill of her dread, and she couldn't shake the feeling that her life, her very soul, was teetering on an unthinkable end. She had become a number, a barcode, a product awaiting its final, dreadful transaction.

CHAPTER SIXTEEN

Earlier, Luca had received a phone call from Rick James. The news was grim: a girl had been found murdered in Bishop's Park. However, Rick reassured Luca that it wasn't Emma Lane. Although relieved it wasn't Emma, Luca couldn't help but feel empathy for the unnamed victim.

Luca co-owned Gianni's, a restaurant in South Kensington, with his brother and sister. Despite the demands of running the business, he had offered to meet Grace during her workday at Gianni's. Fully aware of the emotional turmoil engulfing her, Luca understood the importance of being present, providing comfort, and offering a supportive ear during this trying time.

As Luca embarked on the short journey from the Cortana Club to Gianni's, he reflected on the immense responsibility he had undertaken to help find Grace's missing daughter. Navigating the streets of South Kensington, his mind wandered back to the countless conversations he'd had with Grace over the past few weeks. Her voice, trembling with a mixture of hope and despair, echoed in his ears as she confided in him about the relentless search for Emma. Luca had become Grace's confidant, offering support during her darkest hours with understanding and compassion.

The golden glow of Gianni's interior enveloped Luca like a familiar hug. His nose twitched as he inhaled the earthy scent of garlic and oregano wafting from the kitchen. For a fleeting moment, the tension in his shoulders eased. But as he slid into the leather-bound seat at a corner table, his eyes darted to the entrance, muscles coiled in readiness. The door opened, and Grace stepped in. She paused to allow her eyes to adjust to the light before meeting Luca's gaze. Her eyes—windows to weeks of sleepless nights and worry—locked onto his. With a hesitant smile, she navigated through a maze of tables and chairs to join him. As she sat, Luca caught a slight tremor in her hands. She noticed and quickly folded them in her lap, out of sight. His gut churned; what they had to discuss wouldn't be easy on those trembling hands.

After ordering two coffees and exchanging pleasantries, Luca began, his voice a low rasp. He wanted to reach out, to offer some semblance of comfort before shattering the fragile peace. Grace looked up, her eyes searching his. It felt as if they were both standing at the edge of a chasm, peering down, waiting for the other to jump first. Luca's voice, steady and soothing, filled the restaurant. Each word he spoke was a beacon in the chilling darkness that had swallowed Grace's life since Emma vanished. His eyes met hers, and in that second, something resilient sparked within her—a glint of hope that dared her to believe.

Luca’s phone buzzed. "Do you mind if I take this call?" he said, before rising from the table. He walked away, pulling out his phone as he stepped into the kitchen.

Left alone, Grace's eyes roamed the room, settling on the gallery of faces on the wall in front of her. Each black-and-white photo held a still life: a captured memory, a moment of joy or connection. But it was one photo that caught her gaze and held it. Luca and his late wife, Julia, stood side by side. It wasn't just a picture that captured a moment; it bottled an emotion. Their smiles weren't mere arrangements of lips and teeth but radiant beams of pure, mutual happiness. Even as a mere observer, Grace felt an unexpected pang—a blend of longing and an indefinable ache.

Her eyes lingered on Julia's face, noting the crow's feet born from a lifetime of laughter and the tilt of her head showing her leaning, ever so slightly, into Luca. An irreplaceable bond was immortalised in a single frame. And for a moment, Grace's gut tightened, her flicker of hope obscured by a rising fog of uncertainty. Did she see her own future in that picture, her own happiness? Or was she staring into a past that would always overshadow her, a constant reminder of a space she could never fill? How could she navigate this growing attachment to Luca when she didn't even know where her own daughter was?

Her thoughts churned as Luca re-entered the room, phone pressed to his ear, eyes pinched with new concern. The moment felt suspended; the air taut, like a wire stretched too tight. When he lowered the phone, his eyes found hers, but they carried a weight that hadn't been there before.

Luca sat across from Grace, his heart heavy with the burden of his secret. He knew that revealing his plan to track down Emma using Eddie Ruben would be risky. "Grace," he hesitated, torn between his desire to be honest with her and the need to protect her from the dangerous path he had chosen. "I wish I could divulge every detail of the plan to find Emma, but for certain reasons, I can't reveal everything at the moment," he said.

Grace replied, "That's fine, Luca. I'm so grateful you're helping me."

The darkness of his plan gnawed at him from within as he contemplated involving a violent gangster in their desperate search for Emma. As his gaze locked with Grace's, he saw the toll her pain had taken on her spirit. And as he took Grace's hand in his own, he whispered, "I promise you, Grace. I'll do whatever it takes to bring Emma back home. Just trust me."

Luca and Grace's conversation stretched into the late afternoon, time seeming to stand still within the walls of Gianni's Restaurant. Luca listened intently, absorbing Grace's fears, hopes, and dreams for Emma's safe return. Together, they were forging a bond—an alliance driven by the shared goal of reuniting a mother and her daughter, no matter the obstacles they might face.

CHAPTER SEVENTEEN

The engine's purr dwindled to silence as Terry Gibson switched off the ignition. He looked through the tinted window, his gaze meeting the rising sun that washed the façade of the stately residence. Cheyne Walk had never looked so deceptively serene. Next to him, Roy Knight's fingers drummed on the steering wheel—a steady rhythm that somehow conveyed readiness more than nerves.

Terry glanced at Roy, his eyes locking onto his right-hand man's steel-grey irises. Words weren't necessary; the taut line of Roy's mouth mirrored his internal tension.

The sun's reflection on the Thames glinted into the car for a split second, casting a brief, dancing fire on the dashboard. The phone rang in the console, its abrupt noise shattering the morning's delicate tranquillity. The caller ID read "Eddie." Terry picked it up, his thumb hovering over the green icon before pressing it. The air in the car grew dense; each word from Eddie seared into Terry's ears, his tone laced with an urgency that tolerated no argument. Terry informed him they had just pulled up outside.

As he hung up, the weight of Eddie's summons settled around him like a cloak. Something was wrong—something that demanded immediate attention and carried the risk of an abyss too deep to climb out of. "Lola's in," Terry said; no more words were needed.

Roy nodded, no questions asked. The steel in his eyes hardened further. Together, they opened their doors almost synchronously, their feet hitting the pavement in unison. As they approached the doorway, Terry felt a chilling prickle crawl up his spine. He brushed his thumb over the brass doorbell, hesitating for a fraction of a second that felt like an eternity. But he knew, and Roy knew, that the moment he pressed that button, their world might never be the same again.

During Eddie's numerous incarcerations, Lola adeptly assembled an informal coalition of gangs, forming a delicate alliance aimed at expanding their control over London's most lucrative criminal enterprises. From drug and cigarette smuggling to protection rackets and prostitution, Lola played a pivotal role in growing the city's criminal underworld. Under her leadership, the alliance became increasingly organised, shrouded in secrecy, sophistication, and unparalleled power. Lola shunned the spotlight, having never been convicted or even suspected of any crime. Insiders spoke of her steely charisma, practicality, charm, and exceptional intelligence—all balanced by a ruthlessness that rivalled her male counterparts. In Lola's view, the prostitution trade held particular significance. Men of high standing, whether politicians or industry magnates, inevitably sought the pleasures provided by a prostitute's companionship. Her brothels catered to clients from both ends of the socioeconomic spectrum, and business flourished. In 2015, Lola unveiled Goldie's, a lavish and immensely successful establishment that attracted millionaires, politicians, and even international royalty. Renowned for its high standards and strict regulations, the club became a sought-after workplace in the city.

They found Eddie sitting at his antique desk as they entered the office at the back of the house. Beside him sat Lola, his sister, exuding an aura of elegance and grace that matched the exquisite surroundings. Her eyes, the colour of jet black, met Terry's with a mixture of warmth and intrigue. Terry couldn't help but feel a familiar flutter in his chest—an unspoken connection that had grown between them over the years.

However, any semblance of comfort was shattered by Eddie's growling voice. He wasted no time explaining that he wanted them to find the missing daughter of a friend, deliberately omitting the fact that it was an ex-Detective Inspector from the Metropolitan Police who sought his assistance. Her name was Emma Lane, he said, and she had vanished after a night out on the Kings Road.

Eddie's gaze turned steely as he revealed his intentions to delve into the local Eastern European gangs and their involvement in the dark world of sex trafficking. The weight of his words settled heavily upon the room, weaving an undercurrent of tension that threatened to suffocate them all.

Then, Eddie's voice reverberated around the room in a sudden explosion, causing Lola to jump in her seat. The atmosphere became charged with animosity as he barked, "I won't have these fucking half-wits on my manor, so make it clear to them—I won't fucking have it. And if they do have the girl, I want her back, fucking quick."

Darkness was no stranger to Terry Gibson. Once the head of a notorious Lambeth firm specialising in sadistic torture methods and with Roy Knight by his side, a former armed robber, they knew their work was cut out for them this time. Gibson's previous enterprise had earned a notorious reputation for its barbaric practices, including tooth extractions without anaesthetics.

Justice eventually caught up with him, exacting its due. He spent fifteen years behind prison walls for his involvement in torture and kidnapping. From the shadows of his dark past, Terry emerged, forging a new path as Eddie Ruben's trusted lieutenant.

CHAPTER EIGHTEEN

You'd spot them on New Kings Road, clad in the latest sustainable fashion, their vintage bikes casually leaning against a café's wall. Cycling around was their go-to method of "transporting their creative energies," as they'd say. On the outside, they seemed engrossed in their MacBook screens, sipping ethically-sourced coffee. But look closely, and you'd see they were merely refreshing their Instagram feeds every five minutes.

"Yeah, working on my screenplay, mate," Henry would say, grinning over his fifth flat white of the day. His screenplay, a Word document with exactly three lines, had been in progress for about as long as Brexit negotiations had. If you asked about his income, he'd humbly mention the dole—never mind that his parents' monthly 'care package' was enough to fund a small space program.

Harriet, on the other hand, considered herself an "emerging artist." Her last exhibition was in a friend's basement, attended mainly by other friends and some confused Deliveroo drivers who had the wrong address. But speak to her, and you'd think she was Fulham's answer to Banksy.

Inevitably, these West London aficionados would age, swapping the countryside for the terraced streets of Fulham. There, Henry's screenplay would be forever in 'development hell,' but he'd talk about his "film career" as if he were Quentin Tarantino's long-lost British cousin. And Harriet would be busy decorating their £3 million home with her own "art," of course. But rest assured, they'd fondly recall their countryside days as a "creative boot camp," conveniently overlooking the reality: a lot of posing and little actual composing.

Looking at their Fulham mansions—purchased outright, no mortgage in sight—they'd pat themselves on the back. Ah, the self-proclaimed musicians, artists, and club promoters who never quite promoted anything other than their own inflated sense of importance. But don't worry, they'd still be the first to tell you how they singlehandedly made Fulham the "cultural epicentre" it is—while gazing at their own reflection in a glass of overpriced, organic wine.

But it was all pretence to this new breed of people now inhabiting Fulham. Most of them ignored the fact that three young women had met violent deaths in just three weeks, and a shadow of fear loomed over every corner and doorstep. The real people of Fulham were consumed by a chilling unease that clung to the air like a shroud. Now an ominous darkness had descended upon its streets. Mothers, friends congregated on worn concrete steps, their conversations a lifeline amid the desolation. Men loitered on street corners, their presence a constant reminder of tempers teetering on the edge. Outside dimly lit pubs, they gathered, their souls as worn as the frayed edges of their pockets. In this world of meagre means and scant pleasures, tension simmered beneath the surface, waiting to ignite.

Rumours echoed through the tight-knit community, and neighbours stayed in tight groups, their voices hushed as they exchanged anxious glances and questioned the security they had long taken for granted. The unspoken question lingered in the air: who could be responsible for these horrifying acts that had shattered their lives?

The initial shock waves of the first murder were still reverberating through the hearts of Fulham's residents when the second and third murders took place, each one more gruesome than the last. The police, overwhelmed by the relentless onslaught of these heinous crimes, worked tirelessly to uncover any lead that might shed light on the identity of the killer. They interviewed witnesses, combed through evidence, and chased down elusive threads of information. But as days turned into weeks, the sense of desperation in their eyes mirrored that of the people they sought to protect.

Over the years, the people of Fulham weathered storms, both literal and metaphorical, and understood the fragility of life. They had mourned lost loved ones and witnessed the scars left by acts of violence and war. They were a band of resilient souls who stood united against the darkness that had engulfed their streets. They patrolled the dimly lit alleyways, casting watchful gazes into the shadows, ready to confront any threat that dared to emerge. They spoke with firm resolve, their voices laced with steely determination.

North End Road market, in all its splendour, stood as a testament to a bygone era. Its vibrant tapestry of colours and sounds beckoned visitors to embrace its history, a time when the market was the beating heart of the community. The families who had been part of North End Road since the early 18th century still clung to the market's cherished traditions, even as society had shifted and old values faded away.

On Saturdays, the market truly came alive. Regular traders, hailing from long-established costermonger families, dutifully hauled their stalls to their designated pitches. Lorries rumbled through the bustling streets, making their pilgrimage to Covent Garden, returning laden with the day's fresh fruits and vegetables. Thousands of shoppers weaved their way through the market's maze, relishing the vibrant sights, intoxicating scents, and the comforting hum of conversation. Yet, as the sun dipped below the horizon, casting a golden glow upon the market's hallowed ground, a bittersweet transformation occurred. By six o'clock in the evening, the traders packed up their stalls and departed, their presence dwindling like fading whispers. The once-vibrant streets, now emptied of the merchants' vitality, bore witness to the remnants of their bustling trade—market leftovers scattered like forgotten fragments of a time gone by.

In one corner of this shifting landscape of tradition and change, a young boy named Johnnie Billham traversed North End Road market. Wide-eyed and curious, he observed the stallholders and their families, his heart yearning to be part of it all. His own family, once firmly entwined with the market's roots, had seen the threads of loyalty and belonging fray over time. Johnnie's father, a man with a temper that could ignite the darkest of storms, held both magnetism and darkness within him. His eyes would glaze over whenever anger consumed him. In those moments, Johnnie's mother, with her strength, would usher her children away into their bedrooms.

Johnnie's mother possessed a resilient spirit that matched her husband's volatile nature. Their tumultuous relationship, punctuated by shouting matches, shook the very foundation of their home. In those working-class days, fighting seemed almost natural, a conduit for grievances to be aired in the open. Neighbours peered through the safety of their curtains, their judgment drowned out by the familiarity of their own lives, for they too had their share of quarrels and conflicts.

As Johnnie grew older, the allure of North End Road market continued to beckon him. The families that had once thrived there were dwindling, dispersing like the echoes of a forgotten age. The traditions that once held their community together were being eclipsed by a society driven by different values, leaving Johnnie Billham to yearn for a sense of belonging.

CHAPTER NINETEEN

The dimming sky cast a strange light over North End Road market, leaving vacant spaces where earlier, barrow boys haggled with their customers. The outlines of the abandoned stands cast gaunt silhouettes on the pavement, as if remnants of a lively past.

From a nearby side street, Johnnie Billham stepped into the fading daylight. He surveyed the empty market, his gaze rigid. The same streets that had once echoed with his childish laughter now reverberated with the hollow sound of his footsteps. His eyes, devoid of warmth, scanned the surroundings as though searching for something invisible.

His hands remained steady in his coat pockets, fingering a concealed knife. The boy who had once traded football stickers and raced bikes here had vanished; in his place stood a man, every line on his face etched with purpose. Tonight, nostalgia was a distant echo, smothered by a single, chilling intent: murder.

Johnnie's boots crunched over the grey pavement, each step a deliberate motion, like the hand of a clock ticking away the seconds. The marketplace stretched before him, its emptiness reflecting into his void. Street lamps flickered on, casting a dim glow that seemed almost intrusive in this setting.

He approached a shuttered kiosk, its metallic surface tarnished by years of neglect. This was where he used to buy sweets, where the old owner would slip him an extra toffee for good behaviour. Now, all that remained was a corroded lock and a forgotten sign, faded by weather and time.

Johnnie looked at his wristwatch, its hands aligning like stars in a grim constellation. It was time. He moved towards an intersecting street, knowing his target would be home now. His breathing measured, his pulse an unreadable rhythm. The wind picked up, sending a shiver through the nearby trees, their leaves rustling as if whispering secrets. Johnnie's hand gripped the knife tighter.

The monotonous drone of distant traffic had now faded into the background as Johnnie's senses focused on the eerie stillness around him. The scent of urine, mingled with the acrid odour of desperation, hung heavily in the air—an intense reminder of the decay that had infiltrated every corner of this once-vibrant neighbourhood. Yet this desolation seemed to fuel Johnnie's determination, driving him further into the heart of the darkness that had taken root in his own childhood home at 14a Estcourt Road. His childhood home stood before him, its facade a weary witness to the passage of time. Memories danced like ghosts behind the windows, beckoning him to confront the demons that had haunted him for so long. But these were not memories of joy and laughter; they were memories of pain, betrayal, and a past that had scarred him deeply.

For weeks, he had been meticulously studying her, an enigmatic figure who resided within those cold, lifeless walls where he had once lived as a child. He had memorised her every move. Now, with the moon's silvery glow cascading over the eerie facade of the old Victorian house, he felt compelled by an inexplicable force to approach her. Gaining entry through the kitchen window on the ground floor, he carefully manoeuvred himself inside, adrenaline surged through his veins. He knew the risks, but the allure of getting closer to her was impossible to resist. Each step sent shivers down his spine, as if the house were warning him to turn back. But Johnnie was past the point of no return. He had crossed a line, and there was no going back now.

With every step he took, the floorboards creaked beneath his weight, each sound resonating like a loud proclamation of his presence. Time seemed to slow down, amplifying his awareness of every small detail around him. Memories of the weeks spent trailing her, always at a safe distance, flashed through his mind.

Reaching the top of the staircase, his heart raced even faster. Moonlight filtered through a nearby window, casting a glow on the worn carpet as if to guide him on his quest. He heard her soft, rhythmic breathing as he approached the back bedroom. Pausing just outside her bedroom door, Johnny hesitated, but his heart urged him forward. Finally, he pushed the door open gently, revealing her silhouette against the moonlit backdrop. As he entered the room where his childhood nightmares had once thrived, his mind flooded with images of terrible times. It fuelled his resolve to seek justice, or perhaps revenge, for the innocence stolen from him in his early years.

Inside, the darkness enveloped him like a suffocating shroud. The air felt heavy, laden with the weight of memories he had tried to bury but had now resurfaced with a vengeance, urging him to confront the demons he had tried to suppress.

He stood frozen, his hands still gripping the bloodied knife. The echoes of the violent act he had just committed echoed in his mind, drowning out all other thoughts. He only knew her by name, after he raped her and stabbed her in the chest, neck, and upper back. He also beat her with the table lamp beside her bed. But this wasn't just any life he had taken; it was the death of innocence that had long evaded him, the innocence lost amidst the tormented walls of his childhood home.

As he stared at the lifeless form before him, the realisation washed over him like an icy wave - his actions weren't just a desperate act of vengeance against the world that had wronged him but a twisted attempt to confront the demons that had haunted him from within.

In the aftermath of the violence, the room's silence seemed deafening, and the weight of his deeds bore down on him. The once-familiar surroundings now appeared foreign and distant, like the remnants of a shattered reality. He had sought to extinguish the pain, but he had magnified it instead, allowing it to consume him entirely.

CHAPTER TWENTY

DI Rick Stone's boot met the lino-covered floor with a subdued echo, a sound dwarfed by the looming dread that hung in the room like opaque fog. The moment his eyes fixed on the scene before him, a wave of paralysis seized his muscles, as if the walls themselves forbade him to move. Shadows, elongated by the dim, flickering light, danced across the room, turning innocuous fixtures into monstrous phantoms. Blood—so much of it—had left its chaotic signature on the walls, dripping toward the floor in a grim descent.

The air felt dense, as though he could grasp the horror and squeeze it in his fist. The ferocious beating of his heart filled his ears, a savage metronome counting down the seconds of his resolve. It was as if his very heart had become an accomplice to the room's unspeakable secrets.

His stomach wrenched, a coil of nausea spiralling upward, as if taunting his professional stoicism. He swallowed hard, the act itself a minor victory against the bile that rose to meet him.

Rick had walked through the abyss of human cruelty in his years on the force—unfathomable acts that left scars on the soul. But this room was an entity unto itself, radiating an evil that mocked the laws of man and nature.

Darkness didn't just surround him—it infiltrated him, filling him like ink spreading in water. With every second that ticked by, the boundaries between himself and the room blurred.

Rick beckoned over his seasoned colleague, John Donovan, whose reputation as a grizzled veteran was well-deserved. As Donovan approached, Rick's eyes sought reassurance.

Donovan's eyes widened as he took in the chilling sight. Nevertheless, he mastered the art of concealing his emotions, maintaining an outward calmness that served as an anchor for the younger detective.

Rick spotted a small piece of plastic peeking out from under a splattered newspaper. He carefully approached the item and retrieved it with a gloved hand. The card granted access to a local research institute. The victim's face, now partly obscured by blood, was visible in the ID photo. "Her name is Lisa Jones," Rick read aloud.

As they continued to examine the room, Rick noticed something else peculiar. The patterns formed by the blood didn't seem entirely random. He instructed a team member to photograph the patterns, knowing they might be essential. "Let's get forensics in here," Rick said. "And contact the institute to see what they know about Lisa Jones."

The two detectives stepped out of the room, leaving the grim scene behind. Rick leaned against the wall, taking a deep breath to steady himself. He knew the killer had struck again.

CHAPTER TWENTY-ONE

As the sun dipped below the horizon, casting its warm colours across the city, Luca felt the weight of memories tugging at his heartstrings. The call from Rick James the previous evening had brought a mix of anticipation and trepidation. They had arranged to meet at O'Grady's Club, a place that had witnessed countless tales of laughter and despair. But as Luca strolled along the familiar Fulham Road, his mind was consumed by thoughts of Julia.

It was two years today since she had lost her life in a car crash, leaving Luca shattered and lost. In a world that once seemed full of promise, he now felt adrift in a sea of emptiness and pain. Each day was a battle, a relentless struggle to find a reason to keep going when all he yearned for was to be with her again. Life had become an empty canvas painted in the darkest shades of sorrow and grief, and Luca couldn't comprehend how to mend his broken heart.

The journey to Fulham Broadway was a poignant one, with every step echoing memories of happier times. The city bustled around him, indifferent to his grief, as if life marched on without a care for what he was feeling inside. He questioned existence itself, struggling with the purpose of persisting in a life without the light of Julia. Why should he endure this pain? How could he ever fill the emptiness left behind by her absence?

Tears welled up in Luca's eyes, the weight of his emotions threatening to overwhelm him. Yet, amidst his despair, he made a promise to himself to honour Julia's memory, to carry her love and spirit within him, and to find meaning in the midst of this unfathomable loss.

Arriving at O'Grady's Club, familiar sounds and faces enveloped him. Bernie Montgomery greeted him warmly, a gentle reminder that life carried on, even in the midst of pain. "Lager?" Bernie asked. Luca managed to give a faint smile, his thumb pointing upwards in affirmation. "Cheers, Bernie."

Rick James sat by the window, a contemplative figure looking out onto the bustling chaos of Fulham Broadway. "How are you doing, Rick?" Luca asked, trying to mask the raw emotion beneath his voice.

"I'm fine, Luca," Rick replied, his eyes conveying deep understanding.

"How have you been? It's two years today, isn't it?"

Rick's empathetic acknowledgment of the anniversary brought tears to Luca's eyes once more. But this time, there was a glimmer of comfort in knowing that someone remembered and cared. "You have a great memory, Rick," Luca said, his voice catching slightly. "It's been hard, but I will cope."

Breaking the heavy silence that hung between them, Luca inquired, "Have you any more news on the latest murder?"

Rick let out a sigh, his eyes reflecting the weight of the investigation. "We've interviewed Lisa's friends and family, but no one seems to have any idea who would want to kill her. She had no known enemies, and her life seemed to be going well," Rick explained, his voice tinged with frustration.

Rick leaned back in his chair, contemplating the horrendous crimes. "The police lab examined the clues left behind, but they were unable to identify the killer. The footprints were too small to be of any use, and the hair sample we found belonged to the murdered girl," Rick continued. "Her friends and family painted a portrait of a vibrant young woman, loved by those around her. There were no whispers of grudges or malice, no hint of a motive that could explain her brutal killing. Her life seemed to have been a whirlwind of happiness and success."

Luca creased his brow, his thoughts consumed by the murders. "At what time was she murdered?"

"Sometime between 10:00 PM and 2:00 AM. The killer entered the house through the kitchen window at the back on the ground floor, which was apparently unlocked. She was stabbed 37 times in the chest, neck, and back. The stab wounds were deep and penetrating. She was also hit on the head with her table lamp," Rick said.

Luca's mind drifted to the past, recalling the chilling similarity to the previous murders. "It's got to be the same killer as the other girls?" he questioned, his tone grave.

Rick nodded in agreement. "Almost certainly. We now have four brutal murders: Julie Gadd, found by Hammersmith

Bridge; Karen Tibbs, taken somewhere on New Kings Road; Victoria Peters on the Clem Atlee Estate; and Lisa James on Estcourt Road. We also still have Emma Lane missing. The brutality of the attacks, and the apparent lack of motive, all point to a chilling pattern," he confirmed.

The bar was now buzzing with life and laughter, a lively atmosphere filling the space with chatter and clinking glasses. Amidst the crowd, a group of boisterous builders stood by the bar, their animated banter adding to the atmosphere, and the plaster and concrete on their clothes adding a layer to the carpet in front of the bar.

As Luca scanned the group, a familiar face caught his eye. It was Micky Coomber, an old friend he hadn't seen in years. Memories of their old days in The Bedford pub on Dawes Road and the Clem Atlee in Rylston Road flooded Luca's mind, taking him back to those carefree moments filled with laughter.

Suddenly, Bernie appeared at Luca's side, his eyes slightly misty. "Two years today, wasn't it, Luca?" he said gently.

Luca nodded solemnly, the weight of loss still evident in his heart. "It was, mate," he replied, his voice tinged with sadness.

Bernie's expression softened. "She was one in a million, Luca," he said, referring to someone dear they had both lost. "A real star. I am so sorry, mate."

With those heartfelt words, Luca felt a rush of emotion, and he and Bernie embraced in a warm hug, finding comfort in each other's presence.

Luca's attention was drawn back to the group of builders. He inquired, "Bernie, is that Micky Coomber over there by the bar?" "Yes, you probably know a few of the others too," Bernie replied. "Ronnie Gadd, Gary Hopkins and Alan Ives, all from the days when we drank in the Clem Atlee."

Bernie was right. Luca recognised most of the names. Memories of laughter, shared stories, and camaraderie came flooding back, reminding him of the special bond they all once shared in those iconic pubs.

As the night drew to a close, Luca approached Micky Coomber by the bar. With a friendly smile, he greeted him, "Hey, Micky, long time no see." Micky turned with a surprised grin. "Well, if it isn't Luca Rossi. How have you been, mate?"

The two friends caught up, reminiscing about old times and updating each other on their lives since they last met. It was as if the passage of time had dissolved, and they were back in the Clem Atlee again, surrounded by laughter and good company.

As he exited the bar and stepped into the cool night, Luca felt a bittersweet blend of emotion: sadness for the void left by Julia, but gratitude for the renewed connections with old friends. He walked back home, immersed in his thoughts, yet slightly hopeful that life might offer more shades of light, even in the presence of enduring darkness.

Rick's earlier words resounded in his mind. "Your grief is a testament to your love," he had said. It was true. Despite the pain, despite the sorrow, his love for Julia was a light that would forever guide him. And so, as he walked along the familiar streets of Fulham, for the first time in a long while, he felt a glimmer of hope amidst the night's shadows, a sign that perhaps, someday, he would find peace.

CHAPTER TWENTY-TWO

In the heart of the European Union, amid its bustling cities, a sinister web of exploitation and suffering lurks. Within this dark underbelly, sex trafficking reigns as the most prevalent and devastating form of human trafficking. Ensnaring the vulnerable and innocent in its cold, merciless grip. While the world may turn a blind eye to its existence, the truth remains stark and unbending, haunting the conscience of those who dare acknowledge it.

A haunting statistic looms over this tragic reality, revealing an overwhelmingly female victim composition; a staggering 95% of those ensnared are women. These innocent souls, torn from their homes and dreams, are thrust into a nightmarish existence where their autonomy is stripped away and replaced by the cruel whims of their captors.

Each face tells a unique tale of despair, with hopes shattered and dreams reduced to mere whispers in the dark. Yet, as heart-wrenching as it may be, there is a twisted rationale driving this monstrous enterprise. Among the various forms of modern slavery, trafficking individuals for sexual exploitation stands as the most lucrative. Unfathomable profits await those who perpetrate this heinous trade; each victim generates nearly tenfold the revenue compared to the average exploitation case.

Terry Gibson and Roy Knight pulled the Mercedes to a halt on the busy Shepherd's Bush Road. Eddie Ruben wanted information about the missing girl, Emma Lane. Lola, Eddie's sister, had told them the man they needed to talk to was named Kamil, who she knew was involved in sex trafficking in West London.

They entered the shop through the rear door situated in the small car park. Terry and Roy exchanged a silent nod of understanding before stepping inside. The interior smelled of hair tonic and sweat, and the buzzing of clippers filled the air. As they ventured further inside, their eyes fell upon the colossal figure standing before them. Kamil, the man Lola had mentioned and described, was a hulk of a person—both intimidating and imposing. His unkempt beard and dishevelled appearance, along with facial scars, suggested a man who had been through his share of hardships.

"Kamil?" Terry inquired, his voice steady but cautious.

Kamil's sunken eyes darted towards the newcomers, sizing them up with a hint of suspicion. "Who's asking?" he grunted, his voice deep and rough.

"We're looking for information about a girl named Emma Lane, who's gone missing," Roy interjected.

Kamil's face darkened, and his massive frame seemed to tense. "I know nothing about any girl who's gone missing. Now fuck off out of my shop."

Roy took a step forward. "We're just trying to help someone find their daughter, that's all."

The man screamed, "I said I know nothing. Now fuck off."

Kamil's towering presence loomed, a fractured mountain of suspicion and secrecy. His eyes, wells of darkness, fixed on them one last time before the door burst open. Four figures stormed in, silhouettes against the sickly neon glow from the storefront. No words—just the guttural language of clenched fists and boots on the tiled floor. Every punch thrown was a question; every dodge, an elusive answer. The motives were masked; only the violence was clear.

Kamil hesitated, caught in a crucible of choice. His eyes darted between his henchmen and the desperate struggle that had engulfed his shop. In that split second, his indecision spoke volumes—a narrative of inner conflicts as murky as the fog outside.

Terry and Roy, battered but unbowed, navigated the chaos. Their instincts were sharpened to razor points. Every jab they delivered was a declaration; every block, a testament to their unwavering resolve. But this wasn't their turf, and the odds weighed heavily, like chains pulling them down. Muscles screaming, they carved a path toward the door, their focus steadfast. The adversaries lunged, propelled by a malevolent force that defied reason or restraint. But the duo had gambled on their own tenacity, and as they broke through the throng, it paid off.

The air outside slapped their faces—a harsh but welcome reprieve. A yard's distance felt like a mile as they bolted for the car, its engine a growl of salvation. The tires squealed on the rain-soaked asphalt of Shepherd's Bush Road as they sped off, the murky events of the evening receding in the rear-view mirror but never truly leaving them.

Hammersmith Broadway approached, serving as a stage for yet another act in a drama neither written nor directed by them. They had survived, but at what cost? And behind them, in that dimly lit shop where secrets piled up like so many clipped hairs, Kamil stood alone. His face was a canvas of emotions, each one a brushstroke of a story that wouldn't find its way into words. At least, not yet.

Terry parked the car on Lillie Road, just by the Salisbury Pub and killed the engine. For a moment, the silence in the vehicle felt heavier than the air outside. Both men's chests rose and fell rapidly, their seat belts straining against the movement. Terry's hand shook slightly as he fumbled for his mobile phone in the cupholder. He punched in Eddie's number and waited, his eyes meeting Roy's for just a second—each face a mirror of the other's tension. "Is that you, Terry?" Eddie's gravelly voice came through the speaker.

"Yeah, it's me. Didn't go as planned, mate, there were too many of them."

Eddie's sigh resonated on the other end. "Fuck it. We'll need more faces next time. No more fucking about. Get back here and we will have a chat."

Terry glanced at Roy, whose knuckles were bloodied, gripping the steering wheel. Both men understood the implications of Eddie's words. A "chat" with Eddie was never just talk; it was a directive forged from years on the streets. Eddie knew well enough that there was safety in numbers.

Terry hung up and slipped the mobile back into the cup holder. "Right then, back to the office, for a chat. After tonight, he'll want contingencies for his contingencies," he said, locking eyes with Roy for a second.

Roy started the engine and pulled the car back into the flow of Lillie Road's sparse traffic. "Best not keep the man waiting, then."

The drive back became a journey through unspoken thoughts. Every traffic light at which they stopped felt like an interrogation, every passer-by a potential threat. But they reached Cheyne Walk without incident.

As they stepped out of the car, Terry felt his phone vibrate. A text from Eddie read, "Doors open at the back."

They walked briskly to the entrance and found the door ajar, just as promised. Inside, the air was thick with the musk of old leather and stale cigarette smoke. Eddie sat at his desk, which was covered in papers; a muted CCTV feed played on a monitor behind him.

"You fucking made it then?" Eddie said without looking up, his voice tinged with something that might have been relief.

Finally, Eddie looked up, his eyes scanning both men like an X-ray. "Listen, lads," he began, locking his fingers together on the desk. "Tonight, was a bloody mess, no way around it," Eddie continued, his eyes locking onto each man as he spoke. "But it's also proof, isn't it? Proof that we're knee-deep in something far worse than we initially thought. Emma Lane's disappearance isn't an isolated incident; it's a symptom of a larger disease on our manor."

Terry felt a shiver crawl down his spine. "So, what's the plan now?"

Eddie leaned back in his chair, contemplating the question. "We'll need to up our game. The chat with Kamil didn't go well, obviously, but it served a purpose. We know where to look and what we're up against. We'll need more information, more manpower, and, well, more firepower."

Roy shifted uncomfortably in his seat. "Are you suggesting we turn this into a full-blown war?"

"I'm suggesting we do whatever it takes," Eddie said, his voice tinged with a severity they'd heard many times before. "I'll be pulling in some favours, getting us some backup and some extra resources."

CHAPTER TWENTY-THREE

Strolling down Lillie Road, Luca couldn't miss the neon sign that yelled "Barnies." Regulars stumbled toward the pub, faces flushed and fists clenched, ready for round two. Luca hadn't been in there for years. Inside, the thumping bass was deafening, as if the walls themselves were pulsating. Over in a corner, a group of blokes eyeballed him as he walked in. One of them smirked, revealing a mouth that looked like it had had a run-in with a sledgehammer, while another puffed out his chest as if he were trying to scare off a predator—or perhaps attract a mate.

Luca had arranged to meet Micky Coomber. Upon arrival, he immediately noticed Micky seated toward the back of the bar. As he weaved through the crowd, dodging wayward elbows and half-spilled pints, a loud crash erupted. A glass bottle shattered into a million pieces near the bar; the fragments winked in the disco light like stars. The culprit laughed, his eyes narrowing at his mates in a silent dare to escalate things.

With a pint of lager already on the table, Luca settled into his seat. "Got a bit rough in here now, Mick?"

"Most of them are from the estates around here. The place is full of chavs now, not like in our day, Luca. At least we had some class when we were having a ruck," Micky replied, smiling.

Luca laughed out loud. "Years from now, this lot will graduate—ceremonial ASBOs and ankle tags in tow. Peddling cocaine so diluted, you'd get more kick from a sugar cube."

Raising his glass, Luca asked, "So, how have you been, Mick?"

"Oh, you know, the usual. Plenty of twists and turns, but I can't complain. But enough about me. What have you been up to all these years?"

Over the next hour, Luca and Micky caught up on each other's lives, sharing stories of their experiences, triumphs, and the death of Luca's wife.

As they sipped their pints, Luca asked. "It was great to catch up with some of the old crew at O'Grady's last week. Gary Hopkins and Alan Ives—that's a blast from the past. But Johnnie Billham, why does his name ring only a distant bell? I only vaguely remember him."

Micky chuckled. "Ah, Johnnie. He was always hanging around the Atlee more than anywhere else. He was never out of the place."

Luca nodded. "What was his story?"

"Estcourt Road," Micky said, taking a sip. "Lived there with his parents, which was a bit odd given we were all scrambling to get our own places at that time. Felt like he was clinging to his roots while we were all out there, eager to plant new ones."

Luca's eyes lit up with recognition. "You know what, I do remember him. He was always odd, as I recall. We were quite a group back then, causing all sorts of trouble around Fulham."

"Yeah, those were great days," Micky reminisced. "And you're not wrong about Billham; he's even weirder now. He moved out of Estcourt Road many years ago. He's turned the odd dial up a notch, if you can believe it," Micky said, shaking his head.

"When he left Estcourt Road, he found himself a flat next to my cousin Gary Cutts, on the Aintree Estate."

Curiosity piqued, Luca had heard Estcourt Road mentioned recently but couldn't remember where. "Odd? What do you mean?" Luca inquired.

Micky paused, eyes darting around like a man trying to decide between a doughnut and a diet. "Ah, where do I begin? When he left Estcourt Road, he basically left his neighbourly spirit at the door. Now, he's like a suburban Bigfoot—spotted occasionally but never truly seen," Micky chuckled. "Picture this: we're all out, right? A lads' night sprinkled with a bit of 'better halves' to keep us civilised. There's Johnnie, sitting alone in the corner, just ogling the wives. Our wives have practically formed a Johnnie watch club". As soon as he enters the room, the atmosphere thickens, and you'd think they were picking up frequencies from a ghost detector. Even Karen—and you know she's seen it all—muttered something about him having 'unhinged vibes.' I didn't even know that was a thing!" Micky took a sip of his drink, still amused. "Eccentric? Sure. But these days, he's gone from being the quirkiest bloke at the party to the one who makes you wonder if you should've brought garlic and a wooden stake, just in case."

Luca laughed out loud. "Why do you think he's changed?"

"I wish I had an answer. I suppose we all change as the years go on," Micky said, a hint of sadness in his voice. "Some say he had some personal setbacks that changed him. Whatever the reason, he's become very strange. You said you'd heard Estcourt Road mentioned recently. You probably read it in the newspapers. A girl was found murdered there just recently."

Something clicked in Luca's brain. "You know, Micky, maybe we should pay Johnnie a visit and invite him out," Luca suggested.

A smile tugged at the corners of Micky's lips. "Great idea. I think it's worth a shot. Perhaps a visit from a couple of the old gang would do him some good."

Luca and Micky made plans to pay Johnnie a visit in the coming days.

CHAPTER TWENTY-FOUR

In the back room of a builder's yard on Lillie Road, a single bulb dangled from the ceiling. Its feeble glow barely made a dent in the darkness. Shadows clung to the corners like cobwebs, unwilling to be swept away.

The air pressed down, thick and almost tangible, daring anyone to breathe too deeply. Scrap metal, wooden planks, and unopened bags of cement were piled haphazardly, forming jagged silhouettes that seemed to lurk rather than rest. Each inhalation tasted of dust and latent aggression; it was the kind of atmosphere where grudges fester and cautionary glances speak volumes. The tension knotted itself around the room, ready to snap.

Eddie Ruben's back pressed against the weathered table. His eyes narrowed to slits as they flicked from one face to another. Jimmy Adams, a hulk of a man, lingered just behind him. His hand didn't twitch, but its relaxed position over the bulge under his jacket spoke volumes. In a straight line in front of them stood Terry Gibson, Roy Knight, and six other men. Tattoos snaked out from beneath rolled-up sleeves. One had a nose that veered sharply to the left; its shape was a roadmap of past violence. Another flashed a gap in his grin every time he exhaled a smoke-clouded breath. Their eyes, icy and vigilant, darted across the room, absorbing details but revealing nothing.

These were faces that had seen the inside of a prison cell, fists that had tasted blood and asphalt, eyes that had witnessed transactions best left in the shadows. Each man was a hardened front, a chapter in a larger, grim story written on the margins of society and paid for in scars and missing teeth. The air grew heavy with the weight of their collective past, and everyone in that dim space knew what was expected of them.

Eddie roared, "Tonight, we change the fucking rules. They think they're safe behind their Shepherd's Bush shit tip? Wrong." His voice cut through the room's tension, leaving no room for doubt. A purpose-filled pause followed. "And I want that prick Kamil. I want him fucking here, tonight."

Eddie's men met his gaze, their eyes alight with the urgency his words evoked. They sensed the gravity of what awaited them: not just a raid on a barbershop-turned-underworld-hub, but the capture of a scumbag.

They had been watching the place for days, monitoring its transition from daytime respectability to a nightly den of vices—gambling in the front, whispers of sex trafficking behind closed doors. The atmosphere was charged with the promise of swift, ruthless action. They knew what needed to be done.

As Eddie's men filed out of the room, they did so with a collective air of resolute determination. Each step echoed their leader's sentiment: tonight, was a turning point. Tonight, they would finally pull back the curtain and expose the sordid activities hidden beneath the veneer of a mundane business.

Moments later, the men clambered into the vans, armed with a chilling array of pickaxe handles, hammers, and baseball bats. A pair of sawed-off shotguns lay in the darkness, silent guarantees of additional firepower. Departing the yard at 12:30 A.M., they set a course for Shepherd's Bush Road.

Twenty minutes later, one van discreetly pulled up in front of the barbershop, while the other slipped into the rear car park. The signal to move in was the back door succumbing to sheer force, quickly followed by the front door buckling under a barrage of blows. Almost instantly, the men swarmed the shop, transforming the barbershop into a whirlwind of chaos. Furniture was overturned, glass crunched underfoot, and the confined space echoed with gruff grunts and war cries. In the tumult, the ferocity and violence of Eddie's gang overwhelmed their opponents.

Jimmy Adams headed straight for the office, knowing Kamil would be hiding there. The door yielded easily under Jimmy's forceful push, and there he was: Kamil, his face flushed and his eyes wide in disbelief and fear. "Did you think you could hide forever, you fucking mug?" Jimmy’s voice was devoid of emotion, as clinical as a surgeon's scalpel.

Looking into Kamil's eyes, Jimmy felt a cold satisfaction settle within him. They had struck at the heart of the operation, and now the tremors would be felt throughout their entire network. They would all think twice before crossing Eddie Ruben again. Tonight, a message had been sent, loud and clear. And it was only the beginning.

Terry Gibson, his face a stony mask, took control of Kamil. He led him through the wreckage of the shop, a witnessed to the battle waged. Spent but triumphant, the men regrouped and retreated to their vans with Kamil in tow. They bundled into the vans, their mission accomplished, and returned to their base in the builder's yard on Lillie Road.

Now within the secluded recesses of the builder's office, Eddie loomed like a monument to grit and icy resolve. He held Kamil in his grasp, a man suspected of being a vital source of invaluable information. Committed to exposing the secrets Kamil knew, Eddie was undeterred by the cost. After Roy removed the tape and mask from Kamil's face, Eddie's steely gaze bored into him. The terror in Kamil's eyes was intense—the fear of a man cornered and outmatched. Yet, it was met with an unnerving calm from Eddie, a tranquillity more menacing than any shout. "You will tell me everything you know, you prick," Eddie began, his voice echoing in the vast expanse of the office. The demand left no room for negotiation, no opportunity for mercy. "I want every detail about your sex trafficking ring. But most importantly, I want to know what's happened to Emma Lane."

The words hung heavily in the air—a declaration of intent, an ultimatum. Kamil's terrified eyes darted around, futilely trying to escape Eddie's unyielding stare. Rumours of Eddie's firm was legendary, their repertoire of perverse methods spanned a spectrum of torment, each more disturbing than the last. Their specialty involved procedures that grotesquely mimicked dentistry, using pliers and screwdrivers for tooth extractions. Their sadism extended beyond mock dentistry; they also employed horrifying procedures involving bolt cutters, used with appalling precision for the amputation of toes, fingers, and other body parts.

The cold room echoed with the sinister harmony of silence punctuated by hushed whispers, intermittent screams, and groans. One hour turned into two as they carried out their grim tasks. Eddie watched with unwavering, icy gaze, his determination embodied in his chilling resolve.

Kamil, on the other hand, had been stripped of all bravado. His defiance was the first to crumble, worn down by relentless torture. Each passing moment, each unanswered question, eroded his resilience until, finally, he broke. The admission came in strangled whispers, laden with defeat.

It wasn't just about the trafficking—an underworld network operating in the shadows, trading lives as commodities. Kamil revealed more, his words tinged with dread as he exposed the secrets entrusted to him. More importantly, he spoke of the girls—innocents ripped from their lives and plunged into a nightmare. His voice cracked as he disclosed their whereabouts, locations until then shrouded in mystery. Among them, he confirmed, was Emma Lane. Her name hovered in the air, a poignant reminder of the personal stakes Eddie had in this relentless interrogation.

The room fell silent once more, but the revelations filled the space with an ominous weight. Eddie had achieved what he sought, breaking Kamil's resolve. The secrets lay exposed on the cold concrete floor, testifying to the grim dance between interrogator and captive.

CHAPTER TWENTY-FIVE

Sitting in his office at the Cortana Club, absorbed in reading the morning paper, Luca was interrupted by the buzzing of his mobile phone. Looking down, he was surprised to see Eddie Ruben's name on the screen. "Any news, Eddie?" he asked. His question was met with silence—a silence that suggested more complexity than any straight-forward answer could provide.

"My office, 12 Gun Street, Spitalfields, at 3 PM," was all Eddie told him. The location was familiar to Luca—a blend of old and new London—but Eddie's having an office there was new information.

Leaving Liverpool Street Tube Station at 2:30 PM, Luca walked the rest of the way to Gun Street. The Spitalfields area had recently fallen prey to the encroachment of soulless corporate developments, spreading like a plague from the west. Ugly steel and glass monstrosities clashed with the narrow streets lined with centuries-old brick buildings. Yet, as Luca turned into Gun Street, he was surprised to find early eighteenth-century houses. White marble porticoes adorned the structures, contrasting with the dark-red bricks and black railings—a welcome respite from the cold march of progress.

Standing on the steps outside Ruben's newly acquired office, he rang the doorbell. The heavy door emitted an ominous creak before chiming. The door opened, and Lola Ruben, an intoxicating blend of beauty and danger, greeted him with a smile. Her porcelain skin had a pallid quality, almost ashen, with cold sweat glistening on her forehead. She possessed a timeless allure; her imperfections only heightened her beauty. Her eyes resembled pools of iridescent blue set in a creamy visage. Luca followed her down the hallway, her silky dark hair cascading in lustrous waves over her shoulders.

Upon entering Lola's office, the pungent aroma of freshly brewed coffee wafted through the air, enveloping Luca. The room exuded a serenity that contrasted sharply with the chaos beyond its walls. Spectacular plasterwork adorned the ceilings, and classically inspired furnishings filled the space. Sunlight filtered through the room, filling it with a radiant glow more reminiscent of a luxurious home than an office.

While awaiting Eddie's arrival, Luca observed Lola delicately scanning the pages before her, her eyes tracing the words with grace. Caught staring, Luca quickly averted his gaze, embarrassed by his own audacity.

During Eddie's incarceration, Lola had deftly assembled an informal coalition of gangs—a fragile alliance aimed at expanding their control over London's most lucrative criminal enterprises. From drug and cigarette smuggling to protection rackets and prostitution, Lola played a pivotal role in shaping the city's criminal underworld. Under her leadership, the alliance became more organised, shrouded in secrecy, sophistication, and unrivalled power.

Lola avoided the spotlight, having never been convicted or even suspected of a crime. Insiders spoke of her steely charisma, her practicality balanced by a ruthlessness that rivalled her male counterparts. In Lola's eyes, the prostitution trade held particular significance. Men of high standing, be they politicians or industry magnates, inevitably sought the pleasures provided by a prostitute's company. Her brothels catered to clients from all socioeconomic backgrounds, and business flourished. In 2015, Lola unveiled Goldie's, a lavish establishment that attracted millionaires, politicians, and even international royalty.

Lola playfully blinked at Luca. "What do you think of our new office, Luca?"

"Very classy, Lola. Business must be booming," Luca replied, unable to contain his admiration.

Before Lola could respond, Eddie Ruben stormed into the room. "But it could be better, much fucking better. How are you, Luca?"

Eddie was no longer a young man, but he commanded respect —a respect born not out of admiration but fear. "I'm fine, Eddie. Intrigued to know what the meeting's about. Have you found Emma?"

"Yes, I have. However, we should take things slowly, Luca. I trust you have an appetite. I've booked a table at the Italian restaurant on Artillery Lane," Eddie said, his voice echoing with a powerful undertone.

Luca didn't really feel like eating but decided to go along with it.

Upon stepping into the bustling restaurant, Eddie's stern demeanour immediately caught the attention of a nearby waitress. His voice was coarse as he spoke. "I've made a reservation for two," he stated, asserting his presence.

Recognising his well-known persona, the waitress managed a cordial smile. "Good afternoon, Mr. Ruben. Allow me to guide you to your table," she replied, her tone striving to maintain the required decorum.

As Eddie navigated his way through the restaurant, he took in the scene around him. The atmosphere was saturated with the low hum of chatter—a backdrop of hushed conversations murmuring like an undercurrent. Each table was its own world, cocooned in a sphere of ambient light that lent an intimate touch to every interaction. To Eddie's left, was an imposing figure clad in black. The man's face was hidden in shadow, but even the obscured visage couldn't conceal his dark intensity.

Before he could ponder further, a waiter approached Eddie, deftly breaking his momentary trance. The waiter offered a polite smile and inquired about their choice of wine. After taking their drink orders, he left Eddie and Luca with a pair of menus.

Luca noticed a stocky man enter the restaurant and approach a waitress. Thinking no more about it, he studied the menu in front of him. A few seconds later, his eyes were drawn again to the man speaking to the waitress. The man had wide, hardened features that gave him a miserable look.

He left the waitress and ambled toward where Luca and Eddie were sitting. His footsteps were silent, as if the ground retreated in fear. Stopping in front of their table, he squinted and growled like a distant explosion. "Hello, Eddie. I've got a special delivery for you."

Taking a silver handgun from his jacket pocket, he tilted his head to one side and pointed the barrel at Eddie's forehead. He then pulled the trigger.

Crimson liquid flowed from Eddie's head, splattering blood onto the cream-coloured walls and floor around him.

Luca's brain stalled, every part of him frozen as his thoughts caught up. With the sounds of the day suppressed, there was only silence. This fearful interval was interrupted by the piercing screams of two women who had been laughing just moments before. Chaos ensued as pandemonium broke out, and customers scrambled for their lives. Amid the turmoil, tables and chairs crashed around Luca, and he saw a woman slip and fall face-first onto the blood-soaked floor.

Summoning courage, Luca rose and trailed the gunman. As he nudged the kitchen door ajar, he spotted the man fleeing through the exit at the rear. The man sprang onto a waiting motorcycle, which then roared away into the narrow lanes of Spitalfields.

CHAPTER TWENTY-SIX

When the first slivers of dawn crept into Luca's bedroom, penetrating the crevices of his sleep, he found himself steeped in a chaos of thoughts that refused to be stilled. The turmoil, like a whirlwind, ripped through the calm façade he so often wore. Shaking off the layers of sleep that still clung to him, he rolled out of bed with a determined sigh. He reached for his jogging bottoms and t-shirt.

Soon, he found himself facing the dew-kissed expanse of Eel Brook Common. The verdant green, bathed in the light of the early sun, beckoned him. The air was ripe with the scent of damp earth, the kind that filled one's lungs with a profound sense of life. With quiet determination, Luca stepped onto the path; his shoes crunched against the gravel, breaking the silence. He began to jog across the common, each stride purposeful and strong.

At that point, the events of the previous day were still swirling around in his head. They echoed relentlessly, their horrific reality barely fathomable. Luca found himself grappling with disbelief as he recalled the scene at the restaurant. The memory was painted in stark colours of shock and horror. As he relived the moment, he could almost smell the overpowering blend of expensive perfume, freshly cooked food, and, under it all, the faint metallic scent of blood that marked the end of Eddie Ruben. He remembered the echo of the gunshot, a gruesome note of finality to Eddie's life that sent a shudder of revulsion rippling down his spine. Such a public assassination, such an audacious display of power, was not what he had anticipated when he had left the office in Spitalfields with Eddie.

Eddie Ruben was not a man whose memory would be cherished by the police or law-abiding citizens due to his multiple convictions and alleged ties with other criminal syndicates. Yet, Eddie was on the brink of sharing crucial information with Luca, information that could have led Luca to the whereabouts of Emma Lane and helped the police locate other kidnapped girls. The pressure of finding Emma safe and unscathed was now immense, the stakes even more significant given Eddie's untimely death.

After Eddie was murdered, armed police arrived quickly, swarming the scene. After securing the area, their attention turned to Luca. Questions arose as to why Luca was in the company of one of the city's most prominent criminals at the time of the shooting. The suspicion hung heavy in the air, tainting Luca's reputation as an ex-cop. The questioning was intense, but Luca faced it with composure. He knew the risks involved in associating with someone like Eddie Ruben, but he couldn't turn his back on Grace Lane and her missing daughter, Emma. Luca knew that the lines between right and wrong blurred in the face of human complexity. Although police suspicions lingered, they found no concrete evidence linking Luca to the shooting or any wrongdoing and released him.

As Luca walked away from the police station, he couldn't help but reflect on the choices that had brought him to this point in his life. He suspected Eddie's murder was not random but orchestrated by the Eastern European trafficking gang from Shepherd's Bush. In that cramped and run-down shop, the gang's leader, Kamil, had been subjected to a ruthless pummelling. With Kamil's abduction following closely behind, Eddie's actions had undeniably infuriated the gang. Eddie's murder could be their message of retaliation, a silent vow that they would stop at nothing to guard their secrets.

Luca's feet pounded the path rhythmically, the steady beat of his jog the only sound piercing the quiet morning. His thoughts, however, were far from the serene setting around him, caught up in a tempestuous turmoil of grief and regret. Julia, her face, her voice, her laughter—everything about her dominated his mind. Again, a flash of yesterday's incident coursed through his consciousness like a rogue wave, unyielding and devastating. His heart clenched; the instinctive pangs of guilt and remorse surged through his veins like an electric shock. Yesterday was not just an ordinary day; it was a day when everything that he thought he knew about his life had capsized, leaving him reeling in the aftermath.

Now he was subject to the probing eyes of the law; their questions were piercing. Their scepticism added to the throbbing wound his life had become. He wondered where his life was spiralling toward. The familiar rhythm of his jog seemed distant now, as his life had unspooled into a path he could no longer recognise. The future, once brimming with shared dreams and laughter, now loomed ominously—a blank canvas where the colours of joy and normality had been harshly wiped off. He had lost more than just his trajectory; he had lost a part of himself that was so inherently tied to Julia. His heart, which had once beat in the rhythm of love and contentment, now echoed with the heavy toll of remorse.

Each step he took was a struggle; every breath a fight. But as he continued to jog, he understood that this was his only way to keep moving, to traverse this seemingly unending tunnel of despair, to survive. He yearned for the calm after the storm, a moment of respite in his disarrayed life. His muscles ached; sweat streaked down his face, but he pushed on. With each passing minute, each passing second, Luca was slowly shedding the skin of yesterday. The grief he was suffering over losing Julia was still there, though, as sharp as a shard of glass.

CHAPTER TWENTY-SEVEN

At 6:30 AM, his destination was a modest restaurant on King Street, in the heart of Hammersmith. When he arrived, the chill of the morning air bit into Terry Gibson's skin as he stood outside the dimly lit restaurant on King Street. He squinted, scanning the interior like a hawk surveying its prey. Inside, a dark-haired woman methodically swept her mop across the floor, lost in her routine. Her eyes met his for a brief moment, then darted away.

A silent language of urgency passed between them. Mulling over whether to trust this stranger at dawn, she hastily wiped her hands on a blue towel that had seen better days. The coarse fabric felt like sandpaper against her damp skin. Her hand reached for the door lock, her stomach knotting with a vague, unsettling foreboding.

Terry's voice broke the silence, slicing through her hesitation. "I need to deliver this to Kamil. It's really important." His words dripped with a gravity that made her veins turn icy.

Terry's eyes flickered with an unreadable emotion. Before she could extend her arm to take the holdall, he was already inside. His towering presence filled the small restaurant, eclipsing the morning light that tried to filter through the windows. "And what might your name be, my pretty lady?"

Marie's throat tightened, Terry's words seeming to hang in the air as if they had dark, palpable substance. Her eyes darted to the leather holdall at his feet, a mute enigma that screamed potential violence.

"I'm Marie. Kamil's wife. What do you want? He's not around," her voice barely above a whisper, every syllable soaked in unease.

"Just here for a chat," Terry said, his smile not reaching his eyes, making the hairs on the back of her neck stand up.

As if propelled by an invisible force, Marie's body twisted toward the back door, a path to potential safety. But before she could take a step, a scream erupted from her lips. Terry chuckled, blocking her way.

"Where you off to so quickly?"

His hand guided her shoulder, steering her into a kitchen chair with deceptive gentleness. Sitting down, she felt as though the silence itself was a tangible thing, heavy, almost crushing her. Her heart pounded in her chest, each beat a silent plea for someone, anyone, to burst through the door and end this. Eyes welling up, she let a single tear roll down her cheek. Terry leaned in, still smiling that empty smile.

"Where's Kamil?" Terry's voice cut through the room.

Marie wiped her eyes, her voice shaky. "I haven't seen him in days."

Terry turned his back on her and marched toward the front door, pausing just before exiting. "Almost forgot, Marie. Check the bag; left you a little present." His voice dripped with icy intent as he slammed the door behind him.

Marie felt her breath catch, her body tensing as if preparing for a blow. Every nerve came alive, buzzing with a sense of impending doom. She felt like a wire pulled taut, ready to snap. She gasped, each inhale a laboured effort, like sucking air through a pinhole. Her heart pounded, its beats erratic and unrestrained, echoing in her ears. The restaurant, awash in the glow of midday sun, felt unnaturally still, as if frozen in time.

Taking a hesitant step toward the leather bag, she felt a cold shiver snake down her spine. Her hands wavered in the air for a moment before she mustered the courage to pull the zipper. They were slick with sweat as she parted the leather flaps. Inside, the reality that confronted her struck like a physical blow. Her mouth fell open, her scream slicing through the suspended air, shattering the silence. Kamil's severed head stared blankly at her from the depths of the bag. She buckled at the sight, her legs collapsing beneath her onto the damp, cold floor. Kamil’s lifeless gaze, forever frozen in detached tranquillity, bored forever into her.

CHAPTER TWENTY-EIGHT

Since they last met at O'Grady's Club, Luca and Micky Coomber coordinated their schedules and found themselves standing outside Johnnie Billham's first-floor flat on the Aintree Estate. Micky's knuckles rapped against the fading door, his eyes darting uncertainly to Luca, who stood beside him. After a creaking sound reminiscent of old bones, the door reluctantly swung open, its rusted hinges offering a less-than-warm welcome.

In the muted light filtering from the hallway lamp, Johnnie emerged. Larger and more ragged than they remembered, he appeared like a living relic. As he locked eyes with Luca and Micky, every muscle in his face went taut. His widened eyes flickered, capturing the predatory glint of a hawk that had just spotted a field mouse.

"Luca? Micky?" Johnnie's voice trembled, wavering on the edge of disbelief. He paused, seemingly caught in a silent storm of emotions. His eyes darted between them as if he were trying to piece together a puzzle. "What are you doing here?" His words finally emerged, each syllable squeezed through a throat tightened by disbelief.

"We've come to see you, mate," Micky said warmly.

"Micky, good to see you," Johnnie replied, his voice tinged with rehearsed warmth.

Luca stepped in behind Micky and immediately wrinkled his nose, catching a whiff of something stale and acrid. As the three men settled onto worn-out couches, framed photos from younger days looked down on them, almost like an audience to their trip down memory lane. The atmosphere was dense with echoes of shared laughter and forgotten mistakes. But it was hard for Micky to ignore how different Johnnie seemed. An unsettling shadow clouded his demeanour, as if time had caricatured him. There was no enthusiasm in his conversations about the present, only a subdued eagerness to dwell in the past.

Johnnie leaned back, occupying more space than Luca remembered. Although his frame still carried the bulk of a man who used to command a room, it now felt ominous—fit, but uncomfortably large. And then there was his hair. It wasn't just thinning; it looked brittle, almost fragile to the touch, as if it had forgotten its original colour and substance.

His eyes told another story. They no longer danced with the joy Micky remembered; instead, they seemed to harbour a weight, like the murky depths of a once-clear lake. As Johnnie spoke, Luca couldn't help but notice his beard. It was a dishevelled mess—streaks of grey mixed with patches of colour, the occasional droplet of saliva clinging to the tangled strands. It looked as if his grooming had been abandoned midway, taken over by something—or someone—entirely different.

As Luca stared at Johnnie's face—a roadmap of a life that had clearly ventured into harsh terrain—he knew something fundamental had changed. The Johnnie of the past was nowhere to be found; in his place sat a distorted silhouette, a ghost haunting its own existence.

At times, he looked like a puzzle trying to be solved. Over-complicating things to such an extent that he himself would not understand, mostly he just stared and moved his lips without uttering a single word. Luca observed with a mixture of curiosity and unease how the man he once knew had transformed into an enigmatic figure. A sense of guarded secrecy surrounded him, shrouding his current activities in darkness while freely indulging in tales of the past. It seemed as if he had constructed a fortress of nostalgia to protect himself from any inquiries into his current endeavours.

As they talked, Luca couldn't help but detect an unsettling aura about this changed man. The once-familiar face now bore lines of mystery, and his eyes, though still retaining a glimmer of familiarity, seemed to conceal a wealth of undisclosed secrets.

The more Luca observed, the more he felt instinctively wary. This altered individual projected an air of unpredictability, leaving no assurance that he could be trusted in the company of innocent minds, like those of children. Luca and Micky, once considering him a friend, now hesitated to imagine him in the role of a caretaker for young ones. Despite the distance that now separated them, Micky couldn't help but harbour a flicker of concern for this once-familiar face, now lost amid shadows of secrecy. However, self-preservation compelled him to maintain a cautious distance, for he could not afford to expose himself or others to the enigma that this man had become.

As Luca and Micky departed, a sense of unease hovered over them. The man with whom they had shared laughter and stories was no longer the Johnnie Billham they had known. The transformation was both profound and disturbing, a grotesque metamorphosis that raised more questions than answers.

CHAPTER TWENTY-NINE

The day before her brother Eddie's funeral, Lola Ruben reached out to Luca to arrange a face-to-face conversation. She informed him that she had knowledge of the crucial information Eddie was about to disclose before his fatal shooting at the restaurant. Although wary of a physical meeting for understandable reasons, Luca agreed after Lola insisted that a phone conversation was out of the question—she suspected the police were monitoring her calls. They settled on meeting at the Bluebird Cafe on Kings Road.

The sun poured over Kings Road in Chelsea, casting a golden hue on the glass facade of the bustling cafe. As Luca stepped through the door, a dark-haired woman at the reception counter looked up, her eyes locking onto his. "Good afternoon, sir. How can I assist you?"

"I'm here to meet someone," Luca managed to say. She preempted his next words.

"And the reservation would be under?"

"Most likely, Lola Ruben."

Her lips curved in recognition. "Ah, of course. This way, sir." Luca followed her through the cafe, absorbing his surroundings. Brick walls, stripped bare and authentic, served as canvases for tasteful artwork. Seats upholstered in deep velvet hues beckoned invitingly, and chandeliers hung from the ceiling, their crystals refracting the indoor lights. It was the kind of venue that whispered Lola Ruben—a perfect blend of modern edge and classic sophistication.

Luca extended his hand across the table, and Lola grasped it firmly. As they shook hands, her eyes locked onto his, unyielding, as if pulling him into her very soul. "Discussing Eddie's murder doesn't belong in this restaurant," she declared. Her words were an iron command, yet tinged with an almost imperceptible quiver that betrayed her inner struggle.

Her eyes momentarily flickered to a family enjoying their meal at a neighbouring table before settling back on him. It was more than the devastating loss of her brother that haunted her; it was the complex empire of illegitimate businesses and hidden transactions she had inherited—an empire steeped in a legacy of crime, one she was now responsible for steering.

Reading the complexity of emotions in her gaze, Luca gave a discreet nod, the subtle movement echoing like a gavel in a silent courtroom. No more needed to be said; he had traversed similar emotional landscapes and shared her hesitancy to drag old wounds into the light.

Lola exhaled, a deep and shaky breath she'd been unwittingly holding since their eyes first met. Her shoulders visibly dropped, as if she'd just laid down a heavy burden. "I couldn't agree more," Luca responded, his voice conveying a quiet understanding that reverberated far beyond the clinking of glasses and murmured conversations around them.

Lola picked up her menu, her eyes scanning over the choices but not really absorbing them. "You know, Eddie loved this place," she said, the edge in her voice softening for the first time since they'd sat down.

Luca smiled. "He had a taste for the finer things, didn't he?"

A smile briefly crossed her lips, but it was tinged with sadness. "Always."

A waiter approached, taking their orders. The normality of the action seemed almost jarring after the weight of their earlier exchange.

Luca picked up his glass of water and took a sip. The ice clinked against the glass, a fragile melody in the space between them. "What happens now, Lola?" Luca asked, setting down his glass. "We can't pretend we're just here to reminisce about good times and old memories."

Lola's eyes darted around the room as she sipped her water, her shoulders slightly hunched. "Keeping Eddie's business afloat has been no walk in the park," she said, her voice carrying a weight that hadn't been there before. Luca noticed her clenched fist around the glass.

"He built everything we have from nothing. I owe it to him to make sure it doesn't crumble."

The tension hung in the air before Lola shifted her gaze back to Luca. "You know, before he passed, Eddie shared something with me—something about Emma Lane, the missing girl."

Luca's eyes narrowed, and he leaned in, drawn by the urgency in Lola's voice. "He thought you should know," she continued, her eyes misty but determined. "He believed you'd be the key to finding her, to giving her mother some peace at last."

With that, she slid a piece of folded paper across the table towards Luca. His fingers hesitated above the paper, feeling its weight even without touching it. Finally, he picked it up, stowing it carefully in his jacket pocket without breaking eye contact with Lola. "I hope you know what you're doing," he said, his voice laced with a mix of uncertainty and hope.

Lola leaned back, taking a slow sip of her water. Her eyes met his, unwavering. "I wouldn't be here if I didn't," she assured him.

The room was full of people, yet it felt as if they were enclosed in their own bubble of reality, far removed from the cafe chatter and clinking dishes.

"You will need to act fast," Lola broke the silence, her eyes scanning the room as if expecting someone to jump out at them any minute. "Time isn't a luxury you have."

"Alright," he said, his voice firm with resolve. Luca felt a spark of hope ignite within him. For the first time since Emma's disappearance, he began to think that maybe, just maybe, he could pull this off. But the folded paper in his pocket felt like a ticking time bomb, a constant reminder of the dangerous path he was about to tread.

As he left the café, he felt the weight of the folded note in his pocket. It was a reminder of the responsibility he had shouldered. But no matter how daunting the task seemed, he was ready to face it. Eddie Ruben may have lived in a questionable world, but he'd always held on to his moral compass. It was now Luca's turn to do the same. He stepped out into the afternoon sunshine, onto the busy Kings Road, ready to embark on a quest that would test his determination and courage.

CHAPTER THIRTY

The air in DI Rick James' office was almost too thick to breathe, saturated with the weight of unspoken secrets and haunting cases from the past. The only light that dared to enter the room flickered from a solitary streetlamp outside, casting patterns on the worn-out carpet and the face of Luca, who stood in the doorway. Luca's hand trembled as he extended it, clutching a crumpled piece of paper so tightly it seemed he might never let go. His eyes met Rick's, two stormy seas colliding in a moment of raw understanding. Finally, the paper changed hands. Lola Ruben had given Luca something more potent than a weapon—a catalogue of night-mares neatly jotted down in ink. Ten names. Ten puppet masters in an underworld ballet of human sex trafficking. Rick unfolded the paper, each crease giving way like the breaking of a cursed seal. His eyes flitted over the additional details beneath the names: addresses, phone numbers. The foulness he fought daily was now mapped out before him, each coordinate a den of unspoken horror. But there, at the very bottom, lay the crux—the location where Emma Lane and so many other kidnapped girls were held. Rick's heart pounded in his chest, each beat a tolling bell echoing the gravity of this newfound knowledge.

There was no jubilant feeling of victory, no satisfaction of a puzzle completed. Instead, a knot tightened in the pit of his stomach, a blend of sorrow and rage so potent it nearly choked him. It was as if he could already hear the ghostly voices of the stolen girls, their whispers of lost innocence drifting through the air, enveloping him in their sorrow. Yet mingled with their despair was an urgent plea for justice, for retribution, a cacophonous demand that became impossible to ignore. Rick looked up at Luca, who seemed to be battling his own inferno of emotion. Their eyes locked, and in that charged silence, they made an unspoken pact. The gauntlet was thrown, the quest accepted. The paper seemed to burn in Rick's hands, a white-hot focus for all the anger and anguish that filled the room. There would be no peace, no release, until the men on that list were stripped of their puppet strings, until every stolen girl was returned to a world less dark than the one they'd known. As the weight of the moment settled over him, Rick took a deep breath, filling his lungs with the air of grim resolve that hung heavy in the room. The time for justice had come, and the wheels of retribution were now, finally, set in motion.

Rick studied the note. He knew some of these names. He had wanted to catch these men for a long time. Emma Lane was a name that people knew. Her mother had been on TV, crying for her return. There were other names, other girls who had been taken. The room was quiet. Both Luca and Rick understood how serious this was. The note wasn't just paper. It was a chance to save these girls and a chance to put the gang away for a long time.

Luca sat across the desk, listening intently as Rick recounted the details of a disturbing recent case he had encountered. Rick told him about a girl who was taken by a sex trafficking gang. The girl's name was Elena, a 19-year-old with dreams of a better life in England. She had come from a small village in Eastern Europe, her eyes wide with hope as she arrived in the bustling city of London. Little did she know that her dreams would soon turn into a haunting nightmare. Elena remembered stopping outside a tower block, her boyfriend leading her inside a tiny flat, and then into a back room. The door locked behind her, and she was trapped. The room she found herself in was small and suffocating, with just enough space for a bed, a small table, and a chair. There were no windows, just a single bulb dangling from the ceiling, casting eerie shadows on the cracked walls. She was allowed to leave the room only for basic necessities: the shower or the toilet in the adjacent room. Her boyfriend was from Albania, a cunning man who manipulated Elena's vulnerability and trust.

He would bring her food, just enough to survive, but never enough to feel satisfied. He would tell her that her purpose was to wait for the next man, and there was nothing else she could do. The boyfriend claimed she was in East London, but she had no idea where, exactly. All she could hear were the muffled sounds of the street below, but the window was locked and barred. Days turned into weeks, and weeks turned into months. Time lost its meaning for her as she endured this life of confinement. Every knock on the door sent shivers down her spine, wondering if the next man had arrived, and what horrors awaited her.

Incarcerated in the room, hundreds of men visited and paid her boyfriend £25 to have sex with her. Men were also allowed to beat her, but most were not as aggressive as her boyfriend. He told visitors that they need not use a condom, and when she fell pregnant he punched her so hard she lost her baby.

Rick told Luca, not all the women trafficked into Britain are for sex. Another girl of eleven was exported as a domestic slave from Nigeria to North London through friends of her father. Imprisoned in their home, she was coerced into caring for three children and doing all the household chores. She worked 20-hour days without receiving a penny; she slept on the living-room floor and was never allowed outside unattended.

CHAPTER THIRTY-ONE

He had been watching her for far too long. Like a voyeur on heat, peering into her most private moments. The memory of watching her preen in front of the mirror, undressing, baring her body for her own reflection, sent a thrill down his spine. The way she took off her white lacy push-up bra, her fingers lingering on her perfect breasts, fuelled his darkest fantasies.

But beneath the facade of his infatuation, a void gnawed at his soul - a void born of loneliness, desperation, and the need for control and revenge.

Rosie represented everything he felt he lacked - beauty, confidence, and the ability to captivate others effortlessly. He now lived a life of solitude, existing day by day. In Rosie, he saw an escape, a way to fill the void in his heart and claim the beauty he felt he deserved. His obsession with her became all-consuming, driving him to the edge of sanity.

As he continued to watch her, night after night, he built an illusion of connection, weaving a web of fantasies around her.

He convinced himself that she longed for his attention, that she desired him as much as he desired her. In his mind, he was the hero of his own twisted narrative, the one who would rescue her from the world and claim her as his own.

But Rosie's life continued without interruption, her days filled with the laughter of friends, the joy of love, and the pursuit of dreams. She remained oblivious to the dark shadow that loomed over her, unaware of the extent of Johnnie's twisted obsession. One night, as the moon cast an eerie glow on Rosie's house, Johnnie made a decision that would change everything. Driven by desperation and longing, he found himself standing outside her window, his heart pounding in his chest.

Now in the dimly lit room of the small, nondescript house in Peterborough Road, Johnnie Billham crouched in the shadows, his eyes fixated on the object of his dark desire. Rosie Deane, a young woman who had captured his attention like a moth drawn to a flame, lay in slumber, oblivious to the sinister presence lurking in her bedroom.

His heart pounded with a mix of adrenaline and twisted fascination as he watched her innocent form sprawled on the bed. The oversized T-shirt clung to her curves, revealing glimpses of the white silky knickers beneath, a sight that sent shivers down his spine. He knew it was wrong, an invasion of privacy that only fuelled the darkness that consumed him, but he couldn't tear his gaze away.

In his mind, he justified his actions, convincing himself that his obsession was merely admiration, that he longed to protect and cherish her beauty from afar. But deep down, he was aware of the dangerous path he treaded - a path that led to obsession, control, and the blurred lines between reality and delusion.

Rosie Deans pouty lips, slightly parted as she slept, painted a picture of vulnerability that beckoned to his deepest desires. She looked fragile in her sleep, a vision of innocence and light, yet he could not shake the predatory feeling that consumed him. A sense of entitlement crept into his mind, convincing him that he deserved her attention, her affection, and her body.

He removed one of his rubber gloves, its skin-tight form peeling away, freeing his hand. As if it was something sacred, he reached out, allowing his fingertips to trace the contours of her sun-kissed skin. Her beauty, flawless in its perfection. It was a long-held fantasy; a dream plucked from the ether of his mind and given life. Her hair, a cascade of golden strands, had been lightened by the sun, their textures silk-like, yet possessing the warmth of fine fur. Johnny buried his fingers in the thickness of her locks, their clean scent a soothing comfort on his restless thoughts.

It felt so surreal, so perfect, that for a moment, he allowed himself to believe in the actuality of dreams manifesting into reality.

But dreams seldom stay in their tranquil state for long. The girl's eyes fluttered open abruptly, two sapphire pools reflecting shock and confusion. A piercing scream sliced through the air, the sound hammering against Johnny's eardrums. His pulse rocketed, the beat pounding like a frantic drum in his chest, matching the chaos unravelling before him.

'Get out?' she demanded, her voice a blend of alarm and disbelief.

In an attempt to pacify the situation, Johnnie forced a smile onto his face, 'I chose you from all the gorgeous girls in Fulham. Aren't you happy?' He tried to project an air of nonchalance, but his heart continued to pound a wild rhythm against his ribs.

Her response was another scream, this one even more piercing than the first. It was a distress signal that echoed off the four walls of the room, imprinted into the silent night beyond.

'Shush now,' Johnnie murmured, as he moved to cover her delicate mouth with his own. His breath hitched as their lips met, an illicit contact that sent shivers coursing down his spine. The chaos within him settled, if only for a brief moment, as he sought solace in the warmth of her lips, in the unrealised dream he was desperate to bring to life.

CHAPTER THIRTY-TWO

The dampness of the morning clung to Luca's skin as he ascended the stairs from South Kensington Tube Station. Neon lights from shop windows glanced off puddles on the pavement, but his eyes were on his phone, scrolling through unread messages. Martina and Grace were waiting at the Cortana Club, a cozy sanctuary against the urban chaos. His phone buzzed, breaking the rhythm of his footsteps. Rick. The name on the screen was a sharp contrast to the jovial atmosphere he'd been looking forward to. He pressed the phone to his ear, and before a greeting could even escape his lips, Rick's voice shattered the momentary peace. "Luca, it's happened again." His stomach sank. Rick's voice had that monotone quality reserved for tragedy—a sort of cold detachment that sounded like he was reading an obituary.

"What? Where?" His voice trembled, latching onto the dread he heard in Rick's words.

"Peterborough Road. A young woman. Butchered."

The word "butchered" slithered into his mind and coiled around his thoughts, tightening like a noose. He felt his hands go clammy, his heart rate picking up as if trying to outpace the dark reality.

"Do you know who the girl is?" Luca's voice almost cracked. A part of him wanted Rick to say yes, to offer some kind of closure.

"Nothing yet. We're still at the scene, combing through it. One thing I can tell you, though, is that it's not Emma Lane.

The lights of the Cortana Club shimmered as Luca hastened through its glass doors. His heart pounded in his chest, not from exertion but from the urgency that drove him. He barely registered the tourists and traffic pulsing around him. He made his swift ascent up the sweeping staircase to the first-floor restaurant. In the elegant dining area, the soft, intimate lighting barely touched the corners, creating a subdued atmosphere punctuated only by the low hum of conversation and the occasional clink of silverware. Martina and Grace were already chatting at a secluded table by the panoramic window, their hands wrapped around cups of coffee as they conversed in hushed tones. As Luca approached, he studied them momentarily, his gaze softening. Martina, with her dark curls tumbling onto her shoulders, looked up first, her lively eyes revealing a hint of surprise at his sudden appearance.

Beside her, Grace turned, her soft, almond-shaped eyes clouded with worry. "Sorry I'm late," he murmured, leaning in to place a brief, comforting kiss on each of their cheeks before sliding into the plush seat across from them.

His usual jovial demeanour was replaced with grim determination, his forehead beaded with sweat, betraying the anxiety he was trying to hide. Grace's gaze intensified, the crease in her forehead deepening. Luca was normally the anchor in their trio, the one who maintained a steady calm in the face of stormy waters. To see him like this—it was a signal of alarm that instantly commanded her attention. "Luca, what's wrong?" said Martina, her voice trembling slightly as she reached across the table, her fingertips just brushing his.

She watched him, trying to read the emotions behind his gaze. He had always been an open book to her, his eyes revealing the depth of his feelings, whether it was joy, sadness, or the rare occasions of anger. But now, it was different. He seemed closed off, distant.

"I'm okay, don't worry," he said, trying to offer a reassuring smile that didn't reach his eyes.

Martina didn't buy it. She had been with him through the highs and lows of life, and she knew him too well to believe that. His eyes, usually full of warmth, seemed cold, a veil of worry casting a shadow on his face. His fingers drummed nervously on the table, a clear sign that he was not okay.

She decided to press further, but was interrupted by Luca's next question. "Grace, who had been silent the entire time, have you heard any more from the police, or any other source, about Emma?"

Grace swallowed hard, trying to keep her composure. A sob threatened to escape her lips, but she pushed it down. Her voice came out as a whisper, barely audible. "Nothing. They give me an update every few days, but there's still no news."

The silence that followed was deafening. The ticking of the clock on the wall was the only sound that filled the room. Each tick seemed to amplify the sense of dread that had settled upon them. Martina watched Grace's hands clench into fists. She wished she could do something, anything, to ease her pain. But all she could do was sit there, sharing the silence that echoed their collective despair.

Luca was the first to break the silence. "We'll find her, Grace. I promise. The idea I had when we spoke last time may pay off, but I can't say any more. Just trust me," he said, his voice filled with determination.

Martina knew Luca meant every word he said. He had always been the rock in their family, the one who stepped in when things went wrong. But this time, she noticed a strain in his voice, an undercurrent of fear that she had never heard before. It scared her.

Luca turned his attention back to Grace. Her face was a mask of fear and uncertainty. Her eyes, once full of life, were dull and tired. But there was also a glimmer of hope in them, a hope that refused to die, a hope that Emma would come back to her, safe and sound.

At the heart of her relentless effort to locate her missing daughter, Emma, Grace felt the need to show her gratitude to Luca in the form of a dinner invitation. His consistent support in her desperate pursuit warranted more than just a simple thank-you. However, she was acutely aware that her proposition could be a catalyst for painful recollections, as Luca had been living in the shadow of a personal tragedy. Julia's demise had led Luca into a self-imposed exile, a solitary refuge that shielded him from the harshness of life. The warmth and vibrancy that once flowed through his household were replaced by a quiet solitude, a mirror to the profound void Julia's absence had left behind. The thought of social gatherings, especially dinners, was akin to reopening an old wound. He had come to prefer his own company to that of others, as a means of safeguarding his fragile emotional state.

But as Grace tendered her invitation, her gaze carrying a mix of hopeful expectation and empathetic reluctance, Luca found his usual reticence wavering. Something about her sincere offer nudged at his solitude, prompting him to rethink his response. In a surprise move, even to himself, Luca assented. "That would be nice," he said, his agreement accompanied by a palpable sense of unease.

Yet beneath his grief, he found a faint spark of hope, a longing for the warmth of shared companionship. His acceptance was more than a polite response; it was his first real attempt at bridging the gap between his grief-stricken past and the possibility of a happier future.

CHAPTER THIRTY-THREE

Emma clenched her jaw as another thud reverberated from above.

Her eyes darted toward the ceiling, as if expecting it to betray the identity of the footsteps. But the darkness offered no answers, only amplifying her sense of helplessness. Her hands fumbled in the black void, fingers grasping for the small shard of glass she had found earlier. Its jagged edge pressed into her palm—a sliver of control in a world that had stripped her of it. She tightened her grip, feeling a sting—a small comfort that grounded her in a reality blurred by fear and uncertainty.

A muffled clang resonated from somewhere above—metal against metal. Her heart seized in a staccato rhythm against the unwelcome silence. Was it a lock? Were they coming for her? Each heartbeat blared in her ears like a drum, drowning out distant city noise and becoming the soundtrack of her own suspense. Dread pooled in her stomach, mixing with the gnawing hunger that had become a constant companion. She missed the rhythmic sounds of the city, the predictable footsteps of her daily jog, the aroma of freshly brewed coffee, and the tactile sensation of flipping through a paperback. Those details now felt like luxuries, their absence underlining her disorienting new reality.

In the shroud of darkness, Emma's other senses had become her lifeline. She leaned slightly toward the door, straining to catch any hint of sound. Her entire body stiffened as she made out a faint, yet distinct, scuffle of feet—closer this time. The air grew dense with tension, every molecule weighted with dread. She squeezed the glass shard in her hand, her only ally in a sea of unknowns. It was a meagre shield, but she felt a sliver of courage flow through her veins. If they were coming, she wouldn't be defenceless.

She'd long since lost track of time. There were no windows, no sunlight to mark the passage of the day. Time was instead marked by the irregular rhythm of meals, scant portions of food leaving Emma's stomach aching for the comforting warmth of a home-cooked meal—a stark reminder of the life she had been violently torn away from.

Her heart squeezed in her chest; a sudden rush of emotion overwhelmed her. Emma couldn't suppress the sudden hitch in her breath as she thought of her mum—her mum, who would be alone and sick with worry. The thought of her mum, probably pacing their living room, consumed with anxiety and dread, was more painful than the cold, hunger, or loneliness. Tears streamed down her cheeks as she silently sobbed, the quiet echoes of her distress bouncing off the cold cellar walls.

But Emma knew she couldn't afford to give in to despair. She wasn't the type to sit around waiting for something to happen;

she had to act, had to escape this grim prison. She owed it to herself and her mum.

Her ears became her eyes, mapping out her surroundings through sound. Each creak of the old building, each footfall, every voice, and the jingle of keys became integral parts of her escape plan. Her creative, colourful mind now displayed a sharp contrast in black and white, signifying her present circumstances and her focused goal.

Using her slight frame, Emma began exploring the basement, crawling in the darkness. Her hands bore the brunt of her exploration, skin cracked and bleeding. Yet, she found comfort in the pain—it was a reminder of her existence, of her will to fight.

The cold metal of the stolen fork bit into her palm as she wedged its prongs between the bricks. Her muscles ached; her fingers were stained with a blend of grime and dried blood. But the pain was a footnote, a triviality.

She had found it: a loose brick hidden beside the rust-eaten boiler—a secret vulnerability in her concrete cage.

Eyes darting to the door—a slab of metal bolted tightly—she dug into the mortar, crumbling it into dust. Her heart pulsed in her ears, the rhythm syncing with each meticulous dig, each small triumph pulling her closer to elusive freedom. Her mind flitted to her mother—the unwavering pillar of strength. She could almost hear her saying, "You can do this. I believe in you." The words were a lifebuoy in a sea of despair, pulling her back whenever she felt herself drowning.

Her mother wouldn't give in; so, neither would she. Each new pocket of hollow space behind the brick emboldened her. She was crafting her own destiny with each twist and turn of the fork. It wasn't just about breaking down a wall; she was tearing down her own limitations, fragment by fragment. Visions of her mother filled her thoughts, a dreamy haze in the obsidian abyss around her. She could almost feel the tight, comforting hug that awaited her on the other side of this wall, this prison.

Her body might have been entwined in chains of circumstance, but her heart pulsed with the essence of hope and determination. She clawed out another chunk of mortar, and then another, each crumbling piece another step toward liberty. The fantasy of her mother's arms around her became her sanctuary, soothing the welts on her soul like a balm. Finally, her fork hit emptiness—a hollow sound that resonated not just through the wall but throughout her being. She paused, her body tensed like a coiled spring, her senses sharpened to a razor's edge. Could this really be it? She took a deep breath and pushed the brick. It yielded, falling away into darkness on the other side. A gateway—her gateway.

Freedom was no longer a figment of her imagination. It was real, within arm's reach, just beyond this wall. And so was her mother.

CHAPTER THIRTY-FOUR

As Luca navigated through the streams of people on New Kings Road, his steps were deliberate yet hesitant. The sun had only begun its descent, casting long shadows on the bustling road—an urban scene teeming with life yet feeling alien to him. He was headed toward Putney, to Grace's flat. An unwanted tug in his gut reminded him of the dinner invitation, a social obligation he'd rather avoid. Not because of an aversion to Grace, but because it confronted him with a hard truth: he felt guilty.

Earlier in the day, a fresh wave of grief had washed over him, as it did most days. Like a rogue wave, it toppled his defences, flooding him with memories and pain. His heart, still tender from the loss, felt branded by the unforgiving iron of guilt. He was learning to live again, but with every heartbeat, the question echoed: Was it too soon? The busy pavements felt like a gauntlet. He had agreed to this dinner, yet his reluctance clung to him like a second skin.

By the time Luca approached Grace's flat, the sun had lost its fierceness. The day was giving way to dusk, mirroring his own transition into a new phase of life. He was uncertain, guilt-ridden, but nonetheless moving forward. A firm press on the intercom button produced a deep, resonant buzz, followed by the sound of the front door creaking open. He climbed the stairs to the second floor, each step heightening his anticipation of meeting Grace.

Grace stood a few feet from her door, her anticipation mirrored in her eyes. Dressed in a plain white summer dress that subtly emphasised her slender figure, she was a picture of understated elegance. Her naturally blonde hair, smooth and radiant, cascaded over her shoulders, forming a soft contrast against her bare, tanned skin. Her ocean-blue eyes sparkled with a warm welcome as she ushered Luca into the flat—an inviting space that, like its owner, felt intimate. They walked to the living room, a room filled with carefully curated details that revealed more about Grace than any conversation could.

In a spontaneous moment, Grace suggested they have their dinner on the balcony. Their footsteps echoed in the high-ceilinged apartment as they moved their plates and glasses. From the balcony, they could see the Thames glimmering under the soft evening light, while the lush green canopy of Bishop's Park spread out across the horizon. Its tranquillity served as an ironic counterpoint to the undertow of emotions beginning to surface between them. They settled into the balcony furniture, a profound silence descending upon them. This was not merely the absence of words but the stillness of two people standing on the brink of sharing intimate sorrows, their forthcoming revelations underscored by the rhythmic noises of the bustling city.

The conversation shifted to Julia, Luca's late wife. This wasn't an abrupt change but more like a sigh finally escaping after being held in for too long. His gaze fell on his empty plate, his focus momentarily blurred by haunting memories. The silence that followed wasn't awkward—it was the necessary quiet that gives space to tragedy. He began to recount the day of Julia's fatal car crash, each word coming out slowly, as if lifting a weight off his heart. His tale filled the air, painting a picture of an ordinary day that turned into a nightmare. He remembered the phone call, the frantic rush to the hospital, the despair of loss. His usually confident voice wavered as he described his life after the accident—empty and alien, like a book with half its pages torn away.

In this atmosphere of raw honesty, Grace found herself opening up about Emma, her missing daughter. Her face, usually glowing with motherly warmth, turned pale under the lights. Words tumbled out of her in a rush, like a river of worry breaking its barriers. She expressed her frustration with the stagnant investigation, her sleepless nights filled with worst-case scenarios, and the echoing emptiness of her home reflecting her daughter's absence. Her thoughts spiralled into darker territories, touching upon the grim headlines recently plaguing Fulham: the unknown predator who had claimed the lives of five innocent girls. The unspoken question found its way into the open, her voice barely more than a whisper. She asked Luca if he thought Emma could be a victim of the same criminal.

The question hung heavily between them, a chilling proposition against the backdrop of the sinking sun. It was a harsh reality intruding into their peaceful balcony scene. Their gazes met, not in search of answers but in shared dread and uncertainty. Their individual tragedies intersected at this dreadful juncture. Silence enveloped them, each lost in their thoughts. Luca watched Grace, her eyes brimming with worry, her hands knotting and unknotting the hem of her dress. He felt a deep pit forming in his stomach, the weight of the secret he carried becoming unbearable. It was time to unburden a part of it.

"Grace," he began, his voice shaking slightly with the gravity of what he was about to divulge, "I've got some news about Emma's disappearance." Grace's eyes snapped up to meet his.

"What is it, Luca?" she asked, her voice barely above a whisper. Luca took a deep breath.

"The police have reason to believe she's still in London," he said, deliberately omitting the harsher details of Emma's situation. Grace's breath hitched in her throat.

"London?" she echoed. Hope sparked in her eyes, but it was mixed with a fear that refused to die down.

"The police are doing everything they can, Grace," he reassured her, "They will bring her home." Despite his comforting words, they did little to ease the worry etched on Grace's face.

She nodded, her gaze distant. "Are you sure, Luca?" she whispered, her hands now clenched in her lap. "Are you sure she's still in London?"

"I'm sure," Luca confirmed, again withholding the harsh reality of Emma's circumstances, knowing Grace was already on the brink.

"They won't stop until they find her, Grace. I promise."

The room fell silent, their heavy words hanging in the air. Luca watched as Grace blinked back tears, the spark of hope he'd ignited struggling against her overwhelming worry.

CHAPTER THIRTY-FIVE

Luca's gaze stayed fixed on the pub door. The Mitre, a timeworn establishment in Dawes, hosted its usual hum of chatter, punctuated by the clink of glass on wood. A shaft of fading light burst through the door as it creaked open, momentarily cutting through the dimness.

DI Rick James stepped in, his silhouette sharpened by the light, lending a sombre intensity to his appearance. He locked eyes with Luca for just a moment, the briefest of nods sealing a silent agreement between them.

"Want another one, Luca?" Rick's voice rose over the noise as he sidestepped tables and dodged people, heading for the bar.

With two pints in hand, Rick navigated his way to the table and sank into the chair opposite Luca. Their words, hushed and carefully chosen, clashed with the casual backdrop of regulars arguing about football scores and politics.

Without holding back, Luca asked, "Are you about to act on the information Lola Ruben supplied?"

“Tomorrow, 5 a.m. sharp,” Rick emphasised the time with a determined tap on the table's worn surface, the sound cutting through their quiet exchange like a judge's gavel. “We've got a solid plan to extract the victims. The gang won't know what hit them.”

Luca looked serious. His eyes squinted and his jaw clenched as they talked. Despite being in a relaxed pub, their intense conversation made it feel like they were in a different world. The creases in Luca's forehead deepened. “How's progress on the five murdered girls?” His question hung in the air like a cloud, heavy and loaded with tension.

A weary sigh slipped from Rick, his fingers creating a fortress around his pint of lager. “Still at square one,” he confessed, the edges of his voice rough with frustration. “The only thread that binds them is that they're all young, unattached women.”

Luca nodded, digesting the grim revelation. “I caught up with a couple of friends from the past recently. One of them mentioned he used to live on Estcourt Road.”

Rick's tired eyes sparked to life at the mention of the road. “Estcourt Road?” he questioned, his curiosity piqued. “Lisa James—she was found dead there. Did he say what number he lived at?”

“Number fourteen,” Luca responded. "I knew she was murdered on Estcourt Road, but the house number was kept under wraps by the media."

A murmur of interest swirled around the pub as Rick replied, a hint of shock bleeding into his voice, “Fucking hell, that's where Lisa James was murdered.”

The response caused a stir among the pub-goers; their casual conversations were silenced by the unexpectedly loud comment. Amid the hushed whispers and curious glances, Luca and Rick leaned in closer, a mutual understanding passing between them.

Rick asked, “What's this bloke's name?”

Luca replied, “Johnnie Billham. You don’t think he could be involved, do you?”

“It could be just a coincidence, but I will get someone to check him out.”

Their conversation concluded with a firm handshake, indicating their shared commitment to the cause. Rick disappeared back into the sunlight, leaving Luca alone in the ambiance of the pub. The hum of the pub filled the space Rick left behind, but Luca's thoughts were already miles ahead, thinking of the raids that were to take place the next day.

CHAPTER THIRTY-SIX

Emma's captor loomed over her, his smile warped with malice. But her deep brown eyes, wide with terror yet stubbornly resistant, bore into him. Despite the torment he put her through, he hadn't been able to quash her spirit. His twisted satisfaction faltered at her stare. Her resilience sparked a warmth within her, hope amidst the chilling scene. The man moved back towards the door, cold and predatory, eyes fixed on Emma. However, even in the grip of terror, Emma maintained her resolve. The fear was ever-present, yet it didn't overwhelm her. Rather, it fuelled the resolute spirit within her. She would fight. She would not let these men break her.

A laugh echoed through the dank basement, as the man sealed the exit with a resonating slam, sliding the bolt into place with evident satisfaction. Emma registered the subsequent ascent of the old, creaky stairs, each moaning step a cruel confirmation of her predicament. A second door sounded its closure at the top, met with the finality of another lock engaged. The ticking clock of her captivity was reset, an oppressive silence descending upon her confinement, punctuated only by the distant, muffled hum of the city. Emma counted the seconds in her mind, matching each beat of her heart with the tick of an imaginary clock. The number she sought was three hundred, a cautious five minutes had passed.

Her wait completed, she crawled in the murkiness of the basement. Her fingertips traced familiar paths over the icy concrete floor, the chill seeping through her palms and into her bones. Unseen obstacles that were previously noted were deftly avoided until her touch encountered the rough, flaking surface of the old boiler. Beneath its belly, a small hollow concealed her makeshift tool. Grasping it gingerly, she felt the familiar, cold tines of the concealed fork in her hand, a symbol of her resilience in the face of her dire circumstances. The irregular edge of the metal utensil bore the tell-tale signs of frequent use, indicative of her effort.

Positioning herself beside the brick wall, Emma resumed her painstaking endeavour, each scrape of fork against mortar a whisper of defiance. The wall, once a formidable barrier, now bore an emerging breach, each removed brick a witness to her determination. Behind that wall, the ambient hum of traffic persisted, a constant reminder of the bustling world lying just beyond her grasp. Emma carried on, her hands raw and aching, her spirit unbowed. Every brick, every scrape and every jarring sound of a dislodged chunk of mortar was a piece of her path to freedom.

Emma's concentration was unyielding as she aggressively attacked the brick wall. Every swing of her arm, every scrape of her tool, resonated with an urgency that echoed off the confined space. The rough texture of the bricks abraded her fingers; the persistent dust irritated her throat.

Just as she was about to pause and rest, a sharp gust of cold air hit the back of her hand. Her heart leapt into a sprint in her chest, the unexpected chill bringing an instant rush of adrenaline. Spurred on, she drove her tool into the bricks with renewed vigour. One brick completely gave way to her assault, crumbling into a shower of dust and debris. Her hand immediately shot through the hole, clawing at the brick dust, her curiosity morphing into astonishment.

Now, a hole was revealed where a brick once was. Peering through the ragged opening, Emma could see the world outside. The once faint hum of traffic that barely permeated the wall now escalated in volume. It filled her ears, punctuated by honks and engines roaring to life, their sounds no longer muffled by brick and mortar.

An invisible tide of anticipation surged within Emma. Another brick shifted, scattering fragments onto the dank floor. She stifled a gasp as another loosened, bringing her closer to freedom. Every trembling brick took her a step further from captivity. The sharp taste of dust scratched her throat, but she embraced it, a stark contrast to the stale air she had grown accustomed to.

Her palms planted firmly on the floor, every callus and scar evidence of her relentless effort. With a deep inhale, she mustered her strength, then kicked out. Her boots met the weakened wall with an echoing thud, shaking the foundation. The bricks cascaded onto the floor like a waterfall.

The resultant rush of air was a punch to her senses, yet it was a blow she welcomed. It tasted of wildflowers and rainstorms, a stark contrast to the damp mildew she had grown accustomed to. The gust brought her an affirmation, sweeping away the heavy atmosphere that had been suffocating her for weeks.

Gathering herself, Emma crawled through the gap. She grazed her elbows and knees against the rough edges, but the scrapes were badges of honour, symbols of her strength and resilience. Each move took her further away from her concrete prison, closer to the world she had longed for. The space was tight, but it felt as though she were moving through a gateway, from a place of constriction to one of boundless possibility.

Her first sight was the expansive sky. It was a canvas painted with the fading hues of a setting sun, a spectacle she had only envisioned in her dreams. She inhaled deeply, filling her lungs with the fresh air that smelled of liberation. The fragrance of blooming flowers intertwined with the crisp scent of the approaching night. As she rested on the ground, her muscles trembling from exertion and emotion, she realised that she had done it. The fear and despair that had once been her only companions were now replaced by exhilaration and anticipation for what awaited her in this newfound freedom. For the first time in a long while, Emma felt truly alive.

At the narrow alley's end, a massive barrier emerged. A door, constructed of cold metal, proved to be an unexpected dead end. Escape was futile in that direction. Wheeling on her heel, she sped back along the path from which she had just come, feeling the threatening vibrations of the sounds with each pounding step. Meeting her at the alley's exit was a staircase. Wooden steps, each one bearing the weight of time and disregard, lay before her, leading upwards. Framing her path were walls, a canvas of rusty pipes contorting and coiling in unsettling angles. Each step she took was a negotiation with the treacherous terrain, and the staircase offered no mercy.

Reaching the top, relief was snatched away when a figure lunged forward. A member of the gang. His arms ensnared her like steel traps, cutting short her brief taste of freedom. His eyes were not the welcoming light of solace but the ominous glow of wrath. A visible scar marked its territory down his neck's right side. Its unusual colours of pearl white intertwined with pastel pink were jarring against the mottled skin surrounding it. The off-key discolouration suggested a botched healing process, a grim reminder of the man's capacity to withstand pain.

The lines etched onto his face weren't the wrinkles of time, but the brutal witness of a joyless existence. His face wasn't the flushed red of embarrassment or exertion, but the angry crimson of unchecked rage. With an iron grip, he began to drag her. Each step towards it was a march towards uncertainty. The events of her day were not just a string of unfortunate coincidences but a cruel test of her will to survive. It was not the end, but perhaps, a horrific new beginning.

Emma found herself pulled into a landscape of coarse grey pebbles, the unexpected rough texture scratching against her palms. A scream was ripped from her throat, raw and primal, echoing sharply across the otherwise deserted car park. Without warning, the blaring sound of screeching tires reverberated in the air. A large, black vehicle, gleaming ominously under the streetlight, skidded with reckless abandon and came to a halting stop just a few feet away. The car was a beast of steel and rubber, its engine still growling, a prelude to the terror that was yet to come.

As the dust settled, two figures emerged from the vehicle, their silhouettes imposing against the car's reflective surface. With chilling timing, they advanced on Emma, their hands closing in on her with a sureness that only fed her panic. Their grasp was steel against her skin, devoid of mercy. Emma's captor readily yielded her, a transaction as cold and calculated as the car park's chilling wind. Behind her, the car's boot creaked open, the mechanical sound punctuating her unceasing screams.

The men, with an efficiency that was terrifying in its own right, crammed Emma into the tight, dark space. Her head brushed against the cold metal interior of the boot, her wails bouncing off its confines as the boot door slammed shut, plunging her world into darkness.

CHAPTER THIRTY-SEVEN

In the pre-dawn gloom of 3:00 A.M. Seasoned police officers assembled in a secure room at Victoria Station for a crucial briefing. Their rendezvous had grave importance: to map out a systematic plan for dismantling a human sex trafficking syndicate implicated in transporting underage girls to various European destinations. The police aimed to execute six synchronised raids across London. The strategic importance of simultaneous action was to prevent any leak of their impending arrival, thereby increasing their chances of success.

The room was dim, the faces stern, lit only by the blue glow of the projector screen. Maps and photographs were displayed—addresses, faces, evidence—all scrutinised by each veteran officer in the room. "Remember, timing is critical," the lead officer's words sliced through the silence. "One leak, and we're back to square one. Lives are at stake." No one dared break the tension in the room.

By 4:00 A.M. The room emptied as quickly as it had filled. Riot helmets on, vests secured, batons and shields in hand, the officers dispersed. Their footsteps were hurried yet hushed, reverberating in the empty hallways. They climbed into their vans, each vehicle a fortress on wheels, prepared for chaos.

Outside, the city slept, oblivious. Streetlights flickered as the vans roared through the deserted roads, each directed towards a different map point. Their purpose was singular, their focus razor-sharp; there was no room for error. Inside one of the vans, Officer Sarah Mitchell adjusted her grip on her riot shield. Her mind swarmed with the faces of the girls they aimed to save. Her heart rate accelerated, each beat punctuating the seconds ticking away. "Team 3, approaching target," the radio crackled in her ear, briefly pulling her from her thoughts. Other updates followed: "Team 1 in position," "Team 4, two minutes out," "Team 2, one minute away." Sarah felt the van slow, her body swaying with the shift in speed. She tightened her grip around her baton, adrenaline flooding her mouth. This was it—no room for hesitation. The radio buzzed its final call: "All teams, on my mark." A pause that felt endless. Amid escalating tension, the radio broadcast the long-anticipated command, "Strike, strike, strike." The phrase, though brief, was loaded with urgency, propelling the officers into immediate action.

Speed was crucial. Knowing that suspects might dispose of critical evidence like mobile phones, the officers moved with calculated swiftness. The still morning broke abruptly: van doors flung open, dawn's silence shattered. They moved in synchronised chaos: breaking down doors, swarming rooms, shields up, scanning for threats. This was their moment, weeks of planning culminating in seconds that counted. For Sarah, the faces in the photos transformed into those before her—scared, hopeful, alive. The weight of the mission bore down, matched by the weight of their gear and their resolve. No turning back. Lives balanced on a precipice between nightmare and salvation. And for a moment, as Sarah locked eyes with a young girl they'd come to rescue, grim satisfaction cut through the tension. The message was clear: this ends today.

But achieving their immediate objective was only half the story. In hidden, squalid captivity, the officers unearthed a darker reality that defied description. Eleven young women, aged from a tender 15 to 25, were rescued from barely habitable conditions. Trash littered the floors; the stench of decay filled the air.

However, the operation didn't conclude entirely as planned. One suspect had escaped abroad before the crackdown. Two other individuals remained elusive, triggering a comprehensive manhunt. The apprehended suspects were taken to separate detention facilities, following protocols to ensure the integrity of future interrogations. Communication among the captives was scrupulously avoided to preserve the sanctity of collected evidence.

Back at the raided locations, investigative teams arrived, cloaked in sterile white suits. They meticulously scoured every square inch of the premises. Fingerprints, DNA traces, and other physical evidence were sought to tie suspects to their heinous acts. Digital forensic experts navigated through confiscated electronic devices, piecing together a coherent narrative that now had an international dimension. By the time the first rays of sunlight pierced the city, nine individuals were in custody, a complex web of crime beginning to unravel. Every passport checkpoint, border crossing, and airport went on high alert, part of an intricate web of surveillance. The story was far from over, but the first critical steps had been taken.

CHAPTER THIRTY-EIGHT

Luca gripped the armrests of his seat in the Cortana Club. His jaw clenched and unclenched, a physical manifestation of the unease churning inside him. Conversations buzzed around the room, people laughing and talking, oblivious to the gravity of the moment. To Luca, their voices sounded like a muted television in the background, drowned out by the persistent ticking of the clock on the wall. He glanced at his watch for the twelfth time; the seconds seemed to crawl. Across the room, the door opened, and Rick entered, scanning the crowd. When their eyes met, Rick gave a slight nod. Luca's heart leapt into his throat. Now he would find out if Emma and the other girls had been freed or if the risky strategy he'd been part of had cost them their lives.

As Rick approached, Luca sensed a disturbing shift in the atmosphere. The lines on Rick's face, each a witness to past skirmishes, seemed to deepen. When Rick finally settled into the chair opposite him, his eyes lacked their usual fire, as if life had siphoned away his intensity. "Operation's over," Rick's voice rasped, akin to a shovel on rocky soil. Silence stretched between them, carrying unspoken burdens. "We've lifted the gang."

Exhaling, Luca allowed a sliver of relief to pass through him.

“However,” Rick hesitated, letting the word “however” loom between them, weighted like a pendulum about to fall. “Emma Lane remains missing.”

Instantly, the budding relief in Luca was snuffed out, replaced by a hollow pit in his stomach.

“Listen,” Rick's tone was even, edged with a tightness that bordered on anger. “We had an address in East London. Stormed the place; it was empty. No gang members, no Emma. A hole near the basement's boiler caught our attention.” His eyes locked onto Luca's. “So now we're unsure—did she manage to escape, or did they move her? We're in the dark, Luca.”

Luca stood up, a sudden jolt of energy surging through him, almost electric. He couldn't just sit here, marinating in a blend of frustration and dread. Emma was out there, somewhere. His gut churned at the thought.

His phone buzzed, an unwelcome interruption. It was a text from Grace: “Any news?”

His fingers hovered over the screen. What could he say? That they were at a standstill? That hope was a flickering candle in a tempest? Instead, he typed: “Still working on it. Stay strong.”

He pocketed his phone and grabbed his coat. Its weight offered no comfort; instead, it felt like a shroud, draping him in the gravity of the situation.

As they stepped into the corridor, Luca looked back at the room they'd just vacated. It remained a silent witness to their despair, its emptiness echoing the void they were all stuck in. But an idea flickered to life in the back of his mind—Rick had said the house was awaiting refurbishment. That meant records, workers, perhaps even a stray observation that had slipped through the cracks. Luca was already heading toward the door, his gait heavy but purposeful. Rick caught up to him, tapping him on the shoulder. “Are you okay?”

Luca responded, “Mind if I take a look at Swanfield Street? Maybe there's something your team missed, something minor that didn't seem important at the time.”

Rick looked at him, his eyes searching Luca's face. It was as though he was weighing the sanity of holding onto strands of hope so thin. After what seemed like an eternity, he nodded. “Fine. But be careful, alright? We don't know what we're dealing with.”

Luca felt a knot of tension he hadn't even realised was there start to unspool. It wasn't much—a sliver of opportunity, a flicker of light in the dark—but it was something. And right now, something was all he had to hold onto.

CHAPTER THIRTY-NINE

Johnnie was alone in the front room of the dilapidated Victorian house, which was in his builder's yard, on Munster Road. The quietness of the room seemed to mirror his own deep loneliness, which had grown stronger since his mother passed away. Each thing in the room reminded him of her. They made a sort of living memorial to the woman who was once his whole world. Now, these objects were the only real connection to her that he still had. The room was a sanctuary, a buffer against the relentless sting of his mother's passing, his solitude, and the world's misunderstanding of him.

Aged and frequently handled books filled homemade shelves, acting as Johnnie's solace in the unsettling silence that followed his mother's death. Their presence provided him a small sense of relief amidst the intense vacuum of her loss. Johnnie lingered in the shadowed corner of his personal library, a dark warren where discoloured pages told of forgotten horrors. He traced a crooked finger over worn-out leather spines, each etched with the traces of a disturbing history. His eyes, dull yet intense, sparked to life as they fell upon one particular title - a leather-bound chronicle of the Third Reich's unthinkable inhumanity.

Sinking into his worn leather armchair, Johnnie opened the grim book, his icy gaze drinking in the black and white photographs, the dense, clinical text. The graphic depictions of torment didn't repulse him; instead, they filled him with an unsettling fascination, a hunger to delve deeper into humanity's darkest corners. With each turn of a brittle page, Johnnie's lips tightened, his eyes narrowing as he was transported to concentration camps, the gas chambers, the agonising screams echoing through the silent library. Each meticulously documented account, each raw portrayal of sadistic cruelty added another layer to the intricate puzzle he was obsessed with.

On the adjoining shelves, a myriad of volumes narrated tales from remote corners of the world where civilisation was but a distant echo. Stories of indigenous tribes engaging in cannibalistic rituals filled the air with a heavy aroma of horror and fascination. Unsettling illustrations of body parts adorned some pages, while detailed accounts of ritualistic sacrifices filled others. Johnnie's fingers would often linger on these pages, absorbing the tribal markings, the savage acts, the raw animalistic nature of man stripped bare of society's facade. It was as if he were trying to understand, to dissect the barbaric nature of these acts, to comprehend what drove men to such extremes. On the other side of the room, a massive mahogany desk stood, stacked high with meticulous sketches of human anatomy. Each line was drawn with a chilling precision, a cold detachment. Johnnie had an unusual fixation with these drawings - the sinewy muscles, the complex network of veins, the skeletal framework. The weak light in his eyes mirrored his exploration into the murkier aspects of human nature. Late into the night, he would pore over these sketches, tracing the curves of bones, studying the intricate mapping of veins, and the interlocking puzzle of the human skeletal system. His obsession was more than mere curiosity. There was an unsettling calmness in his examination, a disturbing familiarity with the human body, a man comfortable with the morbidity of death.

Johnnie's world was a chilling masterpiece of humanity's darker shades. It was not a space of comfort or warmth, but a shrine of twisted fascination, a testament to the human capacity for evil. Each book, each sketch served as a disturbing portrait of a man who, though living amongst us, inhabited a far darker and more sinister realm. His dishevelled builder's yard, a mirror to his life, sat as a silent observer of the world, oblivious to Johnnie's solitary existence. People who knew him gossiped about his eccentricity and peculiar habits. To them, he was an outsider, immersed in his own universe. But within his refuge, their chatter barely penetrated. Johnnie was a man drawn towards the grim reality's others chose to avoid. But within his unconventional reality, he discovered comfort. Surrounded by his mother's keepsakes and macabre tales, he unearthed significance in his solitude, his grief, and his existence.

Since the visit to his flat on the Aintree Estate from Luca and Micky Coomber, Johnnie found himself thinking of them continuously. Their presence persisting like the persistent hum of a broken fridge. His mind was a foggy battleground, dotted with the dark silhouettes of paranoia, trepidation, and envy. His thoughts constantly spiralling out of control, like mice scampering in a maze with no exit. The well-worn leather chair beneath him no longer offered the familiar comfort; instead, its touch felt cold, almost hostile. Every noise from the outside world seemed magnified; every creak of the old house sent adrenaline coursing through his veins.

He attempted to picture Luca and Micky, but his mind transformed them and distorted their images into grotesque versions of themselves. Their faces, twisted and unrecognisable, would appear in his thoughts uninvited. His imagination, running unchecked, gave life to the gruesome scenes he painted of them. Johnnie found a dark satisfaction in these images. He could see himself looming over them, a twisted smile playing on his lips. The rich, metallic scent of their blood was intense, staining his hands and the pristine white of his shirt. It was a twisted spectacle, one that he was both the orchestrator and spectator of it.

The laughter—it echoed through his mind—chilling, devoid of any warmth. It was him laughing, a sound that held no joy but was filled with triumph and relief. Through this torment, Johnnie lost track of days, each one indistinguishable from the other. He was trapped in a cycle of his own making, the lines between reality and imagination blurring. His mind a theatre of grim fantasies, casting long, unshakable shadows that tainted his reality. He felt himself sinking deeper into this abyss, the grip of his turbulent thoughts pulling him under.

CHAPTER FORTY

Luca exited Liverpool Street Tube Station, his eyes narrowing as he adjusted to the afternoon light. He navigated through the hustle and bustle of city life, his mind focused on Swanfield Street. He had to see where Emma had been held captive; intuition told him there was something everyone else had missed. After a brisk walk, he reached Swanfield Street. Number 12 stood out like a sore thumb; it was the only house with a skip cluttering its front yard.

Luca circled to the back and found the kitchen door ajar. He stepped inside, his shoes crunching on shards of glass from windows long since broken. Plywood boards had replaced the missing panes, splotched with damp and darkened by rot. The air hung heavy with neglect, pierced only by thin shafts of sunlight struggling past tattered, cobwebbed curtains.

He moved carefully over the floorboards, each step accompanied by a disquieting creak. Dust swirled in the air as his shoes disturbed the untouched surface, lifting for a moment before settling back down, as if the house itself had sighed in resignation. It was a place abandoned by time yet recently disturbed, making Luca's skin crawl. As a former Detective Inspector, he knew that clues often hid in plain sight; he couldn't afford to overlook anything.

In the abandoned house's skeletal framework, Luca moved with deliberate precision. A grim determination was etched on his face, like a hunter painstakingly tracking elusive prey. The traffickers had been there, and so had Emma. He clung to that shred of hope, willing it to lead him to her.

Rick's words echoed in his mind as a stark reminder of their fruitless efforts so far. The forensics team had already combed through this place, their white-suited figures a haunting contrast to the home's otherwise dilapidated state. They had scraped and bagged potential evidence, hopeful for any trace of human touch. But they had come up empty; the traffickers were proving as elusive as ghosts.

The silence in the house taunted him, amplifying the distant sounds of the city. Now armed with a tangible lead, Luca rose, his gaze fixed on the ticket. It was a game of the senses, and he relied on his intuition as much as his training. Every room he inspected was a barren shell, stripped of life, much like Emma's sudden disappearance. But frustration didn't deter him. If anything, it sharpened his resolve, hardened his gaze, and tightened his grip on determination. He knew the world of crime was a labyrinth of dead ends and false leads, a game of shadows and whispers. He was ready to navigate that maze, ready to tear down walls if necessary.

The house might not have yielded its secrets to forensics, but Luca was betting on a different outcome. Armed with unwavering determination, he delved deeper into the grim puzzle that was the house, his mind laser-focused on the task at hand.

Luca completed his meticulous sweep of the house's grim interior. His steps echoed on the empty wooden floorboards as he emerged from the back door into the cluttered car park. Years of neglect had allowed weeds to grow unabated throughout most of the area.

Methodically, he crouched down, his knees sinking into the gravel that crunched under his weight. His hands sifted through the litter: bits of broken glass, discarded bottle caps, and countless unidentifiable fragments. His eyes, sharp and focused, picked out a thin slip of paper wedged between two rocks. Extracting it from its hiding place, he noticed it was a District Line Tube ticket. Flipping it over, he saw a hasty scribble, rushed as if time had been of the essence.

This newfound clue painted a broader picture, hinting at the possibility that the ticket's owner knew they were being followed. It also suggested an escape plan involving the Underground. A city as vast as London provided an easy opportunity to blend in and disappear among the crowd.

Now with a tangible lead, Luca rose from his position, his gaze fixed on the ticket. The quiet hum of the city seemed to fade as he considered his next move. His fingers traced the address one more time before tucking the ticket safely into his jacket pocket. Luca exited the backyard, the crunch of gravel under his shoes echoing his departure.

Luca headed to Liverpool Street Tube Station, his mind racing with the possibilities awaiting him in Earls Court Square. Each new development was another piece of the puzzle, another step toward solving Emma's disappearance. A jigsaw of clues sprawled in his mind, each fresh piece bringing him closer to a resolution. Emerging from the bowels of Earls Court Station, the afternoon light greeted him, a stark contrast to the dank, dimly lit tunnels he had just left behind. The London summer sun imbued everything with a glow, casting long shadows on the streets of busy Earls Court Road.

Earls Court Square is an architectural blend of stuccoed terraces adorned with Italianate dressings and purpose-built apartment blocks. Luca absorbed the setting, its details filing away in the meticulous mental library that came naturally to his ex-detective mind.

The address he sought was a large house, distinguishable from its neighbours only by its boarded-up windows. Strolling past the address, he appeared casual, but beneath the guise of leisurely indifference, his eyes took in every detail: the weather-worn door and the chipped paint on the window sills. Luca spotted tell-tale signs of recent activity and comings and goings. The basement flat was not the end of his journey, but it was a significant step—a lead that held the promise of opening doors and answering questions. He wanted to enter the flat then and there, but he knew he would have to return later that evening with help. And he had no intention of involving the police.

CHAPTER FORTY-ONE

The key grinds against the lock, a piercing noise reverberating throughout the room. Each metallic scrape jolts Emma's pulse, amplifying the pounding in her head. Her gaze sweeps the space, locking onto chipped paint and stained floors. The air itself feels oppressive and weighted. Above, a lamp from another era dangles; its meagre light contorts into ghoulish forms on the walls. A white bucket sulks in one corner, its mere presence an affront to the concept of hygiene. The absence of windows suffocates her, sealing her off from the world.

The distant rumble of tube trains serves as her only lifeline, yet it drones on monotonously, deepening the pit of silence. Memories flood in uninvited: the dark compression of the car boot, muffled voices, and jeering laughter.

Forty minutes, she guesses, but time lost meaning in that confined space. Her ears tingle, catching a distant stir of activity. The sounds are too faint to decipher—a whisper, a footstep? Yet they exacerbate her isolation, leaving her teetering on the edge of dread. She's alone, but not completely. Someone, or something, is near. And it's coming closer.

The heavy thud of footsteps begins to punctuate the air, each step growing louder and closer. Emma's breaths grow shallow. Her hands tighten into fists, her nails digging into her palms. She glances at the door, studying its flimsy structure. It's old and decaying, but probably strong enough to keep her inside. The footsteps halt abruptly. Silence envelops the room again, leaving Emma in a void of anticipation. Her mind races: Is it better for the door to open or to remain sealed in this tomb of uncertainty? Her heart doesn't seem to care; it drums an erratic beat, a cacophony of fear and adrenaline.

A muted conversation seeps through the door. Two voices—foreign, gruff, and low, yet undeniably human—speak in clipped tones. Their words slip past her like vapor, leaving only a chilling sense that decisions are being made and plans formulated. Then a short laugh, devoid of warmth, punctuates the dialogue. The lock rattles. This is it. Her stomach lurches, as though falling through emptiness, and she braces herself.

The door swings open, its rusty hinges squealing in protest. A sliver of hallway light invades the room, cutting through the darkness and settling on a figure in the doorway. He steps in, a silhouette framed by the feeble light, his eyes hidden beneath the shadow of a brow. Emma can't make out his features, but she doesn't need to; the tension in the room merges around him, becoming a real entity. He glances around the room, then locks eyes with her. For a split second, she thinks she detects a flicker of something—remorse? No, it vanishes as quickly as it appeared, replaced by an unsettling calm. "Comfortable?" he says, his voice almost casual, as if inviting her for a walk.

He leaves the room and locks the door. The absurdity of normality in a situation so twisted tightens her throat. Yet she realises that the room, grim as it is, offered a measure of predictability—a known confinement. Whatever comes next is a descent into an even darker unknown.

She shrinks back against the thin, lumpy mattress wedged in the corner. The room closes in on all sides, making her feel cornered. Dank air clings to her like a second skin; the smell of damp stone and rotten wood permeates her clothes and hair. The room is silent except for the noises typical of an ancient, decaying house. A single drop of water echoes at regular intervals, beating an uneven rhythm against the floor. Emma counts the drips in her head; it's all she has to count. This room offers no comfort, just a mattress that is more dirt than fabric. Yet, this is her only reality now; her world has shrunk to the confines of this stifling space. Her skin tingles from the cold, her senses are filled with the musty scent, and her ears strain for any hint of what might be happening above. Emma is not just in the room; she is becoming part of it.

With her muscles trembling from hours of immobility, her lips form a silent prayer, each whispered word a plea for her mother, Grace. She imagines the worry lines deepening around her mum's eyes, the fear choking her. Emma stifles a sob as the reality of her situation washes over her like a merciless tide. Is she terrified? Yes, but more than that, she is determined. Emma raises her chin and takes a deep breath. She is not a victim, not yet. It's a mantra she clings to, a glimmer of hope against the encroaching darkness.

CHAPTER FORTY-TWO

Luca and his brother Franco stepped out of the Cortana Club, the clock striking 2:00 AM. Their minds bore a singular, rigid focus: Emma Lane's rescue from the house on Earls Court Square. For Luca, an ex-Detective Inspector in the Metropolitan Police, the surreal nature of the mission was not lost on him. The prospect was a far cry from the procedural constraints he worked with up until he left the Met. Yet, never in his wildest dreams had he envisaged himself in this role again.

The car boot held tools for a different kind of justice: a heavy sledgehammer, a pair of baseball bats, and a solitary smoke bomb. Packed alongside these unconventional tools were balaclava masks—a stark reminder of the unorthodox route Luca had chosen. Franco wore an uncharacteristic spark of anticipation in his eyes. His almost palpable eagerness, confined within the car, added another layer of complexity to the task ahead. Their mission, fraught with ambiguity, uncertainty, and potential danger, began under the indifferent cloak of night.

At forty-nine, Franco is the eldest of the three siblings. While Franco lacks the physical allure of Luca, his business acumen sets him apart. Known as the 'Bull' amongst friends and family, his massive frame and steadfast courage warrant this nickname. Whether in business or personal matters, Franco plunges into any situation with unbending bravery. His protectiveness has been a constant, ever since he, Luca, and Martina were kids. With a gaze as dark and profound as the night sky, Franco can strike a chord more terrifying than an agitated lion with just one look. He's a towering figure at six feet four, with broad shoulders that lend him an imposing presence. Despite his intimidating appearance, Franco possesses an unexpected soft side, reflected in his full lips that upturn at the corners. Although the intention may be sternness, the resulting expression is endearingly kind. His company is refreshing and engaging, filling any room he steps into with life. Franco's intelligent humour and quick wit never fail to entertain. However, beneath his jovial exterior lies a loyal and warm heart—a rock his family can always lean on. But God forbid, should anyone wrong him or his family, they would have to face the wrath of the Bull.

Luca and Martina are vaguely aware of Franco's ties to certain other Italian families in London, but it's a topic that's generally avoided. Franco, even from his youth, has always made a point to confront his fears, not shy away from them. To him, facing fear isn't just an act of bravery—it's a necessary step towards progress in life.

At 2:15 AM, their car came to a quiet halt on Earls Court Square. With no one around, they slipped out, and opened the boot of the car. Luca's eyes, bloodshot from the day-long stakeout, studied the house. He knew two men spent their time in the front room on the first floor. Emma's location, however, remained a mystery. The once-grand house now sagged in disrepair, forming a foreboding silhouette against the night sky. The house loomed over them, its decline presenting an ominous facade. With each tick of the clock, the stakes for Emma rose. Luca felt the adrenaline in his veins, a tangible sign of urgency rather than fear. Luca tested the boarded window in the basement; it gave way easier than expected. Luca was the first to breach the eerie stillness inside. The cold, stale air held an oppressive quality, wrapping around him in an unwelcome embrace. Franco soon followed. With caution dialled up to the maximum, they manoeuvred through the intricate layout of the house, every sense on high alert for the faintest disturbance.

Luca found Emma quivering with fright in the second room he checked. Her vulnerability affected him deeply, but he set his emotions aside. Time was a luxury they couldn't afford. He knelt next to her, whispering, "My name is Luca, I'm a friend of your mother. We need to leave now."

Emma's eyes, filled with fear yet showing a flicker of hope, met his. As she clung to him, Luca felt an overwhelming need to protect her from the terror that ensnared her. Guiding her with gentle determination, he directed her towards their exit.

Their escape was interrupted by a menacing voice: “Leaving so soon?” Panic tightened around Luca's heart as two large men blocked their path. The eyes of the two men burned with a potent mix of venom and challenge. “Did you really think it would be that easy?”

The words dripped with scorn. “Did you believe you could fucking stroll in here and take the girl? You got no chance.”

Attempting to maintain control, Luca snapped back, "Look, I have no interest in a fight. Allow us to go and our paths need never cross again."

The man on the left barked, "First give us the girl. Then we might consider letting you leave with your face intact."

Emma, in response, gripped Luca even tighter, her body shivering with terror. Despite their fear, Luca stood firm; the defiant look in his eyes was an unspoken promise that he wouldn't be intimidated.

Suddenly, a roar echoed from behind. Franco, who had manoeuvred himself to the rear of the men, swung a baseball bat with all his might. One of the men crumpled to the ground, caught off guard by the surprise attack. Seizing the moment, Luca lunged forward, driving his fist into the other man's jaw with calculated precision. The second man collapsed, knocked unconscious by Luca's powerful blow.

With Emma secure in the back of the car, Luca's foot pushed down hard on the accelerator. Streetlights flashed past as the car cut through the night, the harshness reflected in Emma's wide and fearful eyes. St. Stephen's Hospital loomed in the distance. Emma curled up, arms wrapped protectively around herself. Her skin was ashen, her breath uneven. Luca stole glances at her, his jaw set with concern. Luca picked up his phone, the screen casting an eerie glow onto his stern features. Calling Rick James, Luca held the phone to his ear and waited for the gruff voice on the other end. "Two men down and injured," Luca's voice was succinct and unemotional.

He gave the address in Earls Court Square, pausing for a moment to let the gravity of the situation sink in. There was no room for misinterpretation, no room for unnecessary details.

Franco parked in a side street next to St. Stephen's Hospital. Relief washed over him, but there was a new challenge to face—explaining the night's circumstances to the medical staff. Emma, however, remained quiet. She didn't question who they were, and didn't protest when Luca gently guided her out of the car and towards the hospital's entrance. She was in shock, but she was safe. The automatic hospital doors slid open as they approached, the bright fluorescent lights a stark contrast to the dark world they had just left behind. Franco, lagging behind for a moment, properly parked the car and followed them inside.

The receptionist looked up, startled by the tense appearance of the trio. "What brings you here?" she asked, her eyes flitting from Luca to Emma, and then to Franco.

"Emergency," Luca responded curtly, his eyes never leaving Emma. "She needs to be checked immediately. Possible trauma and dehydration."

Nodding, the receptionist began tapping into her computer, her fingers dancing quickly over the keys. "Name?"

"Emma Lane," Luca answered. A nurse appeared from a nearby corridor, taking quick stock of the situation.

"Follow me," she said, leading them toward an examination room. Emma was quiet, her face as pale as the hospital's linens, but the edge of fear in her eyes had softened somewhat. Luca felt a heavy sigh escape his lungs; they had made it, at least this far.

Luca’s phone buzzed. Pulling it from his pocket, he glanced at the screen—a message from Rick James. “It's done. We arrested two men. They'll be busy answering questions for a long time.”

Luca looked up, meeting Franco’s eyes and nodding slightly. The unsaid words hung in the air, this chapter was closed, at least for now.

Inside the examination room, Emma was being attended to by a doctor and a nurse. She answered their questions in a quiet voice, her gaze occasionally meeting Luca's. Each time their eyes met, he saw a bit more colour return to her cheeks, a bit more life flicker in her eyes.

Emma, now sitting upright on the hospital bed, looked at them, her eyes filled with questions that she wasn't ready to voice. Just then, a nurse walked in. “She's been cleared for transfer to a side room.”

“Thank you,” Luca replied, offering a grateful nod.

Emma finally spoke. “Will I be safe now?” Her voice was tinged with uncertainty.

“You will be,” Luca assured her, meeting her gaze with a promise he intended to keep.

“You're not alone anymore, Emma. You will be safe.”

Franco placed a reassuring hand on her shoulder, “You're tougher than you think. And you've got us in your corner now. Your mum will be here soon.”

Luca and Franco made their way out of the room, down the brightly lit corridor, each step carrying them further from tonight's ordeal but also drawing them closer to a myriad of questions, dilemmas, and perhaps, more danger.

Franco turned to Luca. “Do you ever miss the simplicity of being a copper?”

“Simplicity?” Luca chuckled, the irony not lost on him. “I think we've both learned there's nothing simple about right and wrong.”

“Besides,” Luca continued, “Sometimes it's not about missing what was, but about looking forward to what could be.”

CHAPTER FORTY-THREE

Grace's pulse hammered as she pushed through the door into the clinical white room. The tang of disinfectant stung her nose. She locked her eyes onto the small figure on the hospital bed—Emma. Each day of the past month had stretched into a slow-motion nightmare, her mind stuck in a loop of dread.

Grace's lungs seized, as if refusing to breathe without permission. Emma looked thinner, the light in her eyes dimmed but not extinguished. The mere sight of her was like a lifeline thrown to Grace.

“Emma?” Her voice trembled on the edge of breaking.

“Mum,” Emma responded, her own voice fragile as glass.

Emotion burst its banks within Grace. She closed the distance in three strides and folded Emma into her arms. As they clung to each other, their cheeks wet, it was as if their souls were stitching themselves back together.

"You're safe," Grace choked out between sobs. "Nobody will harm you again." Emma clung back, her grip fuelled by a newfound courage.

Luca and Franco navigated the maze of St. Stephen's Hospital, cups of hot coffee steadying their hands. In the room, Grace sat next to Emma's bed, a tangible aura of concern enveloping her. She lightly stroked Emma's hand, a silent promise of security. Emma's eyes flickered briefly, sensing new energy entering the room. Unaware, Grace remained anchored to her daughter. Luca and Franco exchanged a glance, unspoken words flowing between them.

Soundlessly, they moved towards Grace. Emma watched Luca edge closer, making his way to stand behind her mother. A subtle lift of her eyebrows spoke volumes.

Grace sensed the shift and turned, meeting the familiar faces of Luca and Franco. A rush of relief, almost like a physical wave, surged through her. She let go of Emma's hand and threw herself into Luca's arms, her embrace almost knocking the wind out of him. It was a kind of closeness Luca hadn't felt since losing Julia.

As the seconds suspended themselves, Grace eventually released Luca and turned to Franco, her eyes glistening. She hugged him, a physical manifestation of the weight lifted from their souls.

“How can I ever thank you?” Her words floated in the air, each syllable wrapped in raw gratitude.

Luca and Franco didn't need to speak. Their eyes met, smiles breaking like dawn, and in that shared look, they communicated all that words could not. A circle had closed, a bond forged in the crucible of shared adversity.

Still buzzing with emotion, Grace returned to Emma's side, but not before casting a last, grateful glance toward Luca and Franco. The two men retreated to a nearby set of chairs, giving mother and daughter space yet staying within reach—sentinels in this tender moment.

Grace picked up Emma's hand again, but this time Emma gripped back with a strength that belied her fragile appearance. As their eyes met, Emma whispered, “It's good to see you again, mum.”

Grace nodded, her throat too thick for words. She looked back at Luca and Franco, then at her daughter, and a slow realisation washed over her. “We're not alone, Emma. We never were.”

Emma gave a small, hopeful smile, her first genuine one in a long time. It was as if a string had been pulled tight around them, across months of agony and uncertainty, and finally released, letting them breathe.

In a corner of the room, Luca pulled out his phone, checking for any new updates. There were none, but he didn't expect any. They had done their part, and now it was a matter for the authorities. He looked up to catch Franco's eye. Both men knew they'd crossed some lines, shattered some rules, but neither would ever regret it. Franco got up and walked over to the room's small window. The dawn was breaking. He sighed, aware that while one chapter had closed, another was beginning—both for Emma and Grace and for them.

Grace noticed the pensiveness on their faces and walked over. “Is everything alright?”

Franco turned to her. “We did what we had to do, but it's not over. There will be investigations, legal processes. It's not going to be easy.”

Grace looked at them both, her eyes locking onto theirs. “Whatever comes next, we'll face it. We have something now we didn't have before—hope.”

Emma, overhearing the conversation, chimed in softly but audibly: “And each other.”

Hearing Emma's words, everyone in the room felt a collective shiver, as if a cold breeze had swept through them, dispersing the lingering shadows of the past. They all understood that their journey was far from over, but for the first time in a long while, the path ahead seemed a little brighter, the burdens a little lighter, and the ties that bound them a little stronger.

CHAPTER FORTY-FOUR

Mickey Coomber's hands bore evidence of a life spent wrestling with stubborn planks of wood. A carpenter by profession, his brother Paul shared both the burden and the pride of their small carpentry business on Greyhound Road. Recent months had introduced an unfamiliar discomfort into the Coomber's world. Mickey would often catch Paul's gaze resting on the diminishing stack of jobs. Their once-bustling workshop was now in dire straits. Then an opportunity arrived: Johnny Billham called Mickey a few days after meeting with Luca, expressing a need for custom carpentry for a new development project. It was too good an opportunity to pass up, a possible lifeline for their flagging business.

Mickey glanced at his family photo on the workshop wall—his wife's radiant smile and their children playfully jostling for a spot in the camera's frame highlighted the stark reality of their situation. The Coomber brothers' trade was more than just a means of livelihood; it was the legacy they intended to leave behind, a way to secure their families' futures. With this in mind, Mickey set off to meet Johnny Billham. With the familiar weight of the carpenter's pencil tucked behind his ear, he left the workshop. The breakthrough they'd been waiting for was potentially one successful meeting away.

The aroma of damp masonry mingled with the raw, earthy scent of freshly cut timber and plaster, invading Mickey Coomber's senses as he entered Johnny Billham's builder's yard. Located at the top of Munster Road, its ramshackle appearance clashed with the surrounding stylish houses. Mickey, shifting in his worn work boots, took a moment to survey the expanse. It was a space reminiscent of a bygone era, with rust-speckled machinery scattered haphazardly, their useful days long gone, appearing like carcasses of a forgotten industry.

The texture of crumbling cement underfoot mirrored the unease he felt. Grimy tarpaulins billowed in the breeze, echoing the rhythmic thump of Mickey's pulsing heart. Silhouettes of scaffolding rose against the slate-grey sky, like skeletal fingers. Then, beyond the yard's chaos, stood the house—a Victorian relic. Its battered windows, once its eyes to the world, remained empty, shattered panes glinting ominously under the overcast sky. The exposed bricks told stories of past elegance, now left to decay in silent dignity. Mickey's gaze lingered, unable to shake the impression that the yard, in its peculiar silence, was watching him in return.

Johnny Billham waited, a figure veiled in grime and shadows. His calloused hands clenched around the wooden handle of a well-used shovel, its spade end dusted with dried soil. His gaze was fixed on Mickey. Mickey moved toward the front door, gravel crunching underfoot. Johnny greeted him with a terse nod, his voice a gravelly whisper: “Appreciate you coming, Mickey." His words lingered, an omen of the impending storm.

Johnnie was the first to move, his steps echoing an eerie rhythm, leading the way into the house. As Mickey stepped in, he shivered involuntarily, his apprehension heightened by the creaking floorboards and the echoes of the past. Johnnie led him through the shadowy hallway, towards the ominous opening leading to the basement. It was here, in the clammy confines of the basement, that the rhythm of the afternoon shattered. Suddenly, Johnnie lifted a shovel and swung it at Mickey's head. The chilling sound of metal striking flesh was a stark punctuation, the echo bouncing off the stone-cold walls. Mickey collapsed, akin to a puppet with severed strings, his life seeping away on the dirt-riddled floor.

Johnnie stood, his face devoid of emotion. He gripped Mickey under the arms, his muscles straining as he dragged the body deeper into the darkness. As Mickey's lifeless form disappeared into the basement's obscurity, the builder's yard returned to its quiet slumber, an unwilling host to the afternoon's tragedy.

CHAPTER FORTY-FIVE

The streets of Fulham held their breath once again, as if suspended in time. A stillness that felt as invasive as the river fog seeping into the borough enveloped the area. The shock of Micky Coomber's murder lay heavy in the air. People moved differently, their routines maintaining only a semblance of normality as interactions grew stiff. What were once casual conversations turned cautious, with carefully selected words exchanged in a new reserve.

People walked through the streets of Fulham, their footsteps hesitant, less rhythmic than before. Fog from the Thames rolled in, dampening the pavement and clinging to pedestrians' overcoats, making its presence as clear as the tension that had settled over the area. In coffee shops, eyes met for just a moment before darting away; regulars sipped their espressos silently, as if the very air could carry accusations.

Micky Coomber had lived here, laughed here, and now he was dead. His absence created a void, pulling in the neighbourhood's sense of security and distorting it. Bernard the butcher on Greyhound Road, usually so jovial, kept his banter to a minimum, focusing intently on slicing meat with mechanical precision. At the newsagent, Mr. Dennis handed over the morning papers with a forced smile, headlines screaming about Micky's murder that he didn't want to discuss. The Lillie Road Rec, once bustling with children and dog walkers, had fewer visitors. Those who came kept their children close and their dogs on shorter leashes. Neighbours who used to chat freely over fences now merely nodded, their minds racing with unspoken thoughts and questions too dangerous to voice. So, while Fulham maintained its daily routines, a veneer of normality thinly masked an undercurrent of suspicion and fear. Everyone knew that Fulham had changed, and it wasn't just the fog people felt enveloping them; it was the lingering dread that they might be standing next to the killer and not even know it.

The builders on Orbain Road had started their day like any other, ready to tackle a fresh load of cement and bricks. Their boots crunched on gravel as they approached the skip, expecting nothing more than the usual debris. But as they lifted the sheet of tarp, their eyes widened, freezing them in place. Micky Coomber lay there, lifeless, surrounded by rubble and waste.

Hands that had once effortlessly hoisted concrete blocks now quivered, grasping for something steadier than their fractured routine. The laughter and jests that typically filled the air were silenced, replaced by a hollow echo that magnified their sudden, collective grief. The raw atmosphere, usually saturated with the scent of sweat and dust, now felt contaminated by a darker, invisible force.

Their work came to a standstill; their tools idled beside them like forgotten extensions of themselves. No one spoke. Each man wrestled quietly with the intrusive reality that Micky's life had ended here, reduced to an unwelcome addition to a container meant for builders' waste.

People in Fulham walked faster now, their eyes darting, their heads lowered. School gates, once bustling with chatter, saw parents whispering in tight circles, their glances skimming over unfamiliar faces. On the Tube, commuters buried themselves in their papers, but the hush was different—thicker. The headlines screamed about another girl, another tragedy. Micky Coomber's face stared out from the front pages. No one spoke his name, but everyone felt his absence like a missing tooth—uncomfortable and continually prodded by a tongue that couldn't quite forget. At bus stops, people stood apart, no longer lining up as they used to; their personal space stretched by unspoken tension. Glances met and quickly fell away, questions left unasked, stories left untold. The very concrete of the streets seemed greyer, as if the borough itself had become a canvas for the fears and nightmares it now harboured.

The newsprint left smudges on fingertips, black ink like an indelible stain. People would fold the paper neatly, set it aside, and for a brief moment, catch their reflection in the window or a mirror, as if checking that they were still themselves in a world that had turned alien. No one said it out loud, but Fulham had become a character in a horror story. Not just lines on a map, but a landscape fraught with meaning. Each alley was a paragraph, each street a chapter in a tale they wished someone would close and put away.

They wore their grief visibly; it was in the tightness around their eyes, the rigidity of their shoulders. It was their shield. They would not be broken, not by the horror that had infiltrated the mundane, converting their home into a theatre of dread. Their collective heartbeat was a low drum of resilience, a pulse threading through Fulham and Hammersmith, each throb a silent vow to reclaim their streets, their lives, their narrative. Reporters swarmed local pubs, microphones poised, scribbling notes as patrons recounted tales about Micky. People leaned in, their faces lighting up as they spoke of the last time Micky had raised a pint, singing so loudly that even the darts players stopped to listen. Yet, with each shared laugh, a heavy silence followed, reminding everyone of his absence.

In Fulham, a tension tightened its grip. Shopkeepers peered from behind windows before locking up, glancing at each passing pedestrian as though they might be the next headline. Graffiti that once felt like urban art now looked like coded messages. Parked cars with foggy windows made locals clutch their keys a bit tighter. Inside living rooms, the atmosphere grew stifling. Neighbours who once chatted freely over fences now traded uneasy glances. Television screens flashed with police sketches, CCTV footages, and sombre news anchors discussing Micky and the murdered girls. Crime scene photos replaced family albums on coffee tables, as if the horror had moved in, sitting right there beside the remote control.

A dive into the depths of Micky's life followed, a profound excavation that saw him emerge from the harsh numbers of crime statistics into the warm light of humanity. Interviews conducted, stories shared, all weaved an intricate portrait of a man fondly remembered. Micky, the life of the pub, a pint in hand, his laughter a contagious tune in the air. Fulham was now in the grip of a mystery that refused to leave its shadows, turning its familiar, comforting corners into potential scenes of crime. The image of violence loomed, as Micky's and the girl's murders, stark and unflinching, became the unwelcome guest in every living room.

CHAPTER FORTY-SIX

As Luca's fingers clutched the phone, the tremor in his voice betrayed his fear. "Rick, it's Luca. I've just heard about Micky Coomber."

Slouched amid a formidable sea of paperwork in his office, Rick detected the grave concern in Luca's words. "You knew him, didn't you?"

A pause thickened the air before Luca broke it. "We go back a long time, to Sherbrooke Road Primary. After many years apart, we reconnected recently. Do you think this is connected to the murders of the five girls?"

A sigh slipped from Rick as the phone weighed heavily against his ear; his eyes were anchored to the "Fulham Murders" whiteboard across the room. "We can't rush to conclusions, Luca," he said, careful with his words. "But nothing is being overlooked."

"I might be able to help you. I know most of his contacts."

Rick responded, “Could you meet me in the morning at about 10:00 AM?”

Luca told him, “Shall we meet in the café on Wandsworth Bridge Road?”

“Ok, see you tomorrow.”

In the low light of his office, the daunting stacks of case files seemed less oppressive. Rick felt a rejuvenated sense of purpose. This wasn't about merely solving another case anymore. It was about seeking justice for Micky, for the five girls, and perhaps for a childhood camaraderie that had met an untimely end. Pulsing beams of monotone light flickered against the walls of the surveillance room. An uneasy stillness lay heavy in the air, broken intermittently by the hum of tape decks whirring in the background. The sound of electronic noises sang a solitary tune—a melodic representation of the room's isolation.

Deep within this realm of light and shadow, Detective Inspector Rick James and two of his team sat hunched, their gazes’ firm, riveted to the intricate images displayed across the multitude of CCTV monitors. The broad shoulders beneath Rick’s jacket tightened, carving his silhouette further into the cool, sterile glow of the screens. His unblinking eyes darted from one frame to another—a mixture of ordinary lives embossed onto the glassy panes. These glimmers of existence, flickering with a ghostlike luminescence, held him in their trance. Each car cutting through Fulham's streets, each shadowy figure slipping past the camera’s eye—all potential leads in a game where the rules were as elusive as the objective.

Rick's fingers, calloused from years of service, drummed rhythmically on the scratched surface of the table. The deep beats reverberated through the compact room, the echoes painting a raw portrait of his doggedness. His jaw clenched tighter with each passing minute. The faint aroma of day-old coffee lingered in the background, intermingling with the musky scent of old paperwork and the more recent addition of a cold, greasy takeaway.

A particularly striking image caught his attention: a man clutching a worn leather holdall, his eyes obscured by an oversized hat, striding hurriedly past a pub on North End Road. The angular lines of his hunched figure reflected an uneasy urgency. But was it relevant to his case, or just another phantom of the urban night? Each fleeting image was a potential clue, an integral part of the jigsaw puzzle he found himself compelled to decipher. One false interpretation, one missed detail, could skew the whole picture and misdirect the investigation. Yet Rick embraced the challenge, his mind thriving on the details, distilling the noise to reveal patterns hidden in plain sight.

The hardened exterior of Rick belied the thoughts whirling in his mind. Trained to see beyond the obvious, he constructed narratives from a lone man's lingering gaze, from the quickened pace of a passer-by. Every frame, every fragment of visual information, was inspected with the same relentless scrutiny, the same sharpness that his colleagues often found disconcerting.

Rick leaned back, his posture softening, eyes reflecting the dance of monitor lights. The exterior calm masked an internal tide of realization, a quiet breakthrough. It was in these solitary hours, amidst the glow of electronic screens, that the silent language of the city spoke the loudest. And Rick, in his ceaseless watch, knew just how to listen.

The job demanded patience. It demanded the ability to sift through the mundane in pursuit of the exceptional. And so, DI Rick James continued his watch, his hard-set face basking in the glow of the surveillance screens. The story of the city unravelled before him, frame by frame, as the small hours ticked away into the oblivion of another restless night.

CHAPTER FORTY-SEVEN

In the Tube train's tight confines, Luca was hemmed in by commuters lost in their own worlds of headphones and mobile screens. His gaze flitted to the underground map above the carriage door, mindlessly tracing the colour-coded lines. However, in the corners of his mind, he replayed Mickey Coomber's murder. Mickey's boisterous laughter haunted his memories; he was the epicentre of any gathering. A sudden lurch of the carriage jolted Luca back to reality. Discarded newspapers lay strewn about, and a bold headline about the brutal murder of his friend seemed to leap out at him.

After leaving Fulham Broadway Station following an early meeting at the Cortana Club, he saw them. Dressed in eco-friendly gear, with their old-school bikes propped up outside a café, biking was their favourite way to "move their creativity," they claimed. They appeared busy on their MacBook's while sipping fair-trade coffee, but in reality, they were just scrolling through Instagram. "Working on my screenplay," Jack would declare, sipping his fifth flat white. His "screenplay" had three lines and had been in progress for about as long as Brexit. Asked how he paid his bills, he'd claim he was on benefits, conveniently omitting his parents' hefty monthly handouts. Sarah called herself an "upcoming artist." Her last show had been in a mate's basement and was mostly attended by her circle of friends and some lost Deliveroo drivers. If you talked to her, you'd think she was the next big thing in London. Eventually, they'd grow older and move to Fulham. Jack's never-finished screenplay would continue collecting dust, but he'd still discuss his "film career" as if he were a British Tarantino. Sarah would fill her £2 million house with her own "masterpieces." They'd reminisce about their younger days as a period of "artistic growth," ignoring the truth: lots of show, not much work. Owning their Fulham homes outright, they'd congratulate themselves. They never really achieved anything, but that wouldn't stop them from claiming they'd made Fulham a "cultural hotspot"—all while admiring themselves in a glass of expensive, organic wine.

At 10:00 AM, Luca stepped into Layla's Café at the top of Wandsworth Bridge Road. The heady blend of coffee with hints of fried eggs and bacon greeted him. Slipping between chatting patrons, a few appreciative glances trailed him. The café's illumination accentuated his facial features, distinguishing him from the crowd. Noticing Rick by the window, he promptly ordered a double espresso. Luca studied Rick's weary look: red eyes and a scruffy face. "Rick, you look fucked," Luca observed, a wrinkle of worry appearing on his forehead.

Rick let out a long, laden sigh, his fatigue palpable. Running his scarred hand over his thinning hair, he murmured, "Luca, I'm stretched thin."

Luca's reply was tinged with sarcasm, yet concern lurked beneath. “A peaceful life was never the police’s selling point, was it?”

Rick grimaced, the weight of unsolved cases visibly pressing on him. “It’s not just the usual strain, Luca. The five horrific deaths of the young girls, and now Mickey’s. It’s overwhelming.” Rick’s eyebrow shot up, his voice falling to a murmur. “Mickey Coomber. How well did you know him?”

Luca's answer came after a reflective pause. “As I've said before, we were friends since Sherbrooke Primary School and Henry Compton Secondary School. We were inseparable. But, as the years flew by, so did our contact.” A hint of nostalgia tinged his words. “Our paths crossed again recently. We found ourselves reminiscing over a pint at Bernie Montgomery’s place, O’Grady’s Club on Fulham Broadway. A week after that, we had another meet-up and paid a visit to Johnny Billham at his Aintree Estate flat.” Rick's expression hardened at the mention of Billham.

“That fucking name. It’s continually reappearing,” he grumbled.

Luca bent in, his voice steady but gentle. “Rick, have you run a background check on him?”

Rick shook his head, his eyes suggesting more than his silence. “I haven’t, but perhaps it’s time I did.” He sighed, massaging his temples. “Everything we've found so far indicates that he’s spotless. There's no hint of any tarnish on his reputation.” His voice faded, leaving a trail of unresolved questions hanging in the air.

Rick rested his frame across the table, his hands enclosing his cup of coffee. His brow knitted in a puzzled expression, “What is this Billham character really like?”

Gathering his thoughts, Luca began, “We were mates, throughout primary, and beyond to our teens. But the man I encountered recently? That wasn't the Billham I knew, I didn’t even recognise him when I saw him. He’s transformed, altered beyond recognition. It's not just his appearance and his mannerisms. Once, he had been one of the boys, smart in appearance. He shared our adventures, our laughter, our fights. But now? His eyes have lost their sparkle, replaced by a chilly gaze that felt unnerving. His speech is snappish, devoid of any warmth whatsoever. Honestly, mate, he’s a weirdo.”

Over the next thirty minutes, Luca shared his contacts with Rick. These were mainly people who knew Mickey from the old days, including Bernie Montgomery at O’Grady’s Club.

CHAPTER FORTY-EIGHT

The wardrobe door hinges let out a low groan as they swung open. Suits hung with military precision—greys, blacks, and navies, each having their own designated section. Luca's hand hesitated over the navy suit before grasping it. As he pulled it off the hanger, a subtle yet unmistakable fragrance wafted up to him. He closed his eyes for a second, taken back to the close press of bodies, Julia's laughter in his ear as they twirled on the dance floor. It was the very same scent that had clung to Julia as they danced that final time, lost in each other's arms.

He shook off the memory, pulling the suit onto his shoulders and fastening the buttons. His hands moved to his shoes, each one gleaming black as though just polished. As he laced them up, his reflection in the mirror seemed to waver, replaced for an instant by an image of Julia—her eyes twinkling, a coy smile on her lips. The evening sun sliced through the curtain gaps, casting its orange tint across the room, echoing the warmth of the vision he'd just seen.

His phone broke the silence, emitting a soft, digital chime. The screen lit up; a message from Grace appeared: "See you soon xx." He pocketed the phone and stood up, ready to head out. As he walked towards the door, it felt as if Julia's presence floated alongside him, a shadow in step with his own.

Luca stood on the pavement, eyes scanning the crowd until they landed on Grace. As she walked towards him, her gaze locked onto his, her eyes softening in a way that felt like a warm embrace without the physical contact. A smile tugged at Luca's lips as he gave a simple nod. They walked side by side, soon finding themselves at the doorstep of Le Gavroche on Upper Brook Street. Luca's grip tightened on the cold, metallic handle of the door, his knuckles whitening for a second. Above them, the chandeliers spilled golden light onto the pavement, illuminating the scene in stark contrast to the quiet bustle of the street behind them.

Noticing the tension in his posture, Grace's eyes met his again, conveying silent reassurance. "It's lovely," she said softly, gesturing subtly toward the plush interior beyond the glass.

Inhaling deeply, Luca pulled the door open. A wave of fragrant aromas—rich sauces, hints of truffle, and spices—greeted them, momentarily sweeping away the weight that seemed to hang in the air. As they stepped over the threshold, the gentle lilt of a piano's melody filled the space, whispering a promise of intimacy. Potted ferns stood like sentinels in each corner, their leaves a lush counterpoint to the subdued colours around them. The carpet underfoot seemed to shimmer subtly, its intricate design dancing in the soft light.

A crisp-voiced waiter, in a tailored black suit, approached them. “Good evening,” he greeted, eyes briefly flickering over Luca's face, perhaps sensing the weight of the occasion.

Without uttering another word, he led them through a maze of tables, the clinking of cutlery and murmurs of conversations growing louder. Settling them at a window-side table with a view of the bustling street outside, the waiter gracefully laid out menus in front of them. The soft glow of the table candle-light bathed Grace's face, her deep-set eyes shining with a mix of anticipation and patience.

As Luca reached for his water glass, a small tremor in his hand betrayed his nervousness. Grace, always observant, began light conversation about the history of the restaurant, expertly steering the discussion away from lingering memories and shadows of the past. The elegance of Grace's stance was undeniable, an almost sculpted silhouette against the diffuse light of the restaurant. She wore an age-defying air, as if the decades that had passed were no more than mere whispers against her radiance.

Grace wasn't draped in the gaudy sequins and unnecessary frills that some might favour. Instead, she chose a simple, tailored black dress, its form skimming her toned physique, quietly whispering of the discipline and rigour that kept her looking so youthful. Her hair, a sleek cascade of blonde waves, shimmered under the subdued lighting, framing a face more refined than traditionally beautiful. High cheekbones, a straight, sharp nose, and full, rosy lips curved into a mysterious, yet captivating, smile. The glint of a solitaire diamond caught the light as she raised her hand, the only piece of jewellery adorning her. It was discreet, yet unmistakably expensive. Her immaculate, French-manicured nails clicked softly against the crystal of the glass. Her eyes, blue as an afternoon sky, held a spark of shrewd intelligence.

Luca's eyes were a faded sapphire, scarred with the lingering grief of losing Julia. It wasn't just pain he felt in her absence, but a deep emptiness that Julia's laughter, her kindness, and her very essence once filled. Grace, on the other hand, wore her wounds in the sharp set of her shoulders, and the weary resilience in her blue eyes. Her marriage hadn't ended with a sudden, shocking goodbye like Luca's, but with the slow drip of discontent and disappointment, until one day the love she'd once held for her husband had evaporated completely. The air between them was thick with unspoken words and unexplored emotions. Both knew they were treading a path as beautiful as it was fraught with the shadows of their past.

CHAPTER FORTY-NINE

Amidst the rhythmic din of hammers and drills, Johnnie Billham stood out on Hurlingham Road in Fulham. As he spread mortar on bricks, his bulging arms flexed under the weight. Sunlight struck the mingled sheen of sweat and construction dust on his skin, casting an eerie glow that made passers-by avert their gaze. His face, weather-beaten and lined, showed no emotion. But it was the eyes that people remembered—the slate-grey eyes that reflected the overcast London sky. Those eyes scanned every passer-by, every car that drove by, each movement in the periphery, filing away details with unsettling scrutiny.

A high-visibility vest clung to his chest, concealing something beneath. A quick glimpse would reveal a silver chain around his neck, from which dangled an unidentifiable dark object. A keepsake? A memento? It seemed incongruous in a world of scaffolding and plasterboard.

His hands, calloused and strong, moved with a dexterity that belied their appearance. They were hands that could deftly twist a length of wire, set a wall straight, or lay down a perfect bead of caulk. Yet, their agility suggested other, darker skills—ones that could tighten around a throat or handle a blade with unnerving precision. Even his boots told a story. Worn and mud-spattered, the steel-toed boots had distinctive markings on their soles. Patterns that would not match any other pair, patterns that were deliberately etched—an unsettling signature he left wherever he treads.

To an onlooker from a distance, he might blend into the sea of tradesmen that populate London's ever-changing architectural landscape. Yet, up close, the aura around him was distinctly different—a malevolent undercurrent that suggested his tools were not only for construction but also for destruction. In Johnnie Billham's world, the lines between building and killing had long ago blurred, leaving a disquieting impression that lingered in the busy streets of West London.

Johnnie now at home sank into a worn armchair. His eyes locked onto the rug at his feet, its intricate design mapping out his next move. Cigarette smoke hung in the air, mingling with the weight of his thoughts. He reached for another from the crumpled pack on the coffee table, striking a match and lighting it. The ashtray was a mound of stubbed-out ends, each an hour of meticulous planning, each a moment closer to his dark goal.

His gaze shifted to the photograph next to the ashtray. Younger faces stared back: a snapshot from a day at Southend, with arms slung around Micky Coomber and Luca Rossi. Those were different times, bound by friendship and ignorance. Johnnie's eyes narrowed as they replayed the look of disbelief that had flickered across Micky's face just over a week ago. Micky hadn't seen it coming; the quick, decisive end to their long-standing relationship.

Once Luca was dealt with, Johnnie could refocus. The streets of West London would once again echo with whispered fears about the shadow that targeted its young women.

The chair creaked under him, as rigid and unyielding as his upright back. The knife lay before him on the table, its serrated edge catching the light in flickers. He locked eyes with it, the grey of his irises matching the metallic sheen. For a moment, knife and man seemed indistinguishable—both forged, sharpened, and ready. As he stared, the skin beside his eyes crinkled, casting dark, angular shadows down his cheeks. His face remained unyielding, a bastion against sentiment, contrasting the looming darkness that seemed to crowd around him. His hand moved, fingers closing around the knife handle with a sense of finality.

On the table lay an open folder. Inside, numerous details about Luca Rossi, captured in photos and notes. The photos showed Luca in various places—outside his house, at a Mayfair restaurant with a woman. But it was the one of Luca entering his own home that captured the most attention. He studied the locks on Luca's door, mentally picking each one. His gaze shifted to the windows, noting their type and vulnerabilities. The layout of the house, memorised, played like a silent film in his mind.

A thin line of condensation formed on a glass of water next to the folder, its silent descent marking time. But time was irrelevant; all that mattered was the plan. Every possible scenario had been rehearsed, every outcome prepared for.

The scent of the leather gloves, resting beside the folder, drew his attention next. They whispered promises of anonymity. He reached out, fingertips grazing their familiar texture. In the distance, a clock ticked, its rhythm unbroken. Each second drawing him closer to the inevitable. Luca Rossi, living his life, unaware of the storm on the horizon. But for how long? No emotions clouded his thoughts, no doubts intruded. Only clarity remained. Luca Rossi would soon be a name crossed off a long, meticulous list.

Outside, the streets of Fulham remained oblivious to his deliberations, the humdrum of late-night traffic, the soft patter of rain. A world beyond this one, where Johnnie's purpose didn't reach, at least not yet. The leather gloves beckoned once more, evoking memories of past deeds. They'd seen much and said little, a testament to his skills. Slipping them on, he marvelled at the snug fit, every crease and curve of his hand mirrored in black. A perfect union of flesh and material, they made him whole.

Sounds from outside became more prominent, and the clock's ticking grew louder, more insistent. With each tick, Johnnie was drawn deeper into the world he'd crafted for himself—a world of murder, devoid of hesitation.

CHAPTER FIFTY

Certainly, I've proofread the text and made corrections for spelling, grammar, and punctuation. Here's the revised version with changes implemented:

The heat of the London sun weighed on Luca as he navigated the pavement towards Parsons Green Tube Station. His shirt clung to his back, his skin slick with sweat. Just as he approached the yawning entrance of the station, a vibration against his thigh jolted him. Swift fingers retrieved his mobile from his pocket, and D.I. Rick James' name lit up the screen.

The voice on the other end came through in distorted bursts. "Luca, we've dug even deeper on Johnnie Billham. A couple of petty thefts as a kid. Nothing recent. The bloke's a blank slate."

For a beat, Luca's world went mute. He could almost visualise Rick, hunched over a cluttered desk, eyeing stacks of files and tracing phone records, desperate for anything concrete. Yet Luca's gut churned with an unsettled feeling, an instinct he couldn't shake. As he stood there, clutching the phone in his hand, Luca gazed at the throngs of people milling around him. To them, it was just another sun-soaked afternoon in London. But to him, it was a landscape fraught with invisible perils, hidden agendas lurking behind smiling faces. The Fulham he had once found vibrant now seemed to mock him with its indifference.

"You there, Luca?" Rick's voice intruded again, pulling him back from the edge of his thoughts.

"Yeah, I'm here," he finally replied, the weight of Rick's words settling in like a layer of grit on his already troubled mind.

"Look, if this Johnnie Billham is involved, he's playing his cards very close to his chest. We're at a dead end."

Luca pressed his lips together, a thin line of frustration forming. A dead end. The words hung in the air like smog. His every instinct told him that Billham was a puzzle piece in a picture that was far from complete. Yet, evidence was scant, leads were drying up, and time was a luxury they couldn't afford.

"All right," Luca said, more to himself than to Rick. "Keep digging. There's got to be something you're missing, something buried beneath the surface."

He ended the call, his eyes still fixed on the crowd. But what if they were wrong? What if Billham was as innocent as his empty record suggested?

As Luca descended into the Tube station, the air grew cooler but no less oppressive. And with every passing second, the unsettling notion grew within him: they were racing against a clock they couldn't see, hunting a phantom in a city of millions. The thought twisted in his stomach as he boarded the train, its doors closing behind him like the final notes of a song.

Twenty minutes later, he left South Kensington Tube Station and made his way to Harrington Road. Above, the midday sun, brilliant and golden, cast its glow on the street, making the royal blue facade of Gianni's restaurant gleam as if freshly painted. Harrington Road was alive, pulsing with life. Tourists, awestruck and animated, crowded the pavements, their movements a harmonised dance. Cameras clicked and flashed, capturing mementos of their London journey, the relentless shutters trying to immortalise every second.

Luca strode confidently towards the restaurant's entrance. The glass door, adorned with the golden lettering of 'Gianni's,' swung open with ease. But before it was even fully ajar, a wave of tantalising aromas rushed out to meet him. He inhaled, letting the scents of rich coffee, the earthiness of cured meats, and the all-too-familiar smell of baked lasagne wrap around him like an old friend. It was an embrace that took him back to countless childhood memories.

Inside, Gianni's was bathed in warm, golden light, making the walls appear to glow. The vibrant colours of the interior came alive, creating pockets of cosy nooks amidst the open space. The melodic hum of countless conversations about human connection echoed across the restaurant. Every so often, a burst of laughter punctuated the soundscape, a testament to the joy that good food and company can bring. To Luca's left, a young couple sat, their fingers brushing over a shared plate of garlic bread, their eyes meeting in silent conversation. A little further away, a group of women huddled together, their heads thrown back in joyous laughter, the clinking of their glasses signalling another shared secret.

Behind the counter, Franco was a picture of concentration. His hands, steady and sure, artfully swirled the froth atop a cappuccino, every move a silent dance of precision. At the rear of the restaurant, Martina was deep in animated conversation with two elegantly dressed women. Her hands gestured excitedly, the glint in her eyes revealing the passion she held for whatever story she was weaving. For Luca, this scene was more than just a bustling restaurant; it was a world of memories, of family, and of love. It was another day at Gianni's, a testament to generations of tradition and hard work.

The metallic hiss of the espresso machine subsided as Franco placed two steaming cups on the tray, their dark aroma permeating the air. He made his way to the back office, where Luca was hunched over a desk cluttered with papers. "What's with this Johnnie Billham, then?" Franco asked.

Luca looked up, his eyes shadowed. "Rick says they have nothing on him. But I think there is something. It's like there's a layer to Billham they haven't even scratched yet. The way he looks and that stare of his, it's like there's madness in his eyes. He was never like that. He was always playing the fool and was good company to be with."

Franco's protective instincts flared. "You're not going alone to see him. Not with that gut feeling of yours," he cautioned.

Luca sighed, pinching the bridge of his nose. "I need to do this, mate. Alone."

"At least tell me where," Franco pressed, concern evident in his voice.

"I need to talk to him, to arrange something. I'll probably meet him at O'Grady's. I'll let you know."

CHAPTER FIFTY-ONE

Shafts of dimming sunlight skimmed the walls, casting a soft glow on book spines lined up on the shelves. The room was otherwise still, except for the subdued whir of a desk fan. Luca's fingers hovered over the box's lid for a split second. With a muted creak of its hinges, he lifted it. The fan sent out periodic gusts that nudged stray papers, creating a fluttering contrast to the room's overall stillness. His hands sifted through disorganised stacks of ageing papers and photographs, their arrangement betraying the relentless scrutiny of recent weeks. When his fingertips touched a new photograph, they trembled slightly, hesitating before lifting the image to eye level.

Julia's smile surfaced intermittently from the jumble, each occurrence halting his motions. His gaze would linger, his eyes slightly unfocused, as if travelling somewhere distant. Then, with visible effort, he'd place the picture aside and reach for the next. Breaths seemed harder to come by. The walls appeared to close in incrementally with each photograph sifted and set aside. His eye caught a corner, a fragment of a photograph peeking out from under a rumpled document. A corner he'd learned to recognise. His breath stalled in his chest for a moment before he pulled the picture into full view. There she was, Julia, her eyes gleaming with uncontainable laughter, standing amidst a lavender field.

For a fleeting moment, the scent of lavender filled the room, as though carried by the fan's gentle breeze. It was as though the very air had borrowed the fragrance from Julia, a perfume that lingered in his senses long after their sunlit day had ended. Luca's fingers brushed over the faded photographs, each snap igniting a sensory flashback. Julia's laughter seemed to echo, not in the room, but inside him, filling the hollow spaces. When he touched the images, the tactile memory of her skin—soft, warm, reassuring—flooded back. The room darkened, mimicking the weight inside his chest, while the desk fan continued its monotonous drone, stirring the air but unable to shift the heaviness that settled. He picked up the photo capturing Julia amidst a lavender field and set it beside a lit candle. The flame danced, casting its glow across her captured smile. For a moment, it seemed like she sat there beside him, her absence transformed into a quiet, golden presence. His cheek grew wet; a tear had escaped, a silent yet searing tribute. Love, the one thing time couldn't erode, filled the room and ached within him.

Luca's fingers froze on another photo, pulling it an inch closer. Ten young men beamed back at him, Southend Pier stretching into the horizon behind them. His eyes locked onto each face, recognition flickering. The edges of his mouth twitched upwards, a ghost of a smile that vanished as quickly as it appeared. His brow crinkled. The soft crackle of the glossy paper broke the silence as he held it closer to his eyes. In the photograph, Luca and nine of his old mates from

Fulham, stood side by side, each exuding a sense of friendship. Johnnie Billham stood centrally, a mild, confident smirk playing on his lips. On one side, Micky Coomber, with a cocky tilt to his head, leaned in slightly. On the other, Ronnie Gadd, his expression distant, perhaps lost in thought. The others, Bernie Montgomery, Ray Phillips, Phil Hurren, Pete Galvin, Ronnie Bennett and Harry Noakes, each had their own subtle smiles.

His grip tightened, knuckles whitening. An involuntary shiver jolted down his spine. Micky, now a body in a skip. Ronnie's daughter, throat slashed near Hammersmith Bridge. His thoughts connected dots he'd rather leave un-joined. Breath became a scarce commodity; an invisible weight compressed his lungs. With a meticulous movement, he laid the photograph back on the table, as if it were made of glass. He leaned back, releasing a sigh heavy with unnamed fears. That photograph, its ink faded but its implications indelible, hid something malevolent beneath its glossy finish. An unseen clock ticked louder in his head; he was running out of time to excavate the dark secret buried there before another life was snuffed out.

Luca pushed his chair back, its legs scraping against the floor like a discordant note. He walked over to the window, pulling aside the curtain just a sliver. The city outside was a tangle of concrete and shadows, every alley a potential crime scene, every face a catalogue of untold stories. His eyes scanned the horizon, searching for something he couldn't define. But Fulham offered no comfort tonight; it was as if the buildings themselves were standing in judgement. He returned to the table, passing a hand over his face. Each line on his palm could be a path leading to another dead end. The photograph seemed to taunt him now, its faces frozen in a time when ignorance was the prevailing bliss. The clock on the wall ticked relentlessly, indifferent to his inner turmoil. Time was a luxury he could no longer afford, measured not in days or hours, but in lives that could be lost. With a resigned breath, he knew he had no choice but to dive into the abyss, to dredge up whatever malevolent truths lurked beneath the surface. As he reached for the notebook and pen, he couldn't shake the dread that he was opening a door that couldn't be closed, but it was a door he had to walk through, even if what awaited him on the other side was as dark as the city outside his window.

CHAPTER FIFTY-TWO

The sharp rays of sunlight pierced through the gaps in the curtains, forcing Luca to squint against the unwelcome brightness. His eyes bore dark circles, witnesses to an almost sleepless night. With a heavy sigh, he made his way to the kitchen and brewed a strong black coffee. As he sipped the coffee, the black and white photo on the table caught the morning sun; each face illuminated. Micky's grin looked back at him. Connections needed to be found, and Luca was determined to find them. Leaving the house thirty minutes later, he headed to the O'Grady Club on Fulham Broadway. If anyone had answers, it would be Bernie Montgomery.

Luca felt the familiar buzz in his pocket as he approached the old stone façade of Fulham Library. He pulled out his mobile to see Franco's name flash on the screen. "Franco? It's early for you," Luca commented, looking up at the grey London sky.

There was a rustle, and then Franco's gruff voice emerged. "Have you spoken to Johnnie Billham?"

"Not yet," Luca hesitated, his gaze fixed on the pavement, before adding, "But I may have stumbled upon something interesting."

Franco's impatience was evident. "What?"

Pausing for dramatic effect, Luca finally spoke up. "I found an old photograph from a day out in Southend. All the Fulham boys are in it."

Franco chuckled. "Well, whoop-de-fucking-doo. You found a holiday snap."

Ignoring his brother's sarcasm, Luca countered, his voice tinged with excitement. "But that's just it, Johnnie Billham, Micky Coomber, and Ronnie Gadd are in that picture. Now Micky's dead, and Ronnie's daughter was found with her throat cut."

Franco cut him off sharply, the playful tone now absent. "So, what's your next move?"

"I'm heading to see Bernie Montgomery. He might know where the others are now."

"Just keep me updated," Franco ordered. Especially if you get word from Billham."

The glow of the neon sign—O'Grady's Club—flickered, casting intermittent light over Fulham Broadway. As Luca's hand reaches out to push the entrance door, his mobile buzzes in his pocket. Pulling it out, he sees Johnnie Billham's name on the screen. Raising the phone to his ear, "Johnnie?"

Johnnie's voice carried an unusual urgency. "Can we meet up? I've got something to discuss. It could be worthwhile for you."

Luca hesitates for a split second, glancing at the club door. “OK. Where and when?”

There's a short pause, filled only by faint background noise on Johnnie's end. “My builder's yard. Top of Muster Road. 4 PM.”

Luca narrows his eyes, trying to decipher the oddity in Johnnie's tone.

“That's fine. But Johnnie, give me a hint. What's this about?”

Another pause, longer this time. Finally, in a hushed tone, Johnnie says, “I'm with someone at the moment. Let's talk later.” The call ends abruptly, leaving Luca with more questions than answers.

The O'Grady Club, with its imposing exterior, was a mainstay in Fulham Broadway. By night, its neon lights drew crowds like moths to a flame. But by day, its subdued façade revealed the cracks and wear of a place that held too many secrets. Inside, the wooden floor bore evidence of the previous night's revelry: a forgotten empty pint glass sat on a table next to an overturned packet of crisps. Crumpled napkins and forgotten coasters littered the surfaces. The smell of stale beer mingled with the residue of fried food, carried on the cool morning air that seeped in through the open windows. Mismatched chairs, some toppled, formed haphazard patterns around tables. The leather on the benches seemed more worn, echoing the memories of countless conversations and raucous laughter. By the bar, a solitary barman moved methodically, wiping down the polished counter and clearing away remnants of the previous evening.

Golden morning light filtered through the mullioned windows, casting dappled patterns across the room and illuminating the dusty corners that the evening patrons rarely noticed. In the distance, London began to stir, but inside the pub, there was a brief moment of stillness: a pause before the story of another day began.

Bernie's brow shot up in surprise as he noticed Luca's figure making its way into the club. “Luca? It's the crack of dawn, did you shit the bed?! What's got you up and about, mate?”

Sliding into the seat with a cheeky grin, Luca flourished a photo with dramatic flair, letting it hover for a moment before dropping it onto the table between them. “Recognise this lot?”

Squinting at the image, he laughed heartily. “Southend? That's us in all our embarrassing glory! And is that Ronnie wearing those diabolical shorts?”

Luca chuckled, his eyes crinkling at the corners. “The very ones. That day was utter madness, wasn't it? Wild from start to finish.”

Bernie shook his head in amusement. “Between Ronnie’s fashion disasters and our endless antics, it's a wonder we survived!”

Luca traced his finger over the faded photo, lingering on each face. “That's me, you, Micky, Ronnie Gadd, and Johnnie Bilham. Have you seen or heard from the others lately?”

Bernie took a closer look, his lips curling into a small smile. “Planning a little get-together, are we?”

Luca's gaze sharpened, and his face tightened. “I wish it were something that pleasant.”

Bernie's eyes softened. He took a deep breath. “Phil Hurren, he died about ten years ago.”

Luca's face fell, but he tried to mask his emotion. What about the others?”

“Harry Noakes? Last I heard, he'd gone off to Australia,” Bernie said, his eyes shifting slightly as if trying to recall distant memories. “Ronnie Bennett? He's not too far away. Lives in Worcester Park. Pops in here occasionally.”

Luca looked hopeful. “And Pete Galvin? Ray Phillips?”

Bernie paused, rubbing his temple thoughtfully. “Pete moved somewhere up north. As for Ray Phillips?” He shrugged, looking genuinely puzzled. “Sorry, mate, I'm drawing a blank there.”

“Thanks, Bernie. That information is vital.” Bernie raised an eyebrow, pushing the photo closer to Luca.

“You've been probing quite a bit lately. What's all this about?”

Luca hesitated for a moment, looking at the photo, then back at Bernie. “It's just that I've got this nagging feeling in my gut. I think this photo has something to do with the recent murders.”

Bernie's eyes widened. “You mean the deaths of the girls and Micky?”

Luca nodded. “Especially Micky's and Ronnie Gadd's daughter.”

Bernie looked taken aback for a moment, his gaze fixed on the photograph. “Well, I hadn't thought about it, but now that you mention it, I see what you mean.”

"There's something here, Bernie. I can feel it."

Bernie rubbed his chin thoughtfully. "Like you, I've known Micky for years. The thought that his death might be linked to something bigger," he trailed off, shaking his head.

CHAPTER FIFTY-THREE

Luca emerged from the cool, tile-walled sanctuary of Sloane Square tube station into a world bathed in sunlight. Above Kings Road, the sky unfurled like a cobalt tapestry, transforming the pavement and taxis into a stage lit by golden spotlights. Squinting, he lifted a hand to shield his eyes, giving them a moment to adapt from underground dimness to open-air brilliance. As his eyes adjusted, Kings Road revealed itself—energetic, pulsing with life. Pedestrians donned shades, their shadows dancing on the sidewalk, stretching and contracting as if mimicking the rhythmic heartbeat of the city.

Across the way, Peter Jones department store stood as a familiar landmark, its large glass panes reflecting the scene of life unfolding before it—like a silent observer that had seen decades roll into centuries.

People weaved around him, a river of lives in motion. Some clutched bags emblazoned with designer logos, while others held cups of takeaway coffee. Their laughter, their fragmented dialogues, contributed to the symphony of sounds that was uniquely Kings Road.

Sliding his own sunglasses into place, Luca took a purposeful step forward. Each stride seemed to catch and amplify the day's brightness, as if the sun and he had entered into a silent pact to celebrate the beauty of the moment. Kings Road, an ever-changing blend of history and present-day chic, felt like a stage set just for him—and today, it was a stage awash in light.

The polished glass door of the café swung open, allowing a waft of roasted coffee beans to spill out. Above, a simple, understated sign read "Café Chelsea." Inside, sunlight streamed through large windows, dappling wooden tables and casting soft silhouettes of patrons engrossed in their worlds.

At a corner table, two women leaned in, their heads close, sharing hushed secrets punctuated by laughter. The barista, a young woman with tattooed arms, poured a frothy cappuccino, her concentration evident in the delicate heart she crafted atop the foam.

Grace sat amidst the bustling café, her dark sunglasses a shield against the world. The sun coming in through the window cast playful dapples on her white sundress, and every slight movement of her wrist sent rivulets of light scattering from her gleaming silver bracelet and the pendant that rested just above her heart. From the crowd, Luca moved with a purposeful stride, each step reducing the distance between them. His hand lifted, a simple but deliberate gesture, fingers splayed in a half-wave, half-salute.

She responded by tilting her head upwards and sliding her sunglasses into her hair, revealing eyes that danced with a mix of anticipation and uncertainty. Their gazes locked, as if pulled together by some unseen force, and for a moment, the world around them blurred, leaving just the two of them and the unsaid words that hovered between. "Luca," she murmured, her fingers absent-mindedly caressing the cool metal of her bracelet, as if drawing strength from it. He leaned in, his elbows creating a bridge on the table, drawing their world even closer.

After receiving their coffees, Luca and Grace shared a comfortable silence, punctuated by snippets of conversation about mundane events. But as Luca gazed into the depths of his coffee, a weight seemed to pull at his shoulders. "Ever think about how unpredictable life is?"

Grace's eyes softened, "All the time. Life's got its way of surprising us."

Shaking his head, Luca murmured, "The past two years, they've been unthinkable."

"You and I both," Grace responded, her eyes shadowed by memories. "But dwelling on it won't change anything."

Luca met her gaze, the conflict evident in his eyes. "Every new step, even this coffee with you, feels like I'm betraying Julia. As if I'm forgetting her."

Grace's voice held a gentle understanding, "I get it. When my husband left, it felt like a part of me left with him."

A small smile tugged at Luca's lips, "You've always been resilient."

Grace shrugged slightly, "We don't really have a choice, do we? We've got to live for them. For ourselves."

Taking a moment, Luca said, “It's like stepping into the unknown. An unfamiliar future.”

“Maybe it's about carving our own journey, Luca,” Grace said, her voice resolute. “Not replacing them, but learning to breathe again.”

His voice quivered slightly, “But what if I lose my way?” Grace met his eyes, firm and kind, “You're stronger than you think. And I believe they're still with us, guiding. We've just got to tune in.”

Luca’s eyes brightened just a touch, “You always see the silver lining, don't you?”

Grace reached over, squeezing his hand gently. “We're navigating this storm, Luca. Let’s promise: no letting guilt steer our ship.”

CHAPTER FIFTY-FOUR

Leaving the café, Luca and Grace exited onto the bustling Kings Road. Grace glanced at her wristwatch, her eyes sharp and alert. She hailed a passing black cab and called out, "Knightsbridge, please," as she slid into the back seat. The driver gave a nod, and they sped off, weaving through London traffic.

Meanwhile, Luca turned in the opposite direction and made his way back to Fulham to meet Johnnie Billham at his builder's yard.

Luca's shoes softly scuffed against the pavement of Munster Road, a rhythm so familiar he often lost himself in thought on this well-trodden path. The quiet sounds of the Fulham street mingled with his own reflections; each footfall a memory of the years spent here. There, nestled between the houses he had walked past countless times, was Johnnie's builder's yard. "How could I have missed it?" Luca thought, his eyes narrowing as he tried to reconcile the memory of this path with the reality before him. The sign above the yard, faded and worn by years of London's fickle weather, proclaimed its longevity: “Billham Builders—Since 1979.”

Luca blinked, his eyes searching for relief against the onslaught of sunlight that had no business being this harsh. The rusty jumbles and timeworn stacks of wood glowed with a ghostly aura, and it didn't sit right. The concrete underfoot, scarred and patchy, felt as if it was throwing a dare with every step he took. The old diggers and forsaken lorries didn’t just rust in silence that day—there was a pulse about them, a static charge, as if the yard itself wasn't too keen on having Luca around.

Whispers of wind, tainted with a nostalgic scent of grease and old iron, brushed past him. Off to his left, a weathered tarpaulin, bleached by the sun, gave a rhythmic flap, more like a heartbeat than the work of the wind. The sound rattled Luca’s nerves. Rounding an old tin shed, he found Johnnie sitting there, perched on some relic of a chair amidst a storm of blueprints and mugs that had seen better days. Even beneath the shadow of that tatty cap, those eyes had already taken Luca’s measure long before a word passed between them.

The air between them seemed to crackle; the day’s dazzle was at odds with the storm they were about to wade into. The yard felt like an offshoot of Johnnie himself, and Luca felt it pushing back, sizing him up. Summoning every bit of his grit, Luca shattered the silence. This wasn’t just idle chatter in a yard; he had matters that needed sorting—questions, and Johnnie Billham was the man with the answers.

Johnnie straightened up and glanced towards the house, his eyes gleaming with an invitation. “Coffee's on me,” he murmured. He began walking, with Luca trailing behind. The Victorian structure loomed ahead, its two spires casting eerie shadows against the sky, resembling the kind of house that would star in a Hammer horror film. Johnnie approached the gaping entrance, stepped in, and, with a nod, beckoned Luca to follow. The wooden floorboards creaked under their weight, echoing softly through the house. Johnnie moved with a familiarity, indicating he had trodden these paths many times before. The light from outside revealed old family portraits lining the walls, their faces faded but still visible, watching silently.

Luca hesitated for a moment, taking in his surroundings. The air inside was heavy, carrying the scent of years gone by—a mixture of mustiness and old books. He observed Johnnie walking ahead, seemingly unfazed by the ambiance. In the distance, the soft hum of an old refrigerator broke the silence, guiding them towards the kitchen. A light swayed overhead, the light making the walls appear alive, as if breathing. Johnnie moved toward an old kettle and filled it with water.

The soft hiss of the gas stove caught Luca's attention, followed by the soft blue glow illuminating the base of the old kettle. Johnnie's hands, slightly weathered, manoeuvred the kettle deftly, displaying a familiarity with the outdated stove.

While the sound of the increasing boil murmured in the background, Johnnie reached beneath the window-side table, dragging out two wooden chairs. The legs of the chairs scraped lightly against the worn floor tiles. Luca took the cue and lowered himself into one, noting the slight creak of aged wood under his weight.

“So,” Luca started, eyes darting around the cobwebbed kitchen, searching for a safe topic. “Have you owned the yard for long?”

Johnnie's gaze fixed on the bubbling kettle, his response limited to a slight nod.

“Have you got plenty of work on at the moment?” Luca continued, desperately seeking a foothold in the conversation.

Johnnie poured the steaming water into two mugs, the aroma of strong coffee quickly filling the air. His lips curved into a half-smile, yet no words accompanied the gesture.

Taking a sip from his mug, Luca tried to suppress the growing unease. The sensation was swift and overpowering. As he gripped the table, the edges of his vision blurred. The room seemed to tilt, with every corner shifting out of place. Luca's grip on his mug slackened, and it crashed to the floor, shattering and spilling the remaining coffee in dark tendrils across the tiles. The noise, distorted in Luca's ears, sounded distant.

Luca's eyes darted to the figure opposite him. The name barely escaped his lips, “Johnnie?” His chest tightened, the room seeming to close in on him.

Johnnie's face, however, remained unchanged—like a statue devoid of emotion. As he stood, his every move was calculated, his gaze fixed intently on Luca. The distance between them closed with every deliberate step, the table now a barrier left behind. Frozen, the prickle of fear-induced sweat formed at Luca's nape, cold droplets betraying his mounting dread.

“Easy,” Johnnie's words came out, not loud, but somehow consuming the room's silence.

With each tick of a distant clock, Luca felt time stretch, distorting seconds into minutes. He could hear his own heartbeat, loud and irregular, a desperate rhythm. Luca's attempt to rise was thwarted; his body resisted, weighted and unwieldy. The edges of his vision blurred, darkness encroaching, pulling him towards unconsciousness.

Johnnie continued his unhurried approach, each footfall echoing in the cavernous silence. The muted light from the window cast long shadows across the room, further obfuscating his intentions.

As he reached Luca, he paused, taking in the palpable fear emanating from the man. The briefest hint of a smile touched the corner of his lips, devoid of warmth.

Luca's breathing grew more laboured; each inhale was a struggle, and every exhale was a shallow gasp. The oppressive atmosphere in the room seemed almost tangible, pressing on his lungs, refusing release.

Johnnie's fingers, cool and smooth, brushed against the table. He bent in, his face mere inches from Luca's. "Is this how you imagined our reunion?" he whispered, his breath cold smelly breath against Luca's skin.

The encroaching shadows and the room's stifling silence weighed heavier on Luca, pressing down on him with an intensity he'd never felt before. He tried to summon a response, any words to break the ice, but his mouth was parched, voice lost.

CHAPTER FIFTY-FIVE

Shouldering her way through the bustling streets of South Kensington, Grace's eyes darted past the busy shopfronts. The aromas of freshly baked pastries and roasted coffee beans mingled in the air, leading her closer to Gianni's Restaurant. Each step increased her anticipation. It wasn't just the prospect of a delightful lunch with Martina that spurred her on. No, it was the possibility of seeing Luca.

Taking a deep breath, she entered the restaurant and looked around for Martina—and perhaps for a chance glimpse of Luca.

Inside Gianni's, the mellow conversation washed over Grace, providing a comforting background to the varied mix of modern and vintage décor. In their crisp white shirts, the waiters navigated effortlessly between tables, balancing trays of steaming pasta dishes and colourful salads.

Grace's eyes darted across the room, settling on Martina waving from the back as she navigated her way through the maze of tables. It wasn't Luca seated opposite Martina. The man's dark hair contrasted sharply with the pale blue walls. The way he tapped his fingers on the table—impatient but rhythmic—commanded attention. He looked up just in time for their eyes to meet.

"Hey, you made it," Martina chirped, breaking the spell.

"Wouldn't miss it for the world," Grace replied, though her voice wavered a fraction more than she would've liked.

Martina gestured to the man. "This is Ethan. Ethan, meet Grace. Ethan is joining us as our head waiter." His fingers paused their tapping as he extended a hand. It wasn't the grip of someone trying to prove a point, but firm and self-assured.

"Nice to meet you, Grace," he said, then bid his goodbyes and left.

Grace glanced around the bustling café. "Is Luca in today?"

Martina shook her head, tapping her phone screen to silence an incoming call. "Rang him last night; no answer."

A waiter sidled up to their table as if on cue, dropping off a couple of menus.

"Two lattes?" he asked, already scribbling into his notepad.

"Make mine a tea," Grace corrected, giving him a polite smile.

The waiter nodded and retreated to the counter.

Martina leaned in, her eyes searching Grace's face. "So, how have you been? Must be a big weight off your mind, having Emma back?"

Grace's eyes clouded momentarily, a subtle flinching like touching a bruise. "Incredible, really. Had nightmares for weeks, you know. Expected the worst."

"Can't even imagine," Martina murmured, her eyes softening.

"Yeah," Grace exhaled, her shoulders dropping ever so slightly. "The worry gnaws at you; every phone call felt like a verdict. I wouldn't wish it on anyone."

Martina reached across the table, her fingers gently encircling Grace's hand. "But she's home now, safe."

Grace nodded, her eyes a mix of relief and lingering pain. "She is. And I can finally sleep through the night. But, God, what a horrific chapter to close."

The waiter returned with their drinks, placing them on the table with a cheerful clatter, unaware of the heavy conversation in the air. As he walked away, Grace looked at Martina, her eyes regaining a bit of their sparkle.

"Thanks for this, by the way. It's good to get out and even better to do it with a friend."

Martina smiled back, lifting her latte. "To moving forward."

Grace picked up her tea, the steam rising and curling between them. "To moving forward."

Martina glanced towards the reception area, catching Franco in an animated conversation with one of their waiters. A crease formed between her brows; he'd been clear about spending his day at the club.

Franco finished the exchange with a pat on the waiter's back and turned, making eye contact with Martina as he weaved through tables and chairs like a fat man leaving a buffet. His eyes flickered with a secretive glint that didn't sit well with her.

Franco smiled at Grace. "Nice to see you again, Grace." He smiled at Martina, "Surprised to see me?" he asked, sliding into the chair across from her.

Martina inclined back, her eyes narrowing as she considered the man who couldn't seem to stick to his own plans. "You did say you'd be at the club all day, didn't you?" Martina replied, taking a sip of her water as she studied Franco's face for clues.

Franco rested his elbows on the table. "Well, plans change. Something came up."

Martina's eyes locked onto Franco's, scanning the lines and nuances of his expression as if reading a complex puzzle. For a moment, the restaurant's clatter of dishes and chatter faded into the background. "All right then, since you've graced us with your presence, how about we make the most of it?"

A ripple of ease softened Franco's forehead and brightened his eyes as though a weight had been lifted. "Look, the real reason I'm here is I'm worried. I have been trying to contact Luca since yesterday afternoon and have left countless messages, but nothing."

Martina clutched her glass of water so tightly you'd think it might crack. "Funny you say that. I was telling Grace, I called him four times yesterday."

They both looked down at their phones, sitting silent and useless on the table like two abandoned cars in the middle of nowhere. You could almost hear the tension thickening in the room, every face tightening.

Franco scraped his chair back. "Right, that's it. I'm popping over to Luca's gaff in Fulham. Something's wrong, I can feel it in my bones." He hesitated for a split second. "I hope it's nothing to do with that Johnnie Billham bloke?

Their eyes locked, each not wanting to say what they were both thinking. Finally, Martina breaks the silence. "I hope not. Just be careful, yeah?"

Franco grabbed his jacket from the back of the chair. "Careful is my middle name. Not really, but you get what I mean."

Martina forced a half-smile. "Yeah, just text me when you get there."

He winked his attempt to break the tension only half-successful. "You'll be the first to know

CHAPTER FIFTY-SIX

Franco's knuckles lighten against the steering wheel as he eyes the stubborn red light. The instant it flicks to green, he floors the accelerator. Just as he gains speed, a slow-moving car pulls out in front of him, forcing him to brake. His eyes dart to the rear-view mirror before snapping back to the road. Relief washes over him as he finally makes the right turn onto Parsons Green Lane.

Exiting the car, he shuts the door with a swift, decisive motion and strides towards the front of the house. He raps on the door twice, pauses, then repeats. Silence greets him. Leaning in, his eyes narrow as he listens intently. No sound comes from within the house. His gaze flits from the windows to the letterbox, half-expecting some sign of life. None comes. Pulling his mobile from his pocket, he glances at the screen. No new messages. His thumb hovers over the call button, but he resists. Instead, he pockets the device and steps back from the door, contemplating his next move.

With a sigh, he turns and scans the quiet street. Not a soul in sight. For a moment, he considers going back to his car, but something—perhaps the stillness of the air or the unreadable silence from the house—holds him in place. His eyes return to the front door. He takes a deep breath, as if girding himself for another knock, a louder one this time. Just as his knuckles are about to make contact, he shoulders the door in, putting his seventeen stone behind it.

The relief on Franco's face gives way to a guarded expression. "Luca? You in there, mate?" His voice cuts through the still air. Again, silence greets him.

The hallway is dark, a corridor of uncertainty. He hesitates before taking the next steps. Room by room, he searches—each empty space feeding the knot in his stomach. The air feels heavy, wrong.

His phone buzzes in his pocket, snapping his focus back. The screen displays a text from Martina: "Heard anything yet?"

His thumbs hover over the screen. His mind races; options and scenarios blend into a fog of worry. He begins to type, stops, then starts again: "No sign of him. Something's definitely wrong; I can feel it."

As he sends the message, the name Johnnie Billham flashes into his thoughts, nagging at him. It's a splinter in his mind—out of place yet refusing to be dismissed. Before leaving, he sets about securing the front door.

Franco revs the engine, which hesitantly roars to life, as if dreading the trip to O'Grady's Club. His eyes, once curious windows, narrow into pragmatic slits that break the world down into tasks to complete. Each pothole jolts him; each red light stalls him, as though the universe itself conspires to delay him. Checking the rear-view mirror, he half-expects

Luca's haunting face to materialise, but all he sees are the grey streets behind him.

He parks on Moore Park Road and continues on foot to Fulham Broadway. Inside the club, the air is thick with the musty scent of stale beer. Bernie Montgomery, towel in hand, methodically wipes down glasses behind the bar.

As Franco walks in, his voice is gruff as he greets him. "How are you, Bernie?"

Bernie looks up, breaking his rhythm. "Franco! How are you doing, mate?"

"Been better. It's Luca I'm worried about."

A flicker of concern crosses Bernie's eyes. "What's happened?"

"He's gone missing."

Bernie sets down the glass he was wiping. "You're joking. I saw him just the other day."

"Yeah? Did he say anything, give you any clues as to what was going on?"

Bernie thinks for a moment. "He was going on about Johnnie Billham, reckoned he had something to do with Micky Coomber's murder."

"Sounds like Luca."

Franco's eyes widen, as if piecing together a puzzle. "Did he say what he was planning to do next?"

"No, but he looked rattled. Something wasn't right."

Franco sighs, his fingers combing through his hair. “Luca wouldn’t disappear without a reason. Something’s wrong; I know it.”

Bernie’s gaze turns serious. “Want me to ask around? Some of the regulars might know something.”

“Please do, Bernie. I’ve got to find him.”

“Right, consider it done,” Bernie says, picking up the glass he’d set aside and resuming his wiping with newfound urgency.

Franco looks at Bernie, his gaze steady but weary. “Yeah, do that. But be discreet. If Johnnie Billham is involved, this could get messy fast.”

Bernie nods, understanding the gravity of Franco’s words. “Will do, mate.”

“You watch your back too,” Bernie replies, his voice lowering, infusing the air with a sombre energy that even the thick scent of stale beer couldn’t mask.

Franco emerges from the club, the door swinging shut behind him, sealing out the music and chatter. He feels disoriented, as though each street in the city is another twist in a labyrinth built to thwart him. He climbs into his car, gripping the steering wheel with renewed purpose. As he accelerates, a sense of foreboding settles over him, as if he were steering into an impending storm with no way out. His next destination is clear: the Aintree Estate, on Dawes Road.

CHAPTER FIFTY-SEVEN

Luca's hand trembled as it reached for the frayed edge of his ankle ties. Sweat beaded on his forehead. With each tug, the fibres of the rope frayed a bit more, but so did his hope. He glanced at the steel door; it remained unmoved, indifferent to his plight. The room was silent except for the shallow rasps of his breath. He paused, listening. Were those footsteps in the distance, or just his mind playing tricks? The uncertain sound heightened his senses and narrowed his focus. He pulled at the ropes again—desperation mixing with dread.

A sudden clang reverberated from the door. Luca's heart skipped a beat. He pulled himself into as upright a position as his bindings would allow, his eyes darting to the shadow now spreading across the floor from the widening door gap. Johnnie stepped closer, the weight of his boots echoing in the confined space. Each step seemed calculated, a quiet power play. "Do you recognise where you are?"

Luca scanned the room: Brick and metal walls, the faint smell of damp and rust. It was as though the world outside had ceased to exist. He swallowed hard; his throat was dry. "Should I?"

The tension in the room thickened. Johnnie reached inside his jacket and pulled out a cigarette. As he lit it, the flame briefly illuminated the depths of his eyes. They held something Luca couldn't quite grasp—madness? Regret? Contempt? Johnnie exhaled; the smoke mingled with the murky air before he spoke. "Depends on how much you value your past."

Johnnie flicked ash onto the concrete floor. "You're not very talkative, are you?"

"I could say the same about you," Luca shot back, finding a fragment of courage. "All this mystery. What do you want?"

Johnnie stepped closer, close enough for Luca to smell the tobacco mingled with a hint of sweat. The corner of Johnnie's mouth lifted again, a momentary break in his otherwise stony facade. "What I want, Luca, is simple. I want you to remember."

The room went silent, as though holding its breath. Luca's mind raced.

"Remember what?"

Johnnie stubbed out his cigarette, "Time's ticking, Luca."

Luca's ears throbbed with his own heartbeat, drowning out the world.

Johnnie walked across to the other side of the room, his boots scraping against the concrete. He moved to a metal table where a variety of menacing instruments lay scattered—some sharp, some dull, all ominous.

Picking up an inconspicuous item, Johnnie returned to his position. As he met Luca's eyes, his face betrayed a chilling blend of glee and malice.

Panic tightened around Luca's chest as his eyes flicked to each corner of the room, searching for anything that might be of help. The walls remained bare; the door, impenetrable. Johnnie leaned back in his chair, setting down an indistinct object beside him—close enough to pique Luca's curiosity, but too far for a clear view. The atmosphere in the room grew dense, the silence lengthening with each tick of an invisible clock.

Johnnie folded his hands in his lap, eyes meeting Luca's for a brief, unsettling moment before looking away. Luca felt his throat constrict, the weight of the room settling onto him like a layer of dust. The absence of sound was oppressive; even the shuffle of Johnnie's feet seemed muffled, as though the air itself had solidified.

"Time's almost up," Johnnie said, his voice cutting through the silence but adding no relief. He glanced at the object beside him, then back at Luca.

The corners of his mouth twitched, hinting at a satisfaction he didn't fully express. Luca's fingers clenched involuntarily. His mind raced for options, for anything he could say to break the stranglehold of the room's suffocating tension. But words clung to the inside of his mouth, stubborn and unspoken.

Luca shifted, and the ropes tightened. He tested the ropes around his wrists with a slight flex. His eyes met Johnnie's, probing for a hint of vulnerability in his icy gaze. He found nothing.

Finally, Johnnie broke the silence, his voice cutting through the air like a serrated knife. "Welcome to your new reality, Luca."

The light overhead gave its last flicker before extinguishing, submerging the room in darkness. Yet Luca understood: the darkness changed nothing. Both men remained, anchored in their warped scene, in a world that thrived on uncertainty. Johnnie reached into his pocket, producing a small remote control. With a detached press of a button, a secondary light source activated, casting the room in an unflattering hue. “Comfortable?” Johnnie asked, the word hanging in the air like a noose.

Luca glanced at the ropes, then back at Johnnie, saying nothing. A corner of Johnnie's mouth twitched, almost a smirk. He moved toward the metal table, its surface littered with an assortment of tools, none designed for comfort. Picking up a set of pliers, he weighed them in his hand for a moment, then set them back down, opting for something less immediate.

“Do you know why you're here?” Johnnie continued, his voice void of inflection.

“Fucking enlighten me,” Luca growled.

“The rules have changed, Luca. The old ways don't apply anymore.”

“So, what's the new game?” Luca asked.

“It's that simple, “Johnnie paused, meeting Luca's eyes once again. “Adapt or perish.”

As Johnnie spoke, Luca felt a low vibration beneath him. The chair, the ropes, the room—all seemed to shift ever so slightly, as if aligning themselves to a new reality. The vibration ceased, leaving an unsettling quiet.

Luca absorbed Johnnie's words, understanding their weight. In this room, bound and facing an unclear future, adaptation was more than a choice; it was a necessity for survival.

In the dimness, only their breathing disturbed the silence. Johnnie's breaths were even and steady; Luca's were uneven, punctuated by sharp intakes.

A metallic sound echoed from the shadows. Johnnie was adjusting something, perhaps his tools. With every sound, Luca's imagination spun grim scenarios, each one a sharp edge or blunt force landing on his skin, his bones.

“Still comfortable?” Johnnie's voice cut through the darkness.

The question hit Luca harder than he'd anticipated. “What the fuck do you want?”

“Who says I want anything?” Johnnie's laughter seemed to ricochet off the walls. “Maybe I'm offering you a unique opportunity.”

Luca tightened his jaw, his teeth grinding together. He refused to give Johnnie the satisfaction of a reaction.

Blinking, Luca fixed his eyes on a small handheld recorder next to his chair. “Why the recorder?” His voice was steadier than he felt inside.

“Maybe I want to record your last words,” Johnnie said, casually flipping the device in his hand. “Or maybe it's for something else. You don't get to know. Not yet.”

Johnnie placed the recorder on the table and pushed it an inch closer to Luca. "Any last words you'd like to share? This is your chance."

"I don't play games, you half-wit," Luca responded, his eyes narrowing.

"That's a shame. Life's full of them," Johnnie retorted, picking up the recorder and pressing the record button. "Let's begin, shall we?"

The room seemed to grow colder as the recorder whirred to life, capturing the weight of their words. The tension between them was thick enough to cut with a knife.

"Begin what? Another one of your mind games?" Luca's voice had a biting edge.

"No, not a game. More like a lesson," Johnnie said, eyes locked onto Luca's.

"A lesson in what, exactly?"

"You'll find out." Johnnie clicked off the recorder and pocketed it. "But for now, I think our time is up." The light flickered off again, plunging the room into darkness once more. The sound of footsteps grew fainter, then disappeared altogether. Luca was left alone, enveloped by the dark, pondering the meaning of Johnnie's puzzling words.

CHAPTER FIFTY-EIGHT

In his twenties, Franco was entangled with the Mafia in London. Taking his father's stern advice to heart, he severed those ties swiftly. Thereafter, he worked alongside his father in the family business, learning the ropes and earning trust. When his father passed away, the mantle of responsibility fell on Franco. Known as “Bull,” he had a reputation for strength and zero tolerance for disrespect. Under Franco's leadership, the family business thrived. He implemented modern strategies while retaining the traditional values his father had instilled. Employees respected him, not just for his assertive nature but also for his fair dealings.

Even so, remnants of his past connections occasionally surfaced. Old associates from his Mafia days would show up, testing his resolve. But Franco, the unyielding "Bull," made it clear that those chapters were closed.

He strengthened the business's security measures, both physical and digital. Always vigilant, Franco often found himself scanning crowds for familiar faces from a life he had left behind. He couldn't afford any vulnerabilities, not when the safety of his family and the livelihood of his employees were at stake.

Despite the weight of his responsibilities, Franco managed to be present for his family, just as his father had been for him. Franco's resilience emanated not just from a place of duty, but also from love and a deeply rooted sense of family legacy. Through all the challenges and complexities, Franco never wavered. His reputation as "Bull" wasn't just a testament to his physical strength or his capacity for intimidation; it was an acknowledgment of his unwavering commitment to protect and provide for those who relied on him.

As Franco pulled into Aintree Estate, a gaggle of young lads was engrossed in a game of football outside one of the flat blocks. He skilfully manoeuvred his car into a spot on the left of Aintree Street, all the while trying not to disrupt the ongoing match.

"Oi, lads!" Franco called out, raising his hands defensively as a ball whizzed past him. "Don't worry, I'm not here to join your Chelsea trials. I'm after an old pal of mine who goes by the name of Johnnie Billham?"

One of the cheekier boys smirked, his eyes dancing with mischief. "Johnnie? Oh, he's the local nut job."

Franco grinned, "Oh, you've no idea. I've had the pleasure of his quirks for years."

Another lad, busy adjusting his shoelaces, piped up without looking, "Top floor, next block, Flat 28. You can't miss him—or his strange collection of garden gnomes."

With a chuckle and a nod of thanks, Franco made his way to the next block, looking for Johnnie's infamous gnomes.

As Franco navigated through the concrete jungle that was Aintree Estate, he couldn't help but notice the peculiarities that made it almost charming. Finally arriving at the next block, he gave the building a scrutinising look. A poster near the entrance proclaimed, "Neighbourhood Watch: We're Watching You," as if someone had binge-watched a spy thriller series and suddenly considered themselves Sherlock Holmes. Below the sign, in a much less official tone, someone had graffitied, "Johnnie's gnomes see all."

With no lift in the block, he climbed the stairs. The flats seemed permanently stuck in the 1970s, complete with the aroma of stale cigarettes and urine.

Walking towards Flat 28, Franco began noticing the subtle cues leading to Johnnie's lair. Finally, Franco stood before the famed door of Flat 28. Staring back at him was three garden gnomes stationed as sentinels, their eyes painted in a manner that seemed to suggest it knew all your internet search history.

Taking a deep breath, Franco knocked on the door, preparing himself for whatever brand of weirdness Johnnie was currently marinating in.

Receiving no response, Franco pounded the door with the side of his fist. As he turned to leave, the door creaked open a fraction. Uncertain whether it was his own force or a faulty lock that had caused the movement, he leaned closer to the pale blue, weathered door and peered through the narrow opening. "Anyone in?" Silence greeted him.

Growing impatient, he raised his voice. "Johnnie, you in there?"

When no reply came, Franco nudged the door open with caution. A foul odour immediately assaulted his senses, a vile mix of decayed fish and stale sweat. Franco hesitated, gripped by an uneasy feeling that something was horribly wrong. The smell seeped into his clothes, clinging to him like an unwelcome memory. Taking a deep breath, which he immediately regretted, he stepped into the stinking room.

The sight that met him was one of disarray; papers strewn about the floor, furniture upturned, and dirty dishes piled high in the sink. It was as if the very walls were sagging in neglect. But more than the visual chaos, it was the oppressive atmosphere of the room that unsettled him. It was as if the room itself had swallowed the sound, unwilling to let it escape.

He moved cautiously through the mess, his eyes darting about, half-expecting something—or someone—to jump out at him.

Franco's shoes stuck to the floor with every step. The dim lighting did little to reveal the layers of grime and disarray covering Johnnie's flat. Stray beams of light highlighted the wafting dust in the air. Empty food containers littered the place, and clothes—a mix of laundered and unwashed—made it difficult to make out the carpet beneath.

Among the chaotic sprawl, the walls were a stark contrast. They bore pictures—all of Johnnie's mother. Her stern face, with its piercing eyes, repeated in a monotonous rhythm around the room. It was as if she was watching, always watching.

Franco's heart raced; he had to find Johnnie Billham, and with each tick of the clock, the noose of uncertainty tightened. He rummaged through a pile of paper near the couch. As he moved some old newspapers aside, his fingers brushed against a fabric that felt out of place. Pulling it up, he found a young woman's dress—torn at the hem. His gut tightened. Nearby, half-covered by a stained cushion, lay a photograph. As Franco picked it up, his eyes widened. It was Luca, smiling along with Micky Coomber outside the Wilton Arms in Dawes Road.

Naive to the danger he might be in. Was Luca connected to this mess? Franco's mind was racing. The weight of the situation pressed down on him. Time was running out. As Franco stepped out of Johnnie's flat, he began to pull the door shut. Just then, a voice stopped him. He turned and saw an elderly woman behind him. Her back was curved with the weight of years, and she held onto a tartan-patterned trolley. "Excuse me," she said, locking eyes with him.

Franco released his grip on the door and fully turned towards her. "Yes? How can I help you?"

Her gaze narrowed as it focused on Franco, as if sifting through layers of intent, then her eyes eased. "Would you mind lending an arm for the stairs? My knees are horrendous nowadays."

"Absolutely," Franco said. He looked at the concrete staircase and then back at her. "Ready?"

A sigh escaped her lips, but it was a sigh of relief. "You're a gem, you are."

They descended the stairs together, Franco feeling her weight shift onto her wheeled trolley each time her foot landed on a step. He measured his steps to hers, alert for any wobble or hesitation from her side. At the bottom, he seized the moment. "You wouldn't happen to know when your neighbour Johnnie's back, would you? I've been looking for him."

"I haven't seen him for a couple of days. Though if you're that keen, he has a yard up on Munster Road. He has an old house there too."

"Much appreciated," said Franco.

CHAPTER FIFTY-NINE

Franco's heart ached with an almost unbearable heaviness. Luca wasn't just a brother; he was the very fabric that stitched Franco's world together—he shared laughter, the midnight talks, and the way Luca's eyes twinkled when he smiled. They were each other's anchors, grounding one another in the tempests that life hurled their way. He tried Luca's number again, staring at the screen as it rang. Each pulse of the ringtone pierced him, amplifying the hollow space forming within him. Finally, the call dropped, unanswered, swallowed by the void of uncertainty.

A childhood memory surfaced: a night when they'd built a tent out of bedsheets and spent hours sharing their wildest dreams and deepest fears. Luca had looked at him, his eyes earnest, and said, "Promise you'll always find me, Franco, even if I get lost." Franco had promised, and now that vow reverberated in his mind like an unyielding drumbeat.

The engine roared to life, growling like a beast stirred from slumber. Franco's car shot forward, slicing through the traffic on Munster Road. His mind was a kaleidoscope of fears and hopes, but at its centre, one image remained unchanging: Luca's face, the epitome of brotherly love and friendship.

Franco eased his car into a small gap at the top of Munster Road. The sky above was overcast, an ashy sheet that leached the colour from everything it touched. A dim glow barely revealed the builder's yard of Johnnie—a wasteland of forgotten ambitions.

As Franco made his cautious approach, his footsteps reverberated in the thick air, each echo serving both as an ominous whisper that urged him on and as a warning to stay away. He halted, arrested by the sight of a rusted chain looped around the gates. Its time-worn padlock seemed to sneer at him, as though guarding hallowed ground. “Fuck it,” Franco exhaled, his voice nearly drowned in the oppressive atmosphere.

He felt the unbearable heaviness of lost moments settle on his shoulders like a shroud. Just as he turned to strategise his next move, he collided with a body. Recoiling, he saw a face all too familiar from the photos.

“Mind yourself!” snarled Johnnie Billham, his countenance darkening before recognition set in. “Franco? Long-time no see. How's Luca?”

Standing tall, Franco now loomed over Johnnie, his eyes squinting. "Why don’t you tell me? You’ve seen him recently, haven't you?"

Johnnie’s eyebrow arched, his lips curving into a sly smirk. “What are you on about?”

“Don't fuck with me Billham. Luca told me he met you, recently.”

Johnnie leaned in, his voice an unsettling murmur imbued with a palpable darkness. “It was just a nostalgic little gathering, that's all.”

The air thickened, as if absorbing the tension and becoming heavy with unspoken dread. "Come in, I'll make you a coffee," Johnnie mumbled.

He produced a corroded key from his pocket, its form eaten away by time, and turned it in the ancient lock. The gate moaned as it swung open, as though a long-held secret was being revealed. “After you.” Franco followed him, his gaze flitting uneasily to the windows of the house, which sat in shadow like sightless eyes. “We're not going in there?” Franco asked.

“Nah," said Johnnie, glancing with distaste at his decrepit residence. “The workshop's got your coffee. That place is best left alone—unless you're in the mood for a haunted tour. Go and have a look if you want.”

Johnnie plodded away, leaving Franco standing before the forsaken house, its door ajar in a forbidding invitation.

It felt as though the shadows within were breathing, as though daring him to disturb them. “Kettle's on,” came Johnnie’s voice from the distance.

Gritting his teeth, Franco pushed the door open, the hinges groaning in protest. A musty draft welcomed him—a stifling, unchanging air that seemed frozen in time. Flipping on his phone’s flashlight, it caught on decaying wallpaper and a floor awash in debris. The yard outside lay unnervingly quiet, as though holding its breath. The gloomy atmosphere tightened around Franco as he moved further into the house. The evidence of decline was inescapable: water-stained furniture, empty whiskey bottles and dust. Rodent tracks confirmed that he was not alone in this tomb of a place. 'Luca?" His voice, tinged with growing dread, barely rose above a whisper.

The silence that met him was laden with a menacing stillness. Descending into the basement, the pitch-black void seemed to close in around him. Four doorways loomed before him, like options in a twisted game. When he checked, each room revealed new levels of decay and abandonment—except for one. The chilling discovery froze him to his core. He was jarred from his thoughts by a rustle; a rat disappeared into a hole in the wall, as though running from something even it feared. As Franco made his way back up, the house seemed to almost sigh, as if disappointed.

After leaving the basement, Franco ascended the staircase to the top of the house. The staircase's ornate details were marred by decay, and the wood moaned under his weight. He opened a door on the landing and found a room filled with old clothing and yellowed newspapers, a stained mattress in the corner. The acrid, metallic smell filled the air. A noise from below caught his attention but faded as quickly as it had appeared. The atmosphere seemed to tighten, almost as if the house was closing in on him. Returning to the corridor, he searched through the other rooms. The elongating shadows and ambient noises seemed to grow increasingly hostile. Franco felt observed, as if the house itself was watching him. With each step back down the staircase, time seemed to stretch, until finally, he exited into the yard, the door slamming shut behind him. A sense of foreboding washed over Franco. The answers he sought were buried in that dilapidated house, and he knew he would have to go back, whether he wanted to or not.

Once out in the yard, he felt a renewed sense of looming dread. The questions he had, the revelations he'd stumbled upon, they were all pieces of a malignant puzzle housed within those crumbling walls. And as much as every instinct screamed to stay away, he knew he had no choice but to return. Franco's eyes darted to the workshop, and he strolled over looking for Johnnie, but he was gone.

He looked at his phone and saw there was no signal. Inconvenient, yet fitting. What was the story behind those mysterious photographs? Where was Luca? This was no longer about choices. It was about confronting a necessity born of dark revelations and haunting uncertainties—a necessity that gnawed at his soul, even as it filled him with dread.

CHAPTER SIXTY

A psychopath's thinking is often characterised by a lack of empathy, emotional detachment, and a manipulative outlook towards others. While not all psychopaths are violent or criminal, their thought processes generally deviate significantly from social norms and moral codes. In Johnnie's mind, emotions are just variables to be manipulated, a means to an end. There's a sharp, cold logic to everything he does. He doesn't feel guilt; he calculates risks. He doesn't experience love; he identifies opportunities for gain.

In Johnnie's constructed reality, he's the perennial outsider, always looking in but never a part of anything. His sense of exclusion isn't a wound; it's a badge of honour, a justification for whatever he deems necessary to level the playing field. He sees his old friends not as people who've moved on but as people who've taken something from him—something he's entitled to reclaim.

His sense of revenge isn't fuelled by an emotional grudge but by a calculated desire to take back what he believes has been stolen from him: happiness, family, and a sense of belonging.

In his skewed version of reality, Johnnie thinks of himself as a rational actor in an irrational world. He believes he's not the one with the problem; it's everyone else who doesn't see things clearly. When he plans to target his friends, he's not governed by a frenzied emotional state but by a chilling, methodical planning process. He weighs the pros and cons, considers the risks and rewards, and then moves forward, devoid of hesitation or remorse.

His actions aren't sins or crimes in his own mind; they're simply necessary steps on the path to reclaiming what he's owed. After all, in Johnnie's world, emotions are weaknesses, and he's simply exploiting them in others to correct a world that has always been imbalanced against him.

Outwardly, Johnnie was a successful builder with a good reputation. When working his charming smile rarely left his face, disarming people and drawing them into his sphere of influence. But his steady, penetrating gaze betrayed his constant evaluation, sizing people up. As a child, Johnnie was more observer than participant, treating relationships as transactional. Affection seemed a foreign currency; aggression, a useful tool. Once he hit a friend's sister, baffled when told it was wrong. To him, she was just an object; her feelings irrelevant.

His childhood dreams weren't of monsters, but of violently controlling his father—not nightmares, but affirmations of power. Oblivious to his manipulative tendencies, his parents considered him simply unique.

At eight, a near-drowning in the Thames at Bishops Park, shook him not with terror but exhilaration. Staring death in the face, he laughed. He considered whether different life circumstances would have turned him into something darker, even lethal. It was a thought he entertained but never resolved.

Johnnie had imprisoned Luca, but Luca's brother Franco was emerging as an issue that had to be dealt with swiftly. Johnnie paced the gravel floor of his builder's yard, his boots crunching with each step. Stopping, his hands clenched and unclenched at his sides. A drop of sweat trickled down his temple as he considered the chessboard of his predicament. Luring Franco in was just the opening gambit.

He glanced at the makeshift cell in the corner where Luca was kept, then back to his phone. Johnnie's fingers danced over his phone, crafting a text with the same precision he used for laying bricks at one of his construction sites. "I am sorry I could not stay Franco, I had an urgent call out, on one of my jobs. I have urgent info on Luca. Must discuss in person. My yard. Tomorrow at midday."

His thumb hovered over the send button, after a moment of hesitance, he pressed send. The trap was set.

Johnnie smiled. But the real game would start only when Franco walked into the yard. Until then, every second counted. The trap needed to be fool proof, his actions precise. Time was running out, and Franco was a wild card he couldn't afford to underestimate.

CHAPTER SIXTY-ONE

Franco's Merc roars down Munster Road. The dashboard clock mocks him; each second stretching out as if taunting him. His fingers drum a restless rhythm on the steering wheel. An empty parking space by Johnnie's flat materialises like an oasis. Tyres screech, drowning out the thud-thud-thud in his chest. He bursts from the car, a tornado of urgency. Each step in the stairwell a thunderclap, amplifying his internal storm. He reaches the landing, a momentary pause. His breaths shallow, not from the climb but the electric buzz of expectation tingling his skin. The door to Johnnie's flat is ajar. He pushes in, eyes scanning—living room, kitchen—no Johnnie. His every movement fine-tuned to the razor edge of focus.

His phone vibrates in his pocket, fracturing the silence. A text from Johnnie. His thumb hovers, a brief hesitation. "Alright, I'm interested. We're meeting in your yard again, correct?"

Ping. "Yes, midday tomorrow." He exhales, the text message glowing in his eyes. Shoulders loosen, but not completely. The urgency lingers—palpable, unyielding.

He ransacks the kitchen cupboards. Old cookbooks, loose papers, and then—his fingers snag on a large brown envelope, shoved in the back of a bottom drawer. He yanks it onto the table, tearing it open. Notes scatter like autumn leaves, but it's a black and white photograph that arrests him. Faces from a past he can't sever, staring back. A jolt of recognition—this is what Luca had spoken of.

Names and dates on scribbled notes swim before his eyes. He cross-references, drawing mental lines from name to face, piecing together a jigsaw of betrayal. A breath sucks in, shallow, airless. Realisation lands like a punch to the gut.

He paces, each step a physical manifestation of swirling thoughts, each lap tightening the noose of dread around him. Pauses at the window, staring without seeing. A face reflects back—his own—plagued with questions he fears the answers to. Phone in hand, Martina's number under his thumb. A hesitation, the weight of the room condensed to a single touch. Ringing, then her voice, tinged with anxiety. "Franco, have you found him?"

"I haven't found him, and he's knee-deep in shit. Meet me at Luca's in thirty minutes?"

A hitch in her breathing, a quiver in her reply. "Yes, I'll be there. What's happened?"

He cuts her off. "We'll talk at Luca's. Bring his back-door key, yeah?"

Her agreement emerges as a whisper, heavy with the first droplets of tears. Franco sweeps the notes and the photograph back into the envelope, steps out, and locks the past behind him.

CHAPTER SIXTY-TWO

Franco stands on the pavement, eyes scanning Luca's house. His fingers drum nervously on his thighs. The low rumble of an engine interrupts the silence, and Martina's black Range Rover comes into view. The car parks abruptly, almost skidding, and Martina steps out. Her face is taut, eyes darting from Franco to the house and back again.

"Do you think he's in there?" she mutters, her voice tinged with apprehension.

Franco shakes his head, his lips a thin line. "Doubt it. We're just here for whatever scribbles and snapshots he's got on Johnnie Billham."

Martina fumbles in her pocket and hands over a worn key. "Back door," she says.

They move down the gravel pathway towards the side gate, the sound of their footsteps seeming louder than it should be. Franco unlocks the gate and they both step into the garden. They finally reach the back door.

Franco's hand hovers, trembling subtly, an inch from the door handle. He locks eyes with Martina. No words, but a pact forms in that split second. His fingers grip the cold metal and twist. He turns the key in the lock and the door creaks open, grudgingly breaking its silence. They step over the threshold. Franco's eyes dart around the room, pausing at the kitchen. The hanging utensils cast ominous shadows, as though withholding secrets. Their shoes clack against the lifeless tiles, each echo sharp and accusing, making the emptiness around them almost intense.

Martina's lips part, just barely. Her whispered breath fights against the suffocating quiet. “Office first.”

A single, terse nod from Franco is all the confirmation she needs. They pivot as one, pulled down the narrow hallway as if by a magnetic force. The atmosphere densifies with each step, a mounting pressure that seems almost tactile. Their eyes fixate on the plain door at the end, as if it’s the final barrier to some unbearable truth.

Martina yanks open another desk drawer, her eyes darting like a hawk zeroing in on prey. Papers shuffle and pens roll as she sifts through each item, dismissing each as irrelevant. Franco’s on the other side of the room, nudging books just enough to peer behind them, his fingertips grazing the wood, searching for any irregularities.

The clock ticks, louder and louder it seems, with each passing second. The air’s dense with tension, as if it too is holding its breath for what they might find—or not find. Martina’s hand halts midway through rustling a pile of loose papers. “Franco” she whispers, the word coming out as a stifled gasp. She pulls out a bulky folder, so fat it looks like it's been force-fed its contents.

Flipping it open, her eyes scan lines of text and skip across photos stapled to the sides. Franco abandons his search among the books and comes over, leaning to get a better look. Their eyes meet briefly, a fleeting glance that says, "This is it." Then both sets of eyes are back on the folder.

"Jackpot," Franco says, his voice heavy as if he's just lifted something immense. They both feel it—the weight of the information, the gravity of what they've just unearthed. It's as if the room itself exhales, but there's no relief, only the realisation that they've crossed into dangerous territory.

Martina tugs at the elastic band securing the mound of papers within the manila folder, releasing a scent of old photographs. Franco steps back, giving her room, his gaze shifting to the room's lone window where the curtain clings to the rod like a sentry. Franco takes over and starts leafing through the papers, his eyes narrowing at hastily scribbled notes. Each page he turns feels like peeling back layers of a carefully constructed concealment. Martina watches him, sensing the change in his posture as he delves deeper into the documents. His hands, which had been brisk and business-like, now slow, lingering on a particular photograph.

His fingers trace the outlines of faces, as the air in the room grows dense, laden with the gravity of their discovery. Franco angles the photograph so that he can see it. The faces staring back at them are not unfamiliar, but their arrangement, their presence in this hidden cache, adds a new weight to their mission.

They stand there, locked in that moment, each aware that the folder Franco carefully closes the folder, his hands smoothing over the cover as if he could somehow contain the explosive revelations lurking within its pages.

Martina glances at her wristwatch. “We should go,” she murmurs, her words summoning them back to the immediate urgency of their situation.

Franco presses his lips together and slides the manila folder under his arm. His eyes scan the office one last time—fixing on the worn desk, the stack of papers at the corner. With a mutual, unspoken agreement, they both turn, their steps measured and in sync, just as they were when they entered. They reach for the door handle at the same time, but Franco lets Martina take the lead. The door swings open silently on well-oiled hinges, and they step through.

Once they're in the corridor, Franco breaks the silence. “Cortona Club then? To go through the folder?”

Martina nods, eyes meeting his. “Cortona Club it is. Let's find out what we've got.”

The door clicks shut behind them, sealing off the room that held so much of their focus just moments before. Now, there’s a new task at hand—deciphering the contents of the folder tucked securely under Franco's arm. They walk down the hallway, each step a beat in their unspoken rhythm, already shifting their thoughts to what will come next.

CHAPTER SIXTY-THREE

Martina pushed open the heavy wooden door, its hinges creaking softly, as she entered Franco's office at the Cortona Club. The room was lit, with a small desk lamp providing a circle of warm light amidst the shadows. Franco sat hunched over his large mahogany desk, surrounded by a chaotic sea of photos, documents, and handwritten notes. He scratched his stubbled chin while studying a grainy black and white photo, his brow furrowed in concentration.

“Large Scotch?” Martina asked, even though she already knew the answer.

Franco's eyes flickered up to meet hers, the hint of a grin emerging from his otherwise stoic expression. “Do you even have to ask?” he rasped.

Martina smiled and shook her head, her heels sinking into the plush burgundy carpet as she made her way to the bar. The sound of clinking ice cubes filled the silence as she poured the amber liquid into each tumbler. She brought the glasses over to the desk, nudging aside a stack of papers to set one down in front of Franco.

He immediately lifted the glass to his lips, closing his eyes as he savoured the smooth burn of the alcohol. Martina perched on the edge of the desk, swirling her own drink casually.

"Grace called again," she said after a moment. "Asking about Luca."

Franco's steely gaze remained fixed on the items on his desk. "We'll call her back later," he murmured, his gravelly voice tinged with urgency. "I think we're finally getting close to cracking this thing wide open."

Martina nodded slowly and took a sip of her Scotch. She knew when Franco got that look in his eyes, it meant he was really onto something. All other concerns would have to wait. Martina nodded, her eyes meeting his for a moment before they both dived back into the chaotic world spread out on the desk, each buoyed by the silent promise that tonight could be the night they found what they'd been searching for.

The largest photo on the table, yellowed by age and creased at the edges, showed ten young men. All friends, smiling, arms around each other on the beach by Southend pier. The sea stretched infinitely behind them, oblivious to the darkness that would later envelop these men's lives. Luca, whose eyes met the camera with an unreadable expression, is now missing without a trace. Johnnie Billham is the only one who seems to be forcing a smile. Micky Coomber, standing slightly apart from the others, was found dead under circumstances that spelled murder. Ronnie Bennett and Bernie Montgomery are in jovial spirits, perhaps sharing a private joke. Ronnie Gadd's laughter reaches his eyes, belying the future tragedy that would claim his daughter's life. Phil Hurren and Ray Phillips stood shoulder to shoulder. Pete Galvin appeared to be saying something to Harry Noakes, who was laughing in response. This wasn't just a photograph; it was a Pandora's box. The air in the room seemed to thicken as if it too sensed the undercurrents linking the men in the frame.

Someone had once said, "Photos never change, even when the people in them do." But looking at the faces captured in that moment, it was hard to shake the feeling that the photo itself had changed. As if it whispered secrets and unanswered questions; as if it demanded scrutiny, begging someone to dig into the interconnected tragedies that marred the lives of those men. The photo didn't just represent a happier time; it was a haunting jigsaw of lives that had spun out of control. Every smile masked a story, every pair of eyes hinted at a drama yet to unfold.

Franco shakes the photo towards Martina and says, "There's got to be a link. This bloody photograph practically screams it."

Martina studied the photograph and then looked up at Franco. "So, do you recognise everyone in the photo?"

Franco glanced at the photo again. "Yeah, they're all faces from Luca's circle. But it's been years since our paths crossed."

Martina slid open a desk drawer and pulled out a magnifying glass. "Know where any of them might be living these days?"

Franco shrugged, his hands in his pockets. "Couldn't say."

Martina looked closer, inspecting some of the notes. "Look here. Luca jotted down some scribbles about the lads in the photograph."

Franco leaned over to take a closer look, his eyes widening "Ah, Bernie Montgomery. Luca mentioned he'd got some information from him. This must be it."

They exchanged a quick, understanding nod. This was a puzzle piece they hadn't anticipated, but one that might bring them closer to solving the bigger picture.

Franco straightened up and paced around the room, his eyes narrowing as he thought. "So, what's the next move then? We can't just sit on this information."

Martina browsed the papers in front of her to see if there were any more notes. Finding nothing, she set it back on the desk. "First, we need to figure out what these notes actually mean. Then, maybe we should try to find these people."

"Sounds like a plan," Franco agreed, coming to a stop and crossing his arms.

Martina agreed with a nod. "Absolutely, we need to be on the same page, every step of the way."

Martina's darted across Franco's face. "Do you reckon it's time to call in Rick Stone?"

Franco's jaw set hard, as his fists balled up. "Rick Stone? Are you having a laugh? The bloke's as useful as Anne Frank's drum kit."

Martina's eyes sharpened to slits, lips compressing. "We're out of our depth, Franco. We need to hand this over to someone who knows what they're doing."

He let out a derisive snort. “Relax, I've set up a meeting with Johnnie Billham for tomorrow.”

Her eyes blew wide, the pitch of her voice squeaking upward. “Johnnie Billham? Are you mental?”

Franco crossed his arms, the corners of his mouth twitching upwards in a maddening smirk. “Chill out. Johnnie knows a lot more than he’s letting on.”

Martina's cheeks flush, a deep red that could give a double-decker a run for its money. “He’s a lunatic, Franco. If he's involved, we might as well put your head on the chopping block now.”

Franco's eyebrow arches, completely unshaken by her display. “A lunatic? You think a clueless copper would be any better?” Franco shakes his head, locking eyes with her. “I’ve got to do this my way, Martina.”

Neither of them blinks. The room fills with a tension. Each one doubts the other's sanity, if not their loyalty.

Martina clenches her fists, her nails digging into her palms. “Your way? You mean the reckless, no-looking-back way? That's gotten us into a mess before, Franco.”

Franco straightens up, his smirk fading into a grim line. “It’s also gotten us out of messes. You know that.”

She glares, her jaw quivering. “This isn’t a petty street fight; this is serious, Franco. One wrong move and it’s game over.”

Franco shrugs in a casual, dismissive motion. “All the more reason not to bring in some clueless outsider who could fuck it all up.”

Martina lets out a harsh laugh, devoid of any real humour. "Or all the more reason to bring in someone who knows what the hell they're doing, unlike you."

Franco's eyes flash for just a second, stung. "I know what I'm doing."

"Do you?" Her voice is a low, challenging rumble. "Because from where I'm standing, it looks like you're just one step away from blowing it all to pieces."

He scowls, opening his mouth to respond but then closing it again. Instead, he just shakes his head. "If you don't trust me, fine. But I'm meeting Johnnie Billham tomorrow."

Martina stares, a mixture of disbelief and dread pulling her features taut. "Don't say I didn't warn you."

Franco's gaze hardens, locking onto hers. "I won't need to."

They remain like that for a few seconds, their eyes battle-grounds of unspoken tension and fraying trust. Finally, Martina turns, walking away with a frustrated shake of her head.

"God help us," she mutters, loud enough for him to hear.

Franco exhales a long, heavy breath he didn't know he was holding. He watches her leave, her words hanging in the air, an ominous cloud neither can escape.

CHAPTER SIXTY-FOUR

From a young age, Franco displayed an unmistakable hunger for the unknown. While his peers hesitated on the diving board, he was already soaring through the air, hitting the water with a splash of daring. He seemed to understand that bravery wasn't a choice; it was a requirement for a fulfilling life.

Franco captivated everyone. He brought life to any room, effortlessly combining humour, intelligence, and quick wit. Family members counted on him for his steadfastness and warmth. Yet, anyone who threatened Franco or his loved ones quickly realised they had made a grave mistake.

Franco and Lisa, his wife, live a child-free life above Gianni's restaurant. She's a local girl, as reliable and grounded as Franco is daring. Together, they make an unforgettable pair.

The door closed with a soft click as Franco entered his flat above the restaurant, dropping his keys onto the table. His jacket flew onto the back of a chair, serving as a makeshift coat hanger. He navigated through the organised chaos of his workspace before plopping down into his chair. Shoving an empty coffee mug aside, he booted up his laptop.

The screen flickered to life, illuminating his face while casting shadows across the room. His eyes darted between a tattered notepad and a group photo displayed in front of him. Ten young faces grinned back, as if sharing a secret, he was yet to discover. The bullet points scrawled on the notepad hinted at Martina's hunches and observations.

His fingers danced across the keyboard, moving through social media profiles, online forums, and public records. The room remained dark, the lone light emanating from the laptop screen. Time blurred; the night stretched long.

Then the tension in his shoulders lifted. “Pete Galvin,” he murmured, as the name, a phone number, and two addresses flashed across the screen. He scribbled them down on a yellow sticky note, which he slapped onto the edge of his monitor. He exhaled, savouring the small victory. The computer’s digital clock blinked 4:47 A.M. The chase had eaten into the night, but it had borne fruit. Franco retreated to bed, slipping under the covers next to a snoring Lisa.

His eyes closed for what felt like minutes rather than hours. When they opened again, Lisa’s rhythmic snoring still filled the room. Quietly, he disentangled himself from the bed covers and slipped out of the room.

In the kitchen, Franco brewed a pot of coffee, the aroma filling the space. As the coffee trickled into the pot, his mind shifted gears. He thought about Pete Galvin, recalling a foggy memory of him downing pints at the Clem Atlee with Luca and the gang. According to Luca’s notes, Pete had moved north. Now, Franco had found a Peter Galvin listed as a plumber in Birmingham. He connected the dots: Pete had been a plumber back in Fulham, running a small outfit on Dawes Road.

Sipping his coffee, Franco felt a tingling sense of anticipation in his veins. He had a name, a face, and now, a location. The day ahead offered a meeting with Johnnie Billham and the promise of answers. He was ready to chase them all down.

Franco glanced at the clock, noting the time: 9:10 A.M. He picked up his mobile and entered Pete Galvin's number. He pressed "call" and waited, his fingers tapping against the table. After three rings, a professional, feminine voice answered, "Galvin Plumbers, how can I assist you?"

"It's Franco Rossi," he began, trying to keep his voice calm. "I need to speak with Pete. It's important."

The voice on the other end hesitated for a split second, a hint of caution evident. "Could you let me know the reason for the call?"

He sighed, frustration bleeding into his tone. "It's personal. Pete and I go way back. Just get him on the line for me."

There was a soft sigh from her end. "One moment."

Silence settled; the weight of Pete's revelation hung heavy between them. It was broken by a familiar voice, deep and roughened by age. "Franco? Luca's older brother?"

Franco smirked. "The one and only." But before he could say anything else, Pete interrupted, urgency evident in his tone.

"Is Luca okay? Did something happen?"

"No, no," Franco replied, sensing Pete's anxiety.

"Luca's good. Been a while, Pete. How have you been?"

A noticeable tremor crept into Pete's voice. "Not great. Lisa, my daughter, she was murdered a few weeks back."

Silence settled; the weight of Pete's revelation hung heavy between them.

It took a moment for Franco to gather his thoughts. "Oh, God, Pete... I... I'm at a loss for words. I'm so sorry, mate."

Pete's voice cracked, but he continued. "It's been hell, Franco. I took some time off, this is my first week back."

Franco chose his next words carefully. "Where was Lisa living?"

"In Fulham, Estcourt Road." Pete answered.

"Was she married?"

Pete let out a weary sigh. "She was married once. Got divorced last year."

"What name did she go by then?"

"Jones. Lisa Jones." Pete's voice held a steady, distant quality.

Franco's face drained of colour. He blinked slowly, trying to process the information. "Lisa Jones? The same Lisa Jones who was..." he trailed off, not wanting to say the words.

Pete replied, "Yeah. One of the five girls recently murdered in Fulham."

Franco swallowed hard, glancing at the photograph on the table. Another friend, another victim.

CHAPTER SIXTY-FIVE

Moisture oozes from cracks, leaving dark, damp patches. Luca's breathing is uneven; each inhalation is a struggle against the musty, stale air that fills the room. He shifts his weight, and the ropes binding his wrists and ankles tug against the metal chair to which he is now fastened. The sound reverberates, briefly drowning out the distant hum of what might be a generator. His limbs ache from hours of immobility; the skin is chafed and bruised where the rope meets his flesh.

A tray of untouched food sits on a table to his left. The colourless slop has started to congeal, and the water in the plastic cup beside it is tinged with the brown of rust and dirt. He turns his head away; the smell assaults him, mingling with the odour of mildew and his own unwashed body.

The place feels like a relic, as if time itself has stopped. A high-pitched wail of sirens slices through his thoughts. Two years ago—same sound, different context. His eyes tighten, the scene unfolding uninvited: mangled cars, flashing lights, and Julia. He squeezes his eyes shut, teeth grinding together.

His jaw pulses with tension, as if he were physically restraining the emotional mess knotted inside him. It has been two years, but still, the knot remains—an unopened box of memories and a wedding ring he hasn't had the courage to remove.

He takes a deep breath. When he opens his eyes again, they fall upon the door—scratched, old, but a portal nonetheless. A gateway to an uncertain freedom. The face that flashes before him now isn't Julia's; its Grace Lane's. Her laugh seems to echo faintly, the crinkles by her eyes almost visible. Warmth begins to seep through the cracks of his emotional barricade. But then comes the guilt, a swift jab to the gut, as if his newfound warmth were an act of betrayal. The room seems to shrink; the walls edge closer, mirroring the internal battle that leaves him disoriented and trapped. There it is: his past and a flicker of the future, standing at odds, both demanding his emotional allegiance. He remembers Grace's touch, so different from Julia's, yet somehow comforting in its own right. The moments they've spent talking, really talking, as if she could see the cracks in his façade. Luca realises that his feelings for her are deepening, whether he likes it or not. And the awareness brings both relief and a sense of loss, as if acknowledging the possibility of a future means losing a part of his past. He tightens his fists, nails digging into his palms. Time to let Julia rest; time to let himself live. All he has to do is get through that door—physically and metaphorically.

If he could just break free, in every sense of the word, he could finally give himself permission to move on. And in that moment, despite the walls, the darkness, and the weight of the past, Luca felt the first stirrings of hope.

His eyes moved back to the tiny window, to the sliver of daylight that reached him. The quality of light changed, dimming slightly. Perhaps it was clouds, or the angle of the sun—a subtle marker of the passage of time. He counted his breaths, each cycle a minor victory of will. He listened for footsteps, for voices, for any indication of what might come next. Yet the only sound that filled his ears was the muted growl of the generator, punctuated by his own breath and the occasional creaking of his chains.

Uncertainty gnawed at him, but he kept his face impassive, schooling his features into an expression that gave nothing away. He had learned that much. A dull pain pulsed in his temples, marching in time with his quickened heartbeat. He flexed his wrists subtly, testing the ropes. They held firm. All his senses were sharpened to a razor's edge, but there was little to perceive, little to know, and nothing to do but wait.

CHAPTER SIXTY-SIX

Martina's gaze flicked to the computer clock—11:00 AM. Her hand hovered over the mouse, trembling slightly before clicking "Compose." A new email window popped open. "DI Rick Stone," her fingers flew across the keyboard, typing, "I can't ignore this any longer. Attached are scans of evidence we uncovered at Luca's and Johnnie Billham's properties. Please, you need to look at these immediately."

Sweat dampened her brow as she attached photographs of Luca and Micky Coomber and their friends, faces frozen in pixels, alongside scribbled notes that seemed to connect them to the recent string of murders. She then finished the email, "Luca thinks this is somehow connected to the murdered girls and Micky Coomber's death. Now, Luca himself is missing. Franco is meeting Johnnie Billham at midday, today. At Johnnie Billham's builder's yard on Munster Road. I'm worried about Franco and Luca both. Please act fast." A final click on "Send," and her pulse raced as if trying to outrun her fear.

She watched the attachment bar fill up, the blue line inching its way to completion. "Email Sent" flashed on the screen. Martina pushed away from the desk, her eyes stinging, not just from the computer glare but also from the weight of what she'd done. It was now in DI Rick Stone's hands. Martina leaned back, staring at the screen's reflection of her drawn face.

The room around her was dark, except for the artificial glow from the computer screen, which cast long shadows on the walls. She felt isolated, cornered. The seconds dragged on, amplifying her solitude and heightening her nerves. Sending the email to DI Rick Stone was like throwing a stone into a dark pond; she couldn't see the ripples, couldn't gauge the impact. She set the phone back down, resisting the urge to call Franco and tell him what she had done. If she did, would she be putting him at greater risk? Could she trust the police to act on her email promptly?

At 10:15 A.M., a beep broke concentration. An incoming email notification popped up on the corner of her screen. It was from DI Rick Stone. Her pulse quickened as she clicked to open it. "Received your email. We are assessing the evidence and will act accordingly. Keep your phone on. Updates coming soon." Brief. To the point. Yet the words carried weight. They meant that someone else was now shouldering part of her burden. But as the seconds ticked into minutes. Her brothers Franco and Luca, and now DI Rick Stone, were all intertwined in a timeline that seemed more fragile with each passing moment. She forced herself to stand; her legs were shaky. The room felt constricting, suffocating. She needed air. Martina walked over to the window, her hands trembling as she drew the curtains apart.

Minutes later, her phone rang on the desk behind her, jolting her nerves yet again. It was a call from a number she didn't recognise. Her hand hovered over the phone, hesitating. Then, with a deep, steadying breath, she answered it, her voice barely rising above a whisper. "Hello." In that instant, Martina felt the axis of her world shift, uncertain what the voice on the other end would bring: a reprieve, a tragedy, or another thread in a rapidly unravelling story.

The voice on the other end was gruff, tinged with the bite of urgency. "Martina, this is DI Rick Stone. We're acting on the evidence you sent. Officers are en route to Munster Road. We've also initiated a search for Luca."

For a moment, Martina's breath hitched in her throat. A torrent of questions swelled, wanting to spill forth, but she caught herself. Instead, she managed a shaky, "Thank you. Please find them."

"We're doing everything we can," DI Stone assured her, but his voice carried the strain of someone who had seen too many outcomes, not all of them good.

"As I said, could you please stay by your phone? We may need more from you."

The call ended, and Martina set the phone back on the desk, her fingers lingering on the cool screen. The gears of justice were in motion, but the wheels sometimes ground too slowly. Her mind raced through countless scenarios, each more frightening than the last. What if they arrived too late? What if Franco had already met with Johnnie Billham, and something had gone horribly wrong? And what about Luca, missing but clearly embroiled in this web of chaos? Martina felt a shiver crawl up her spine, and she wrapped her arms around herself as if that could ward off the terrible possibilities blossoming in her mind. Martina slid back into her chair, gripping its armrests as she nudged it closer to the desk. Her eyes bore into DI Stone's succinct email on the monitor. The screen's cold light flickered but added nothing to the sparse lines of text before her. Her eyes narrowed, as if she could force the pixels to rearrange into something—anything—more reassuring. Yet the words sat there, immutable, reflecting her mounting dread. Her phone buzzed abruptly on the desk, making her jump. Swiftly, she grabbed it. Franco. Her thumb hovered over the screen as she opened his text. "Won't make it to the yard until 15:30. All still good."

Each repetition gnawed at her, as if taunting her very understanding of "good." She looked back at her phone, her thumb still lingering. Was it even Franco who had typed those words? Her trust frayed with each tick of the clock, leaving her strung tight between dread and the frailty of hope. Sitting there, in a room that felt too quiet, too still, Martina felt the weight of each second that passed—each one a lost chance for someone to say something, do something. In that lingering silence, she found herself stranded, painfully aware of how brittle hope could be when stretched too thin.

CHAPTER SIXTY-SEVEN

The streets of Fulham were paved with memories of Franco's and Luca's shared childhood: skinned knees, laughs, and lessons learned. Whenever a shadow cast doubt or an unexpected menace approached, Franco's jaw stiffened, his posture straightened, standing as a living barrier between the world and his younger brother. Luca, on the other hand, would flash his eyes with a challenging glint, never wanting to be seen as just the little brother but always eager to stand shoulder to shoulder with his big brother Franco. Without words, they had established their roles in each other's lives. Franco was the steadfast wall, absorbing shocks and bearing the weight of protection. Luca was the fire, the spark, bringing energy and passion to every escapade they embarked upon. Their brotherhood wasn't just an indication of blood or childhood memories. It was evident in their daily actions, their gestures, the silent way they looked out for one another. Their love was palpable, a force as tangible as the streets beneath their feet.

Before their midday meeting, Franco sat in his car, eyes trained on the rusty gates of Johnnie's builder's yard. The dashboard clock flicked from 11:29 to 11:30. He drummed his fingers on the steering wheel, tension filling the car like an intense fog. If Luca was being held in that yard, Johnnie would likely use the time before their meeting to ensure Luca remained securely detained. The thought made Franco's grip tighten around the steering wheel.

When he arrived, the gates were open. He then saw Johnnie walk out. Franco felt his pulse quicken, not because of Johnnie but because of what—or rather who—might be hidden behind those gates. Johnnie paused to light a cigarette, looking around suspiciously before heading back into the yard. Franco seized the moment. He stepped out of the car, locked it, and slipped into the yard through a hole in the fence he'd noted earlier. Once inside, he had to move quickly.

Franco weaved through the labyrinth of bricks, wire, and gravel cluttering the yard. His eyes darted around, scouring the maze for any sign of Johnnie. A knot tightened in his stomach with each tick of the invisible seconds.

A voice sliced through the air. "Trying to outsmart me, Franco?" Johnnie emerged, his face twisted into a menacing grin, a crowbar gripped in his hand. "You thought you'd waltz right in?"

Franco's eyes flicked toward the house, calculating distances and chances. The tension was electric. His eyes locked onto a shaky stack of wood. With a burst of movement, he lunged, his arms pushing against the planks. Timber toppled toward Johnnie, who let out a curse. The wood crashed into a dusty heap, but Franco had gained the seconds he needed.

He sprinted toward the house, boots churning up dust, each stride increasing the space between him and Johnnie. Behind him, Johnnie's roar erupted, each footfall a thunderous echo of his rising frustration. But Franco had counted, had measured the ground, had timed the chase in his mind. Reaching the house, he vaulted over a low wall, landing on the other side with a muffled impact. No time for triumph; he threw open the door and vanished into the maze of hallways and rooms of the derelict Victorian mansion.

Johnnie's eyes darted around the darkness as he stood at the threshold, crowbar clenched in his grip. Banging it against the wall, the clang echoed through the empty space, amplifying his frustration. Seconds ticked by until Johnnie's gaze finally landed on Franco, hidden awkwardly behind a frayed sofa. As their eyes met, Franco's skin paled. With the crowbar in hand, Johnnie locked eyes onto Franco. The weight of the metal felt right, like an extension of his own arm. He swung it downward, every muscle committed to the strike. Franco shot up from his hiding place, his reflexes firing. The table lamp teetered and fell, glass exploding upon impact with the floor. Their feet pounded the hardwood in a chaotic rhythm, filling the narrow corridors of the decrepit house. Mould on the walls seemed to close in, as if the very building were gasping for breath.

Franco glanced over his shoulder; Johnnie was closing the gap. He veered left into another hallway, hoping to lose him in the complex layout. Every doorway he passed was either boarded up or gaping open like an orifice of darkness. Johnnie saw Franco's wobble as they rounded a corner. A smirk tugged at the corner of his mouth. He knew this building better than anyone. For Franco, every turn was a gamble; for Johnnie, each was calculated.

Franco's eyes flicked to a door on his right—not boarded and slightly ajar. Without breaking stride, he pushed it open and burst into the room. It was an old laundry area. The smell of damp and mildew intensified. Johnnie skidded to a halt just outside. His nostrils flared; then he stormed in. In that cramped, dingy room with its stagnant air, both men knew only one would walk out. And the crowbar, still clenched in Johnnie's grip, gleamed with an ugly promise.

The door had barely clicked shut when the crowbar burst through, wood shards flying in disarray. Cornered, Franco's heavy breaths filled the air as he looked up. The crowbar descended—metal into flesh, a nauseating crunch, against Franco's jaw, shattering it. The crowbar then crunched down with blinding force onto the top of Franco's head. Then again and again. Each impact was measured, the methodical rhythm of Johnnie's unyielding anger. Franco's head vanished in a red mist. Franco then bled out, the stink of copper his only companion. Finally, Franco lay there dead—a battered, formless mass on the floor. Johnnie stepped back, his breath less erratic, crowbar hanging idle by his side, dripping with Franco's blood. Silence then settled over the room.

CHAPTER SIXTY-EIGHT

The wail of sirens shattered the late morning, each note a spike of urgency that jolted Rick Stone's nerves. Hands tight on the steering wheel, he swerved the police car through Fulham's busy streets. In the rear-view mirror, the glaring lights of two squad cars followed; their strobing blues painted intermittent chaos onto the tarmac.

Muscles rigid, jaw clenched, he felt his pulse match the blare of the sirens. Every twist and turn ramped up the pressure, like a screw tightening its grip.

Up ahead, Munster Road unfurled into an arena of disarray. Firemen wrestled with hoses; their movements were precise yet frantic—a choreographed dance with no room for error. The spray of water arced through the air, creating a temporary rainbow in the sky. Rick's eyes darted to the crowd, penned in by a wall of police tape. Faces—some slack with shock, others alight with a grim sort of thrill—peered from behind screens. Smartphones hovered like a forest of digital eyes, all trained on the turmoil before them. His gut twisted. The voyeuristic assembly grated against his professional resolve. The world had its stage, and today, he was an unwilling actor.

Rick's eyes narrowed, locking onto the task at hand. The sense of duty hardened within him, as immovable and cold as steel. For him, this was not a spectacle but a life-altering event in the lives of his fellow Londoners. It was a scene that had to be contained, a story that had yet to reach its end. Rick, at the helm, felt the weight of its unwritten chapters bear down upon him.

Rick pulled his car to the kerb; the engine idled as if holding its breath. The other police cars followed suit, aligning themselves in a grim procession. They parked twenty yards from the site, a distance that seemed to stretch with every heartbeat. For a moment, the world seemed suspended in brittle silence, as though even the sirens sensed the heaviness that weighed down the air.

“Let's go,” he muttered to his team, his voice tinged with weary resignation, and they exited the vehicles to confront whatever awaited them in the yard ahead.

Rick's boots hit the pavement, each step an echo in the still air as his team closed in behind him. The firemen were shouting now, directing jets of water at an unseen blaze hidden behind a wall of smoke and orange light. He glanced at his team; their faces etched with lines that extended beyond the physical toll of the job. It was a map of a different kind of exhaustion, one that had settled in their souls over the years.

“DI Stone, what have we got?” One of the firemen broke through his thoughts, his uniform smudged with soot and sweat. Rick met the fireman's eyes, seeing his own weariness mirrored back. “We're still piecing it together.

Any casualties?"

The fireman shook his head, his expression one of grim relief. "No, but we haven't searched the building yet; it's a very large property."

Rick's eyes tightened, and he nodded curtly before moving away.

His radio crackled to life. "DI Stone, we've got a possible lead. Witnesses spotted someone fleeing the scene in a white van."

Rick picked up the radio, his thumb hovering over the transmit button. For a brief second, he hesitated, as if holding his breath before plunging into deep waters. "Understood. Keep me posted."

As he turned to re-join his team, the smell of burnt wood and melted plastic filled the air, mingling with the stench of disillusionment that had long since become a part of him. Each step toward the blaze felt like a step into a darkness that grew with every case, every unanswered question. But for Rick and his team, the only option was to move forward, because standing still was a luxury they could never afford.

Rick moved through the dense haze of smoke, his eyes stinging but focused. The sharp outline of his deputy, Sarah, came into view; she was speaking hurriedly into her radio, jotting down notes on a pad. As he approached, he caught the tail end of her conversation. "...Right, keep the perimeter tight. We can't let anyone compromise the scene," Sarah ordered, disconnecting the call as Rick closed the distance between them.

Her eyes met his, and he could see the unspoken questions swimming there. He offered a terse nod. "Witnesses?"

Sarah replied, "Two so far. Both claim to have seen a white van hurrying away just as the fire started. Vague descriptions, though."

Rick sighed inwardly; vague was not what they needed, but it was better than the complete absence of leads they'd had in their last few cases. "Security cameras?"

She shook her head, her expression souring. "Either non-operational or conveniently facing the wrong way."

The tight knot of frustration in Rick's gut tightened. Of course. Nothing was ever straightforward in this line of work. He looked back at the smouldering ruin, at the firemen who fought to subdue the final pockets of flame. His eyes settled on a charred piece of wood, its edges still glowing with embers. It was as if even the remnants of the building were resisting surrender, defiant to the end.

His radio buzzed again. "DI Stone, they've found something you'll want to see."

Rick took one last look at the expectant faces in the crowd. The media would be here soon, feeding off the drama, spinning stories that ranged from the factual to the speculative. He dreaded the impending circus but knew it was an inevitable part of the grim theatre that was his job. "All right, let's go," Rick told Sarah, not waiting for her reply as he turned and made his way toward the back of the smouldering building.

The world around him felt like a mass of frayed threads, each one threatening to snap, each one demanding his attention.

And as he moved, one foot in front of the other, Rick couldn't shake off the feeling that the thread was about to unravel entirely, and he was woefully unprepared for the chaos that would ensue.

CHAPTER SIXTY-NINE

Navigating the maze of charred debris and damp ash, Rick reached the rear of the smouldering building. A fire officer met him there, his yellow reflective stripes dulled by soot. His face was taut, his eyes weary from more than just the fire. “We've found a body on the ground floor,” the officer announced, the edge in his voice cutting through the acrid air.

Rick looked at him, his eyes narrowing. “Was the body burnt?”

The officer shook his head, the weight of his response evident in his drooping shoulders. “No, he was in a room untouched by the fire.”

The surrounding wreckage seemed to absorb the officer's words, each burnt timber and shattered window a silent witness to the unspeakable irony. A life lost amidst chaos, yet untouched by the flame that had devoured everything else. Rick's gaze shifted to the building's scorched silhouette, its skeletal frame looming like an accusing figure. The untouched room the officer mentioned felt like a cruel joke, a grim pocket of normality in a theatre of ruin. It seemed as if fate itself was mocking them, as if saying that the fire was not the only purveyor of doom that day.

“Do we know who he is?” Rick inquired, his voice tinged with a bitter expectancy.

The fire officer shuffled through a clipboard, his finger tracing lines of hastily written notes. “Still working on identification.”

Rick clenched his fists. The inconsistency gnawed at him, a jarring note in an already tragic composition. But what could anyone expect? The world seldom offered answers wrapped in neat packages of logic or justice.

“Let's see the room,” Rick finally said, ready to face the grim scene that awaited him.

Leading the way, the fire officer guided him back through the unstable ruin, each step a negotiation with the unpredictable footing. As they reached the hallway, Rick's eyes found the room in question—a distressing oasis amid devastation. The door was ajar, its wood stained but unscathed. Rick took a deep breath before stepping inside.

There, on the floor, lay the body. A man, middle-aged, was dressed as if he had been in the middle of an ordinary day. His face wore an expression not of terror, but of resignation, as if he had been waiting for this inevitable moment.

The ground beneath him had absorbed the scarlet pool spreading from the wound at the back of his shattered head, akin to a dropped porcelain bowl. The stark contrast of red against the cold, grey floor added primitive punctuation to the tragedy.

Rick swallowed hard, feeling the lump in his throat grow larger. Each detail—Franco's dishevelled hair, his clothes sticking to him at awkward angles, even the way his wrist-watch had stopped ticking—served as a silent testament to the abrupt halt of a life that had once been so full of verve and laughter.

He couldn't tear his eyes away from the devastation. A shiver crawled up his spine; the scene before him was a screaming silence that filled his ears, drowning out the world around him. Even in the chaos that followed, with people rushing and sirens wailing, Rick stood immobile, trapped in the finality of the moment. Franco Rossi had been here, full of life and plans for tomorrow. And now he wasn't. The grim reality settled in Rick's chest like a block of ice, making it harder to breathe with each passing second.

Rick looked at the fireman. “And the rest of the building? It's cleared?”

The fire officer tapped his clipboard, skimming the lines. “For the most part, yeah. A couple of hot spots we need to monitor, but no signs of anyone else.”

Rick looked over his shoulder at the charred skeleton of the building. “How did it start?”

The fire officer locked eyes with Rick. “Looks like arson, we found accelerant near the back entrance.”

“Security footage?”

“None that we've come across.”

A silent beat passed between them, heavy with unspoken implications. Finally, Rick let out a barely audible sigh. "All right, keep me updated."

The fire officer nodded and jotted down a final note on his clipboard. "Will do."

CHAPTER SEVENTY

Rick Stone's sweaty fingers gripped the steering wheel. Traffic on Fulham Road crawled, each car an obstacle in his inevitable quest. Pedestrians darted past, their faces smeared by the setting sun into streaks of meaningless colour. None of them looked his way; none knew the weight he carried.

Ahead, brake lights flared up like glowing eyes. A visceral knot tightened in his stomach as if those lights could see right through him—laser-focused on his hesitation and dread. Every inch forward felt like a step closer to a precipice he couldn't avoid. This wasn't just about delivering news; it was about shattering a world. For that, there was no turning back.

Switching on the radio, the sombre notes of a violin concerto filled the car, but they did nothing to ease his tension. Soon enough, he turned into the side street next to the Cortana Club, its neon sign a misplaced invitation to enjoyment. He killed the engine, pocketed the keys, and, for a moment, sat contemplating the weight of the words he was about to utter.

Inside the club, Martina sipped her coffee, her hand cradling the warm ceramic mug. The aroma mingled with that of freshly baked pastries and the underlying tinge of burnt espresso from the machine. Grace Lane, her friend, sat across from her, flipping through a fashion magazine. Martina smiled, but her eyes were distant. Her phone lay on the table, screen down, as if she were half-expecting a call. It was odd, she thought, how her intuition prickled at her; a spider sense leaving her unsettled.

Grace looked up, catching the nuance in Martina's expression. “Everything will be fine.”

Before Martina could reply, the ambient chatter dropped a notch. She turned to see Rick Stone walk in. The atmosphere seemed to fold in on itself, retracting into a tighter, denser version.

Rick caught Martina's eye and approached; his solemn face drained the colour from her cheeks. Each step seemed to add gravity to the room, as people’s conversations grew quieter and their laughter stifled.

Martina's hand trembled as she set her coffee cup down, the liquid sloshing over the rim. A tight knot formed in her stomach, and she glanced at Grace, who was now staring at Rick with a mixture of concern and confusion.

Rick arrived at their table, his eyes meeting Martina's. For a moment, time hung suspended. “I need to speak with you, Martina,” he said, his voice just above a whisper but carrying a weight that Martina felt in her bones. “It’s about Franco.”

Rick pulled out the chair next to Martina, its legs scraping against the wooden floor in a grating dissonance that seemed to punctuate the heaviness in the room. He sat down, his eyes never leaving Martina's. Martina felt a knot tighten in her throat, choking off the words she might have said. Her gaze flickered toward Grace, who had set aside the fashion magazine and was looking at both of them with growing apprehension. Rick bent in closer, his voice quivering despite his best efforts to maintain a professional tone. "There's been a fire at the Munster Road builders' yard. Franco… he didn't make it, Martina. I'm so sorry."

A numbing wave washed over Martina, her vision blurring as her eyes welled up. Her phone on the table, once a banal object, now felt like a ticking bomb that had just detonated, shattering the life she knew. The ambient noise of the café seemed to fade into an incongruent backdrop, a cruel contrast to the heart-wrenching news.

For a moment, she felt detached from her own body, observing the scene from afar. She saw her own hands, pale and trembling, clutching the edge of the table. She saw Grace's face contort in an expression of unspoken grief, her own eyes brimming with tears. And she saw Rick, his shoulders hunched, as if he were carrying a burden too immense to bear.

Martina asked, "have you told Lisa, his wife?"

Rick nodded, "We have just spoken to her at her mother's house."

Then the emotional wall Martina had built crumbled. A sob escaped her lips, resonating with the raw anguish she felt, filling the room in its haunting echo. Grace reached across the table, clutching Martina's hand in a warm grip, trying to lend her strength through the simple touch. But Martina felt as if she were spiralling into an abyss, every comfort slipping through her fingers like grains of sand.

Rick looked at Martina, his eyes tinged with a sorrow that not even professional detachment could fully conceal. He knew that the hard part was not over; in fact, it had just begun. There were questions that needed answering, a crime that needed solving. But for now, in this intimate bubble of grief, the quest for justice was eclipsed by the unvarnished humanity of loss.

Slowly, Martina looked up, her eyes meeting Rick's, and in that second, an unspoken agreement passed between them. The questions, the investigation, the long journey to understanding what had happened—they would come. But for this fragile moment, they sat, suspended in mutual acknowledgment of a life lost and the irreversible change it had brought.

CHAPTER SEVENTY-ONE

Johnnie Billham's boots crunched on the gritty Fulham pavement, echoing in the tight alleys like a muffled drum. His eyes flicked from shadow to worn brick to scuffed doorway, not just looking but scanning, calculating. Each step, each turn, was weighed and measured in a split second, as if a wrong move might cost him more than just a moment's delay.

He pivoted sharply into Walham Grove, his pulse thrumming in his ears. Was that a footstep behind him? He whipped his head back—nothing. Just his own reflection in a broken window pane, pale and distorted. He took a steadying breath but kept his hand close to the inside pocket of his jacket.

The door of the weathered house loomed in front of him. As nondescript as the hundreds he'd passed, this one, he knew, was a sanctuary—at least for now. He glanced one final time over his shoulder, then ducked inside. The door clicked softly shut, sealing away the night, the fear, and—for now—the relentless hunt.

Inside, a musty odour of damp wood and stagnant air encircled him, clinging to the walls. His nose wrinkled in distaste at the dimly lit hallway, cluttered with bags of plaster and discarded tools. The floorboards creaked and groaned beneath his weight; each footfall sent a hollow thud echoing up the rickety staircase. Signs of neglect were evident, bearing witness to the passage of time and the settling-in of indifference.

Ascending to the first floor, Johnnie's hand dipped into his pocket, retrieving a jumble of keys. Fumbling momentarily, his fingers eventually found the right one, worn and tarnished from repeated use. The key slid into the lock with a raspy scrape, and a heavy click marked the disengagement of the mechanism. The door to the rear bedroom swung open, revealing a space that seemed to have weathered its own share of hardships.

The sparse furnishings bore the marks of time's uncaring touch—faded upholstery, chipped edges, and worn surfaces. The window, once an inviting source of natural light, now served as a portal to a world that seemed to mirror the room's desolation. As Johnnie entered the room, a sigh escaped his lips, laden with the weight of memories and regrets.

“Comfortable?” Johnnie asked, leaning against the door frame, his tone dripping with sarcasm.

Luca's muffled attempts at speech vibrate through the gag, but Johnnie remains unmoved.

The room is silent, except for the distant hum of traffic and the occasional creak of the old house settling. Luca's eyes dart around the room, a mix of defiance and desperation in them. Johnnie's gaze drifts to the window, observes the slight sway of the tree outside, then returns to Luca. "You know, I had hoped it wouldn't come to this," he remarks, with an air of detachment. "But you just couldn't mind your own fucking business, could you?"

Inaudible sounds come from Luca again, more insistent this time. Johnnie steps forward, pulling a small knife from his pocket and begins to clean his nails with it. "I'm in a good mood today, so I'm going to give you one chance to tell me what I need to know," he says, never taking his eyes off his nails.

Luca's breathing quickens; his chest heaves against his binding ropes. The weight of the situation is intense; the tension in the room almost unbearable.

Johnnie flips the knife closed and pockets it. He strides over to Luca, kneels down to eye level, and yanks the gag from his mouth. "Speak. One chance."

Luca coughs, gasping for air. "I don't know what you want me to say. You won't fucking get away with this."

"Ah, the cliché line," Johnnie mutters, standing up. "Disappointing, really. I expected something more creative from you."

Struggling to break free, Luca shouts, "So it's all about that fucking picture, is it? Why?"

Johnnie yells back, "You lot had it all—family, love. I had nothing."

"What are you talking about?"

"You all had the perfect life—wives, kids, love. I had nothing. I was willing to leave you alone because you'd lost your wife. But you couldn't leave well enough alone, could you? So now I've at too take something from you."

Luca narrows his eyes. "What do you mean by that?"

"Let's just say, your brother won't be sending you a Christmas card this year."

Luca's eyes harden, the weight of Johnnie's words sinking in. "You're saying you did something to my brother?"

Johnnie smirks. "Fuck me, you're quick."

A chill courses through Luca. "You sick bastard. All this over envy? Over a picture?"

"It's more than a picture. It's about fairness. It's about taking something back."

Luca sniffs, a sharp sound cutting through the air. "By ruining lives? You call that fairness?"

Johnnie's shoulders lift and fall in a dismissive shrug. "Life's not fair. I'm just resetting the scales, that's all."

Heat surges through Luca's veins. "As I said, you won't get away with this."

"Who's going to stop me? You?" Johnnie scans Luca's bound hands and feet.

"Seems like you've got your own problems to sort out."

Luca's lips pull back, a low growl in his voice. "People will notice. Questions will be asked."

Johnnie interrupts him, getting closer until Luca can feel the warm air of his near-whisper. He draws an object from his pocket. "Take a look. It's a gold St. Christopher—Franco's."

"That means fuck all. You're lying. You think you're invisible?" Luca's voice is steel. "Someone will connect the dots. They always do."

Johnnie steps back, his eyes a calculating blend of scorn and self-assurance. "Time will tell." He turns, his footsteps receding, leaving Luca alone to grapple with his restraints and the haunting implication of his brother's pendant.

Johnnie's boots thud on the worn wooden floor as he approaches a decrepit dresser, its paint chipped and hinges rusty. He slides open the top drawer, revealing its cluttered contents: a jumble of forgotten keys, crumpled receipts, and other neglected items. His hand sifts through the mess, finally landing on a roll of duct tape.

"You had your chance to make this easy," he mutters, almost to himself. A quick flick of the wrist and the tape unrolls with a sharp, ripping sound. He presses a strip over Luca's mouth. Instantly, the room's ambient noise dims to a series of muffled grunts and futile struggles against restraints.

Johnnie steps out of the room, making sure the door clicks locked behind him. Down the staircase he goes, his boots crunching on fallen plaster and sidestepping an obstacle course of bags and tools strewn about. Reaching the bottom, he exits onto Walham Grove, blending seamlessly into the maze of backstreets. The house stands still, exhaling a quiet emptiness in his wake.

CHAPTER SEVENTY-TWO

Martina's eyelids snapped open, jolted by a shard of sunlight stabbing through the window. The alarm clock glared 7:30 A.M. back at her. Her fingers clenched the duvet, which had become less a comfort and more a paper-thin shield against the crushing weight of the day ahead.

In her dreams, she had escaped—albeit momentarily—to a place untouched by yesterday's horror. The murder of Franco remained an unreal, distant nightmare. Her heart hammered against her rib cage, its rhythm disjointed, much like her thoughts. The allure of that dream world tugged at her like a black hole of escape. She yearned to sink back into it and evade the searing pain awaiting her in consciousness. But the sun's invasive glare and the unyielding digits on the clock chained her to a reality she wasn't ready to face. With each passing second, the sanctuary of her dreams receded further, leaving her stranded in a waking world she no longer recognised.

The weight of the day ahead settled on her like a wet blanket, extinguishing any lingering wisps of joy from her dreams.

Unlike the relief that usually accompanies waking from a nightmare, Martina felt a sinking dread as her feet touched the cold floor. She stared at her reflection in the mirror, her eyes tracing the dark circles that had deepened over the last 48 hours.

Making coffee in the kitchen, Martina stared vacantly at the empty chairs across the dining table. Franco's chair, forever imprinted with the wear of years, remained untouched—a silent witness to his sudden absence. Luca's chair, slightly askew as if he had just stood up and would return any moment, served as a haunting reminder of uncertainty.

Her phone vibrated on the kitchen worktop. The screen displayed a message from Grace: “I'm outside. Ready when you are.” She took a deep breath; her chest tightened as if an invisible hand squeezed her heart.

For a fleeting second, she imagined Franco bursting through the front door, filling the room with his contagious laughter and questionable jokes. The fantasy evaporated as swiftly as it had formed, leaving behind only a biting emptiness.

She grabbed her coat and bag, took one final look around the room, and stepped outside to join Grace in the car. The engine roared to life, carrying them toward a destination no one wants to visit, to confront a reality she still hoped was a nightmare.

The outside world, a blend of grey concrete and the now-overcast sky, mirrored the hollowness inside her. Her eyes lingered on the mortuary sign, the letters stark and unforgiving. Beside her, a half-empty water bottle wobbled in the cup holder, contrasting with the stagnant air that filled the car. Martina glanced at it, then back to the mortuary doors, as if the distance between the two were an uncrossable chasm. Her hand paused over the door handle. It felt cold and impersonal, much like the building that awaited her. The seatbelt across her chest suddenly felt like a restraint, holding her back from a reality she wasn't ready to face.

Her mobile phone vibrated in her handbag, offering a brief distraction. She ignored it; the world outside was still pressing in. In that moment, the car was both her refuge and her prison, shielding her from and trapping her within her own apprehension. Martina couldn't move, suspended between the life she'd known and the abyss of the unknown that lay beyond the car door.

The phone vibrated again, a muted vibration against the fabric of her bag. This time, she took it out. A text message flashed on the screen, from her sister-in-law Lisa: "Are you okay? Thank you for doing this for me. I will never forget it. Lisa xx." Simple words, but they cracked the shell of Martina's inertia. For the first time, she felt the dampness on her cheeks, realising she'd been crying without even noticing.

Her thumb hovered over the screen. Could she say she was okay when every fibre of her being screamed otherwise? She put the phone down, unable to reply. With a deep breath, she finally unlatched her seatbelt. The door creaked open, admitting a gust of cool air that swept through the car's interior like a sobering slap. As her feet touched the ground, Martina felt the gravel beneath her heels, unsteady and fragmented. She shut the car door with more force than she intended; the sound echoed in the still air. It was a punctuation mark, separating her from the sanctuary of her car and thrusting her into a reality she could no longer evade.

Her eyes caught a glimpse of her reflection in the glass doors —dishevelled hair, eyes red and swollen, a face bearing the indelible marks of a sleepless night and a torrent of tears. She looked like a stranger to herself, a hollow vessel stripped of its vitality.

Walking side by side, Grace put her arm around Martina. Inside, the antiseptic smell hit them immediately, erasing any remaining sense of normality. The lighting was subdued, casting the room in a soft, pallid glow. A receptionist glanced up from her computer, offering a smile that was both sympathetic and rehearsed.

Martina and Grace approached the desk. Martina's voice trembled as she stated her purpose for the visit. The receptionist nodded, already pulling out a clipboard with papers that needed signatures—another layer of cold formality to what was an unbearably personal ordeal. Completing the form felt mechanical; each stroke of the pen conflicted with her emotional turmoil. She handed the clipboard back, her hands trembling slightly. Her trembling signature at the bottom of the page acknowledged a reality she hadn't fully accepted.

The receptionist directed her to a door down the corridor. "Take as much time as you need," she said softly, the words floating in the air as Martina walked away.

Detective Inspector Rick Stone was waiting outside. With a deep, steadying breath, Rick opened the door. As it swung inward, Martina felt the last barricade crumble, exposing her to the unyielding truth of what lay inside. And as she crossed that threshold, she knew there was no turning back. The door closed softly behind her, sealing her into a new chapter of life, one not written in the ink of possibility, but in the indelible strokes of loss and remembrance.

CHAPTER SEVENTY-THREE

The ropes bit into Luca's wrists, each coarse fibre a biting reminder of his restraint. With each flicker of his fingers, he sifted through the knot, as if solving a riddle only he could understand. Hours had blended into a smear of darkness, punctuated only by the quiet resistance of the rope against his touch.

A slight give. He felt it more than heard it—a minute loosening, as if the rope had exhaled. It was like cracking a safe's combination; every minuscule shift setting the stage for freedom.

The final loop surrendered, tumbling to the ground in silent defeat. Shoulders that had been knotted with stress eased back into place, sinking as if unshackled from an invisible burden. He opened and closed his hands, savouring the alien sensation of skin against air, muscle against bone, unobstructed.

Eyes darting to the door, he could almost see the outline of Johnnie materialising, filling the frame with inevitable surprise.

In his mind's eye, he watched Johnnie's eyes widen and saw his jaw slacken. The thought drew a tight line of expectation across his own features.

He was a coiled spring, a predator in the dark, poised for that one priceless moment when realisation would dawn on Johnnie's face—the ropes were empty, and their captive was no more.

While waiting, Luca's thoughts ricocheted between despair and memory. His eyes, tired and filled with grit, shifted to the dirty floor, unable to focus on anything for long. Each moment stretched on, punctuated by his thoughts and the muffled sounds of footsteps beyond the door.

Grace. The thought of her infiltrated his mind unexpectedly. He remembered the lift of her laughter, the warmth in her eyes. The way she listened—truly listened—when he spoke. She had a vitality that defied the mundane, an effortless allure that he found himself drawn to, despite his reservations.

But then, like a match struck in darkness, Julia's image ignited in his mind. His late wife still occupied the quiet corners of his thoughts; her absence a constant undertone. She had been his rock, his love, the compass by which he navigated life. Two years gone, yet she felt interwoven into his very being, as inseparable as his own shadow.

Guilt swelled within him, making the air in the room feel even heavier. How could he contemplate new love while tethered to a past that still consumed him? It felt like a betrayal, a violation of an unspoken oath. But even in that moment, trapped and uncertain of his future, he couldn't deny the emerging truth: life was beckoning him forward, even if he wasn't sure he deserved to move on.

Julia would want him to be happy; of that much he was certain. But would she understand his feelings for Grace, a woman so different yet eerily similar in ways that seemed to matter? Would she see it as an act of moving on, or as an act of forgetting? But even as he turned to confront whatever awaited him, the emotional calculus continued to churn deep within, unresolved, like an equation missing vital variables. Whether he wanted it or not, life was pulling him in new directions; he was left to grapple with the dissonance, caught between the love he had lost and the love that might yet be.

The door hinge creaked, grating sounds punctuating the air as Johnnie Billham's key forced its way into the lock. A click signalled its surrender. In a dim corner of the room, Luca's chest heaved; each heartbeat was a violent drum solo against his ribs. The red welts on his wrists and ankles contrasted sharply with his pale skin. Frayed rope fragments lay like fallen soldiers around him. His muscles coiled, every fibre taut, his eyes narrowed to slits as he peered through the gloom. Johnnie pushed the door open; its base scraped against the worn, bare floorboards. His gaze immediately latched onto the empty chair in the centre of the room, surrounded by stray bits of rope. A smirk crawled across his lips, twisting them upwards. He stepped in, confident of his victory.

In that heartbeat of distraction, Luca pounced. His arms wrapped around Johnnie's neck and shoulders from behind, pulling him backwards. The two men crashed to the ground, a jumble of limbs and raw energy. Skin scraped against splintered wood, grunts mingled with curses. Luca's arm snaked free, and his fist collided with Johnnie's jaw—a solid thud that sent vibrations up his arm. "You prick, I'll fucking kill you!" Johnnie spat, fire flaring in his eyes. His hand scrabbled across the floor, closing around a shard of glass. In a swift, arcing motion, he lunged at Luca, aiming for his face. Luca's eyes locked onto the gleaming shard. His hand shot out, gripping Johnnie's wrist with a steel clamp of muscles. The shard quivered in the air, inches away from Luca's neck. For a moment, everything stilled—the shard glinting, the room draped in shadows. Then Luca twisted sharply, wrenching Johnnie's wrist. The glass shard skittered across the floor.

In a swift motion, Luca swept his leg behind Johnnie's knees, unbalancing him. Johnnie hit the floor with a thump, his breath expelled in a sharp gasp. Luca pivoted toward the door, nearly reaching it when his momentum halted. Johnnie's hand had latched onto his ankle, gripping it like a vice, and Luca fell to the floor. For a brief moment, their eyes met, and the room seemed to narrow to just that connection. Peripheral vision caught Luca's attention—another shard of glass. He extended his arm, his fingertips barely grazing its jagged edge before seizing it. Without hesitation, he drove the shard into Johnnie's gripping hand. A scream—guttural and ragged—reverberated through the room. Johnnie's grip slackened, and Luca yanked his ankle free.

Now both on their feet, Johnnie circled Luca like a shark smelling blood. Johnnie lunged at Luca, aiming to overpower him. Luca deftly sidestepped to his left, driving his elbow into Johnnie's face. Shrugging off the blow, Johnnie retaliated with a forceful left hook that sent Luca stumbling sideways. Luca recovered just in time to evade Johnnie's next attack.

Capitalising on Luca's brief imbalance, Johnnie unleashed another left hook that landed on Luca's ear, quickly followed by a right-hander to the jaw. He rained down a flurry of blows, punch after punch. Blood trickled from Luca's lips and nose, but he showed no other signs of distress. From then on, Luca shifted his strategy to evasion, nimbly dodging the ceaseless barrage from Johnnie.

Johnnie's eyes darted around, momentarily unfocused. Luca's muscles tensed; every fibre of his being was coiled and ready. In a split second, Luca unleashed an uppercut with explosive force. The collision was unmistakable: a raw, crisp smack resonated as Luca's knuckles found their mark squarely on Johnnie's exposed chin, the sound of bone meeting bone cutting sharply through the air.

Johnnie swayed on his feet, his eyes cloudy. Luca sidestepped and landed a crisp right hook to Johnnie's jaw. The impact snapped Johnnie's head to the side, his legs buckling beneath him. A split second later, Johnnie was sprawled on the dusty floor, unconscious.

Wasting no time, Luca untangled the ropes that had chafed his wrists. With deft movements, he redirected the rope toward Johnnie, securing his wrists and ankles with swift, taut knots. A brief glance confirmed their snugness; they wouldn't give easily. He dropped to one knee beside the prone figure; his hands patrolled the fabric of Johnnie's jeans and jacket. His fingers brushed against something solid, tracing its rectangular outline. Extracting the mobile phone, he weighed it in his palm for a fraction of a second before thumbing it to life. Luca keyed in "999," his gaze never leaving Johnnie's immobile face.

After a few minutes, Johnnie's eyelids flickered open, his gaze blurry. He mumbled something incomprehensible, his words tangled in his groggy state. As he felt the ropes digging into his wrists and ankles, his consciousness snapped into focus. Johnnie locked eyes with Luca, who was standing a few feet away. "You," he snarled, the fog lifting entirely. He yanked at his restraints, muscles straining, face flushed red. "I killed your brother, and I'm going to fucking kill you." His voice escalated into a scream, filled with a rage that echoed through the empty room.

Luca met Johnnie's glare steadily, a hint of anticipation in his eyes. "Are you done?" His voice cut through the air, cold and sharp. Johnnie's muscles quivered, and the ropes bit into his wrists. The strain was evident in the bulging veins on his forehead and neck.

Luca told him, "The police will be here soon. You should save your energy for them. My plan was to kill you, but unlike you, I have things to live for."

The tension in the room hung heavy, punctuated by the distant wail of approaching sirens. Johnnie's eyes narrowed, and his options were evaporating as quickly as his strength. Luca walked over to a chair and sat down, never taking his eyes off Johnnie. The sirens grew louder, close enough to signal the imminent arrival of the police. Johnnie glared at Luca, any pretence of bravado now gone, replaced by the cold, hard reality of his situation. "Do you have any last words, Johnnie?" Luca asked, as the blue lights began to flash through the windows. It was clear neither of them had anything left to say.

CHAPTER SEVENTY-FOUR

The door burst open with a deafening crash, splinters of wood flying through the air. Armed-response police officers in ballistic vests poured into the room, their weapons trained forward, eyes shielded behind ballistic glasses. Their boots thudded on the hardwood floor, echoing through the tense air. "Police, get on the floor and spread your arms," the lead officer shouted, laser sights dancing on the figures in the room.

Luca, standing over Johnnie, lay down and spread his hands. His face was ashen, his eyes wide with a mix of relief and fear. Johnnie, bound with rope, looked up. Sweat and blood mixed on his forehead, matting his hair. The officers swiftly moved into position, securing Luca with quick, professional movements—hands pulled behind his back, cuffs locked into place. One officer checked the ties that bound Johnnie, while another kept an eye on Luca, whose rapid breathing filled the room. "All clear and secured," an officer finally said, his voice carrying a weight of authority as he surveyed the scene.

The room, smelling of sweat and fear, seemed to exhale, releasing its tension as the law reasserted control. With Luca restrained and Johnnie beginning to regain his composure, officers started their preliminary checks—weapons were holstered but still at the ready, eyes alert for any unexpected moves. As Johnnie's gag was removed, he coughed, taking in large gulps of air. His eyes met Luca's for just a second; it was a complex exchange that only they could fully comprehend. The scene was secure, yet the emotional currents running through the room were far from settled. Each person present—Johnnie, Luca, and the officers—was steeped in their own mix of adrenaline, relief, and unanswered questions. But for now, the immediate threat had been neutralised, and that was enough.

The sound of footsteps approached from the corridor, measured and assured. DI Rick Stone walked into the room, his face a mask of stern professionalism. His eyes scanned the scene—armed officers, a bound Johnnie Billham now being lifted to his feet, and Luca, cuffed and lying on the floor. "Stand down," he commanded, locking eyes with the lead officer, who nodded. DI Stone moved straight to Luca. "Uncuff him," he said, his voice carrying authority. The officer who had initially restrained Luca glanced at Stone for confirmation, then promptly unfastened the cuffs. The metal clicked open, and Luca's hands were free. Stone helped him to his feet, taking a moment to look him in the eye. "Officers, this is Luca Rossi," Rick clarified to the room, keeping his tone level.

A murmur ran through the ranks of the armed police. Stone didn't wait for questions. "Take him," he nodded at Johnnie, who was being helped to his feet by another officer, "down to the station for questioning."

Officers quickly moved to comply. As they escorted Johnnie out, his eyes met Luca's once more. This time, it was harder to read what lay behind them. Johnnie was led away, his steps uneven but defiant. DI Stone turned to Luca. "Come on, we need to talk." Luca nodded, flexing his wrists to shake off the lingering sensation of the cuffs.

As they exited the room, he cast a final glance back. The air still hung heavy, but for him, at least, the ordeal was over. Both men moved towards the unmarked police car parked outside. The engine started, the gears shifted, and they pulled away, leaving behind a room now empty but fraught with the echo of unfolding lives.

The unmarked police car pulled into the reserved spaces at the station. The engine cut off, leaving behind a brief silence that seemed heavy with unspoken words. DI Rick Stone opened the door and stepped out, followed by Luca. They walked through the glass doors of the station, past the front desk and into the maze of hallways. Finally, they reached an unremarkable room labelled "Interview 2." Rick flicked on the light and gestured for Luca to sit. He closed the door behind them, sealing them in with the beige walls and the lingering scent of stale coffee. "Luca, we've got some bad news," Rick began, his voice tightening with an emotion he rarely let surface. "Franco has been murdered."

"I know," Luca replied, his face impassive but his eyes filled with a storm of conflicting emotions. "Johnnie told me. I wasn't sure if he was lying to mess with my head."

Rick nodded, taking a seat opposite Luca. "It's true. Franco was murdered at the builder's yard on Munster Road. Johnnie Billham is our prime suspect."

Silence filled the room, punctuated only by the distant chatter from the corridor outside. Luca gripped the arms of the chair, as if anchoring himself to the moment. "Does Martina know?" Luca's words cracked as he spoke, his eyes narrowing as if bracing for impact.

Rick hesitated, his gaze drifting to the floor before lifting to meet Luca's. "Yes, she knows. His wife, Lisa, too. Martina... she was the one who had to ID him."

Luca's body recoiled as if slapped, and he sank into the chair, his fingers clutching its arms. His face contorted, every wrinkle and line magnified by a heavy weight—some cocktail of loss, regret, and raw vulnerability that comes with being a brother. As Rick rose to leave the room, Luca looked at him and nodded, acknowledging not just the arrangements but also the fraught emotional terrain that lay ahead for both of them. Their eyes met, and in that moment, both men were united by the gravity of loss and the difficult path that lay ahead.

Rick reached for the door handle but paused, letting his hand hover for a moment. He turned back to Luca, who was still sitting, his gaze fixed on the table top as if searching for answers in its worn surface. "You've been through a lot, Luca. I won't lie; the path ahead is tough. But we'll navigate it. Together," Rick said, his voice coloured by an earnestness that had evaded him for much of his career. "We do what we can to protect our own. But some things are out of our control. Franco…" His voice faltered, revealing a crack in his otherwise stoic demeanour.

"Yeah, Franco," Luca echoed, each syllable tinged with regret. "He was so proud of the family name, of the traditions. And now, my brother is gone. What about Billham? What's going to happen now?"

"We'll build the case," Rick assured him, his grip tightening as if trying to transfer some of his own resolve into Luca. "We'll make sure he can't hurt anyone else again."

Rick finally released his grip and stepped back, opening the door. "I'll go arrange for a car to take you to see Martina. Take a few moments here. Gather your thoughts."

As Rick exited the room, Luca found himself alone, enveloped by the stillness and the magnitude of what had transpired. For now, though, he was free. And with that freedom came an obligation to honour the name and memory of his brother. It was a tall order, but one he was now fully committed to fulfilling.

CHAPTER SEVENTY-FIVE

Martina saw Luca's hunched shoulders long before he reached her. As he walked up Kingwood Road, each step seemed to weigh him down, drawing his brows together in a tight knot. When he finally stood before her, they embraced. Their arms clenched around each other, neither willing to be the first to let go. It was as though they were trying to wring the pain out of each other's souls.

Stepping into the house, they moved through an atmosphere that seemed to catch in their throats. Eyes traced them from framed photos on the walls—Franco's eyes, forever frozen in a happier time. The very walls of the house seemed to tighten around them, as if even the plaster and wood were in mourning.

Martina gestured wordlessly toward the living room. When Luca spoke, his voice barely rose above a murmur. "The police have Billham at the nick."

Martina stopped before a photo on a side table. Her fingertips ghosted over the image, barely making contact. There they were, all three of them: a sunny day on Leysdown Beach, Franco in the middle, smiles all around. “This day... remember?”

As she said it, a tear broke free, tracing a wet line down her face. Luca looked at the photo, then at his sister's tear-streaked face. It was like someone had scraped the inside of his chest with a rusty knife.

Luca took a deep breath, the weight of the day resting heavily on his shoulders. “I can't believe Billham was one of ours, you know? Grew up on these very streets,” Martina nodded, her fingers absently playing with the frayed edge of a cushion.

“I played football with him, drank in the Clem Attlee with him. It's surreal. How does someone from our own childhood do this?”

Silence hung in the room. The ticking clock on the wall seemed louder, counting down seconds that were heavy with memories.

Martina huffed sharply, holding back another wave of tears. “I just wish we could've protected him, been there for him. Like he was always there for us.”

Luca reached out, taking her hand in his. Their fingers inter-laced, finding strength in each other. “We always did our best. And Franco knew that. This pain won't go away overnight, but we have each other and the rest of the family. And we have our memories.”

She rested her head on his shoulder, drawing comfort from his warmth. They sat like that for a while, lost in their thoughts, united in their grief. Outside, a light rain started to fall, tapping softly on the windows, like memories knocking gently on their hearts. They sank into the old couch, their voices soft but relentless. They talked of school days, of long summers filled with the chime of ice cream vans, Bishop's Park, and children playing in the streets of Fulham. Of a community where every face was known, where the idea of someone like Jonnie Billham lurking among them was unimaginable. Yet, here they were, bound by grief, finding a flicker of warmth in a world that had suddenly gone cold.

CHAPTER SEVENTY-SIX

Luca pushed open the heavy glass door of the police station and stepped onto the pavement. His breath misted in the frigid air, condensing into a small cloud before dissipating. Around him, the city lived its cacophonous life—taxi horns blared in impatient bursts, people chattered as they passed by, their words intermingling in an incomprehensible murmur. A couple laughed heartily at a shared joke from a nearby café.

But Luca barely registered any of it. It was as if he were wrapped in a shroud that dulled the world's colours and muted its sounds. His eyes focused, almost unseeing, on the pavement beneath his feet, each step heavy and deliberate. As he walked, his mind churned over the name that had haunted him for weeks: Johnnie Billham. This name seemed to cast a shadow darker than the approaching evening, clouding Luca's thoughts and filling him with a growing sense of dread. He envisioned Johnnie's face, a picture from the case file, and the unsettling calm in those eyes made his stomach churn.

At the traffic light, he stopped. Not because he noticed the red light, but because his legs felt as though they would no longer carry him. He leaned against the cold metal of the lamppost, the chill penetrating his coat and matching the icy sensation that gripped his insides. A siren wailed in the distance, snapping him momentarily back to reality. The light changed, the little pedestrian figure glowing green. People moved past him, their faces a blur, their lives untouched by the haunting investigation that consumed his own.

On his way to meet a friend, he hailed a black cab. Luca muttered, "Stevenage Road, please." Reaching his destination fifteen minutes later, Luca exited the cab and paid the burly driver. Ahead, the sprawling Bishop's Park beckoned as a refuge.

Luca made his way to a wooden bench over by the Thames, his legs almost thankful to escape the relentless march. The wood felt hard and unyielding beneath him, just another extension of the world he found himself increasingly disconnected from. He pulled out the photograph and held it up to the sunlight, as if hoping to extract some hidden meaning from the pixels and colours.

Just then, a child's cry tore through the park, shattering the calm. Luca's head snapped up, his eyes scanning until they locked onto a little girl who had tripped and fallen, her balloon escaping skyward. Her mother rushed to comfort her, the scene playing out in a world that still felt light-years away.

As the summer sun danced on the Thames like a ribbon of light weaving through London, against the backdrop of this golden canvas, a woman strode along the path towards him.

The hem of her light-blue summer dress brushed against her knees in a whispering stroke.

Her blonde hair, reminiscent of sunlit wheat fields, flowed freely, cascading down her shoulders in waves of gold that seemed to dance with each step. She exuded a quiet kind of elegance—not loud or demanding, but there, distinct like a melody you can't quite place but won't forget either.

The wind subtly shifted, as though deciding to be her companion, carrying the scent of nearby blossoms and the ambient notes of the park. It teased her dress, offering a brief caress before moving on, as she continued her unhurried journey beside the Thames. There was an aura of serenity about her; a calmness that transcended the ordinary. Passers-by couldn't help but steal glances, captivated not just by her beauty but also by the emotion she exuded. It was as if she wasn't just walking through the park, but floating, drifting like a summer dream, blurring the lines between reality and fantasy.

The gentle afternoon sun streamed through the gaps between the tall trees, casting playful shadows on the paved path of Bishop's Park. Luca's eyes scanned the park, catching a glimpse of Grace's familiar silhouette near the riverside. Her gaze was fixed on the gentle ripples in the water, a clear reflection of the deep thoughts swirling within her.

With each step he took toward her, the soft crunch of leaves underfoot echoed the palpable anticipation hanging in the air. As he approached, she turned her head slightly, the wind tousling her hair and revealing a smile.

"Grace," he greeted, his voice carrying the weight of a thousand unspoken words.

She turned fully now, the corners of her eyes crinkling as her smile grew wider. “Luca,” she replied, her voice a soft lilt, almost lost amid the distant cries of seagulls and the gentle lapping of the river's waters.

They began to walk side by side; the River Thames flowed parallel to their journey, reflecting the London skyline.

“Do you ever think about it?” Luca asked after a moment, his voice hesitant yet hopeful. “About us, and the life we could have?”

Grace looked over at him, the reflection of the sun in her eyes giving them an ethereal glow. “Every day,” she admitted, taking a deep breath. “I dream of a quiet house, laughter echoing in every room, and nights spent under a blanket of stars.”

Luca's fingers brushed against hers, entwining them gently. “I’ve imagined waking up, where we could be free to dream and chase every one of those dreams together.”

A thoughtful silence enveloped them, punctuated only by their synchronised footsteps and the distant hum of the city. The riverside lights began to flicker to life, casting a warm, golden hue over the water and their entwined shadows.

Grace squeezed his hand, her face turning toward the horizon where the sun had nearly set. “Let’s promise each other,” she whispered, “that no matter where life takes us, we'll always chase those dreams together.”

Luca nodded, pulling her closer, sealing the promise with the gentle warmth of their shared embrace as the River Thames flowed on, a silent witness to their dreams and hopes.

The End

Printed in Great Britain
by Amazon